"Jane, I want you."

"Thought I was just the help?" The walls around Jane's heart started to slip; she felt it in the way her body sagged against Brock. Already he'd noticed things about her nobody ever had, and he'd fed her, and he was helping her, and he was beautiful."

Was it so wrong to want that? For herself? Once in her life?

"You're more than that, and you know it." His eyes locked on to hers as his deep voice washed over her.

"You're getting auctioned off in two weeks and you know it."

He paused, his expression going completely ice-cold before he looked away and then back at her. "And if I wasn't? What then?"

"Then . ." She bit down on her bottom lip. "I'd ask you to kiss me again."

PRAISE FOR *The Bet* SERIES

THE WAGER

"Rachel Van Dyken is quickly becoming one of my favorite authors and I cannot wait to see what she has in store for us in the future. THE WAGER is a must-read for those who love romance and humor. It will leave a lasting impression and a huge smile on your face."

—LiteratiBookReviews.com

THE BET

"I haven't laughed this hard while reading a book in a while. The Bet [is] an experience—a heartwarming, sometimes hilarious, experience... I've actually read this book twice."

—RecommendedRomance.com

"If you need a funny, light read... I promise you this is a superb choice!"

—MustReadBooksOrDie.com

"Friends-to-lovers stories... is there anything better? And when told in a fun, light manner, with a potential love triangle with lovable characters, well, how can you not enjoy it?"

—TotallyBookedBlog.com

THE *Bachelor* AUCTION

RACHEL VAN DYKEN

FOREVER

NEW YORK   BOSTON

Copyright © 2016 by Rachel Van Dyken
Excerpt from *The Playboy Bachelor* copyright © 2016 by Rachel Van Dyken
Cover design by Elizabeth Turner
Cover photography by Claudio Marinesco
Cover photograph © Trinette Reed/GettyImages
Cover copyright © 2016 by Hachette Book Group, Inc.

Forever
Hachette Book Group
1290 Avenue of the Americas
New York, NY 10104
forever-romance.com
twitter.com/foreverromance

First Edition: October 2016

Forever is an imprint of Grand Central Publishing.
The Forever name and logo are trademarks of Hachette Book Group, Inc.

The publisher is not responsible for websites (or their content) that are not owned by the publisher.

The Hachette Speakers Bureau provides a wide range of authors for speaking events. To find out more, go to www.hachettespeakersbureau.com or call (866) 376-6591.

ISBN 978-1-4555-9871-7 (mass market edition)
ISBN 978-1-4555-9870-0 (ebook edition)

Printed in the United States of America

OPM

10 9 8 7 6 5 4 3 2

To the Cinderellas of the world…
May you find your prince…
Preferably one who knows how to clean
better than Brock.

THE *Bachelor* AUCTION

CHAPTER ONE

He's senile. Last night he asked if I believed in unicorns."

Brock suppressed a groan at Bentley's insensitive statement. No doubt about it, or way around it. Their grandfather, the CEO of Wellington, Incorporated, was losing his damn mind.

But still, someone should come to the old man's defense, and ever since he was twelve years old, that someone had always been Brock. Always.

His younger brothers—twins—were a united front against anything and everything that happened, not only within the family, but especially with Brock. It had always been them against the world, leaving Brock the awkward job of defending them to his grandfather while simultaneously living with the ever increasing aggravation of their sex- and alcohol-filled lifestyles.

"His medication…causes…" Brock clenched and unclenched his fists, mainly so he wouldn't do something stupid like punch one of them. Sleep. He needed more sleep, and a life outside of running a company he'd never wanted to run in the first place. "Visions," he finished. Bitterness took hold like it always did when he thought of the company, his grandfather, and the heavy weight of the world on his shoulders.

"You think visions of unicorns is bad?" Brant, the younger of the twins, gave Brock a disgusted look. "Just last week I found him skinny-dipping in the pool."

Brock frowned as the elevator doors opened to the main offices of Wellington, Inc. "Why is that strange?"

"Alone," Brant said. "Who skinny-dips *alone*?"

Bentley smirked, pushing past both of them. "Not you... clearly."

Brant's lips pressed into a smug grin. "Jealous?"

"Of the skank from last night?" Bentley snorted and sent off a text, most likely to the very same girl who had left Brant's bed the night before. Always a competition with them. "Hardly."

"Hello, boys." Mrs. Everly, their grandfather's secretary, was like family. She refused to acknowledge the brothers were well past the "boy" stage and had been for years.

"Hello," they all said in unison. Bentley reached for her hand and kissed the top of it.

"You get younger every day. Amazing, almost like you're aging backwards." He winked.

Brock's patience was already on edge. Running the company for his grandfather was one thing. Keeping the twins from making asses of themselves was another.

"Bentley." Brock gripped his brother's shoulders with a jerk and shoved him toward the door. "Don't keep Grandfather waiting."

The twins exchanged an eye roll.

"So responsible," Brant said under his breath. It wasn't meant to be a compliment.

"So...old," Bentley added, because that's what he did. "Brock, when was the last time you even got laid? If you say anything past seven days I may need to disown you."

It had been more than seven.

Way more than fourteen.

But with a company to run...

And two brothers to keep under control...

Not to mention the accident that had nearly taken his grandfather's life this last year. Resentment washed over him.

When would he even have time?

For fun?

Sex?

Women?

Anything?

"You're not getting any younger," Bentley interrupted Brock's depressing thoughts. "Aren't you turning thirty-five this year?"

"I saw a gray hair when he turned his head," Brant added. "Depressing as hell."

"It's not gray," Brock snapped, clenching his jaw so tight his teeth ached. "And if you haven't noticed I've been busy."

"Boys?" Brock flinched at the sound of their grandfather's booming voice. "Boys, is that you out there?"

"He may be losing his mind but he sure hasn't lost his vocal cords," Bentley murmured as all three of them stepped casually into the office and shut the large wooden door behind them.

It closed with a resounding thud and Brock felt an ominous current of anxiety travel down his spine.

It was the same feeling he'd had when he was twelve and his grandfather had told him his parents had died in a plane crash.

The same feeling he'd had last year when he'd gone head to head with his grandfather over an acquisition—and won. The board had approved his decision. And less than twenty-four hours later, he'd almost lost his grandfather in a car accident.

As if reading the direction of his thoughts, his grandfather winced. The pain was still there, Brock knew, even if Grandfather refused to admit it.

Charles Williams Wellington the Third was seated behind his desk as if he sat on a throne, his mass of silver hair flowing into a deep curl that fell over his forehead. His wrinkled and tanned face didn't look older than seventy, though he was pushing eighty-two, only weeks away from celebrating his birthday.

"I have decided"—he paused and stood to his full height of six-four—"to have an auction."

"Oh?" Brock was the first to speak. Business he could deal with. Numbers he could process. Anything outside of that and he was going to need a drink.

Or ten.

"What would you like to auction?" He pulled out his iPhone and started a new note. "One of your houses? A few of your stallions? Titus Enterprises had a car auction last year that was extremely profitable."

Grandfather's face transformed into a wicked grin. "Maybe the other two should sit down."

"I think he means us," Bentley said under his breath, while Brant shot Brock a worried glance.

"I mean to auction..." Grandfather took a deep breath and raised his finger to point at them. "You."

Brant, the fastest of the bunch, jerked his chair to the right. "He's pointing at Bentley."

Bentley, never the more clever of the two, faked a

coughing fit and fell forward in a vain attempt to kick Brock's chair closer to the middle.

Rolling his eyes, Brock said, "He's pointing at all of us."

"Actually..." Grandfather's voice deepened. "I was pointing at you, Brock."

Brock had always done everything his grandfather asked. When he graduated from high school he'd been pressured into going to Harvard, because wouldn't it be so wonderful to go to the same school as his father? In honor of his memory?

Football, not basketball.

Chess, never checkers.

It was easier to keep the peace, to keep the smile on his grandfather's face. And because he'd do anything to keep the old man from more grief and sadness. He'd seen those emotions on his grandfather's tear-stained face when he'd told him his parents were dead. And ever since, Brock had said yes.

To Harvard.

To football.

To business school.

To taking over the company.

To the women his grandfather thought it best he be seen with.

But this? This was too far.

"Auction a person?" Brock tried to clarify. "Why?"

Immediately relieved they were no longer the focus of attention, both of his brothers had already directed their attention to their phones.

Not even paying attention.

Story of his life.

Grandfather limped around his massive desk. Guilt slammed into Brock's chest in perfect cadence with his increasingly erratic heartbeat.

With a curse, Grandfather grabbed his cane and wiped his brow with the back of his hand.

His eyes locked in on Brock. "Please."

Brock opened and closed his mouth.

"It's for a good cause." His grandfather didn't blink, just kept limping toward Brock until he had to crane his neck to stare up at the man he'd do anything for and had sacrificed everything for.

The final nail in the coffin was when the older man lowered his chin and humbled himself by uttering, "Do it for me."

Fuck.

CHAPTER TWO

Jane!" Esmeralda shouted. "Hurry up! You're taking way too long! We're going to be late to the party!"

"Maybe you should just go without me," Jane offered in what she hoped sounded like the perfect balance between depressed and content. She was exhausted from work—the last thing she needed was to babysit her sisters while they drank their body weight in vodka tonics.

Esmeralda's voice was loud and clear as day. "Jane! If you don't come who's going to fix my dress if something happens? Or watch over Essence; you know how she gets shy with guys! And you're the best wingman."

Jane clenched her teeth together. What girls actually had their own personal scamstress? Though Jane was really more of a jack-of-all-trades. And she was probably the worst wingman in history.

"You girls ready?" Essence asked.

"Jane! Hurry up! We don't want to arrive too late. It's rude, and he may not notice us."

Jane barely managed to hold in her gasp as Esmeralda

and Essence tumbled down the stairs and presented their dresses.

Esmeralda's tight black dress had just enough fabric to cover her surgically enhanced boobs and barely covered her ass.

Essence's was nearly the same style, except it was white.

One wore purple lipstick, the other had on gray; they were always on top of the newest trends even if the trends were stupid—and ugly.

At Fashion Week, they could get away with it.

In Phoenix they just looked like Bratz dolls.

"Yeah, I think"—Jane coughed into her hand—"he'll notice."

"Aw!" Esmeralda clapped her hands and flicked her dark hair over her shoulder. "That's so nice of you to say."

"Yes." Essence twirled a few times to show off her dress to full effect. "How sweet of you, Jane." With her eyebrows drawn in perfect arches, it was amazing she could even move them. "Jane, why aren't you dressed?"

"I think I'm just going to stay in," Jane answered, tugging at her dress self-consciously. It was the best one she could find at the last minute. She hadn't even known about the party until an hour ago, and the best she'd been able to scrounge up was a dress she'd borrowed for prom four years ago from one of her sisters.

She'd tried her best to make the black cocktail dress appealing.

But you couldn't fix plain.

And that's what it was.

What Jane was.

Plain Jane.

Her sisters gave her the same empty-eyed stare. Arguing with them was completely useless. When it was two against one, she never won, not that it mattered in the long run. Her sisters typically got their way regardless of what Jane said. They were pushy—but they were family.

Swallowing back her insecurity, she nodded quickly. "I'll just grab my purse, then."

Her sisters whispered under their breath, though Jane heard every mean word.

"Doesn't she have any other dresses? Poor Jane."

"Hey, I offered to help her shop and she said no."

Jane snorted quietly. She'd said no because Essence's shopping style was more like buy everything name brand and go into major credit card debt. At one point, Jane had had to use all of the money her parents had left them to pay off the bill.

"Poor Jane," Esmeralda said again.

She hated pity.

Especially theirs.

She would move out of the house if she thought her sisters wouldn't starve without her. Well, that and the fact that they were family and family stuck together. Even if family exhausted you, stressed you out, and made you want to scream at least ninety percent of the time.

"Let's go!" Esmeralda clapped her hands loudly and they were off…headed to a party that Jane didn't even care about.

CHAPTER THREE

Admit it. This is one of the best ideas he's had in years. The sheer publicity alone is priceless." Bentley tossed back his third drink of the night and slapped Brock on the back then showed him his phone. "Hey, look, you're trending."

"I will literally break your phone in half with my bare hands if you show me one more tweet with my name and 'auction' in the same sentence." Brock barely managed a polite nod in his grandfather's direction as he greeted people filling the large downtown nightclub for the annual Wellington party.

He tossed back a gulp of whiskey, watching as his grandfather winced in pain after a particularly hearty handshake from a journalist champing at the bit to get in on the story of the century. Brock grimaced. The press had gone wild when they'd caught wind of the auction.

CNN.

The World News.

The *New York Times*.

God, every damn newspaper in the universe thought

the auction was the most newsworthy thing they'd ever heard of.

One of the country's richest bachelors was allowing women to bid on him.

And allowing his grandfather to pick a winner from the bidders.

A winner that Brock would date—and even potentially marry. That was the worst part about the press: give them a crumb and they'd make a feast.

Brock sure as hell hadn't agreed to marry anyone.

One of the newspapers had hinted at a future Mrs. Brock Wellington.

And they'd taken it and run.

Date a stranger? He could do it. For the good of the company. For the press. And most importantly, for his family's reputation.

His grandfather had informed him that the board didn't trust his brothers to do anything right—hell, he agreed with that assessment—but Grandfather had also let it slip that they were starting to doubt Brock's ability to be a team player.

Because he wasn't a team player.

He kept to himself.

He made them hundreds of millions.

And they still weren't happy.

He stared into his empty glass.

"Do it for me and for your reputation in the company." *Grandfather had slapped him on the back. "You're a stick in the mud. Hell, have you ever even been to any of the company baseball games?"*

No, because he hated baseball.

"Fine," he'd whispered while his hands shook, with rage, with the need to hit something that would break.

The only silver lining was that the money that would be raised was going toward cancer research—one of his passions—so there was that, at least.

It was stupidity at its finest, but Brock had agreed to do it. Maybe because he was just as insane as his grandfather. Or, even worse, maybe because he was convinced he would never find love, nor cared to.

Because what his brothers said was true.

He *was* getting older.

And he'd yet to find a woman who wanted him for who he truly was.

Then again, did he even know himself anymore?

He'd allowed his protective love for his grandfather to decide how he would live his life, his future, his everything.

With a groan, he stole Bentley's drink straight from his hand and downed the entire thing.

"Cold feet?" Bentley teased.

"Go to hell," Brock fired back.

Bentley, as if sensing how pissed off Brock really was, quickly grabbed a flute of champagne from a passing waiter and shoved it into Brock's waiting hand. "Look on the bright side. Grandfather said if you married the girl he picked he'd give you the ranch as a wedding present, so there's that."

The ranch.

Their home.

Their safe haven after their parents had died, where their grandfather had pushed aside his own grief to give them the best life possible. Shit, he was screwed.

"Hell." Bentley let out a low whistle. "I'd even sleep with *her* for the ranch."

"Who?" Brock was too busy chugging champagne to notice anything except the constant beat of the techno music and bright red and white lights flashing around them. He really was getting old.

"Her." Bentley glanced at Brock's empty glass and handed him another from a passing waiter. "Her lipstick's purple."

"How…exciting." Brock actually flinched when the woman waved his way. "She looks like she should be poking her head out of a limousine screaming, 'What up, bitches?'"

"Oh God, I'd sell my soul to hear you say that exact same phrase in a high-pitched voice while you rip at your shirt. Please, it's just what this party needs."

Brock's lips twitched into an amused smile as he let out a bark of laughter. "What? And steal her moment?" He nodded at the woman, who had just started convulsing on the dance floor with a friend. "I think I'll let her have the spotlight."

Bentley grinned. "Imagine how they dance when they're drunk."

"Are you under the impression they're sober?"

"Either way. Bad choices."

"Oh, shit!" Brock choked on his third drink. "They just saw Grandfather."

Brock prayed to God that his grandfather wouldn't send the girls his way. Time slowed as Grandfather turned, made a face, and dismissed them.

Both Brock and Bentley exhaled loudly.

"Drink," Bentley encouraged. "Maybe the caterpillars will turn into butterflies. Whiskey encourages these things."

"I'm only taking this drink." He gripped it between his hands. How many had he just downed, anyway? Four? Five? "Because I see no other option. And believe me, I've done nothing but try to think of a way out of this."

Bentley crossed his arms. "What about no?"

"No." Brock shook his head vehemently.

"You have no problem saying it to me or Brant on a daily basis, yet the minute Grandfather turns his furry eyebrows in your direction you turn into this...robot."

Brock stiffened. "Robot? Hardly." He'd been called worse. But that was beside the point.

His brothers didn't get it; they didn't understand the power behind a simple word, and how it was Brock's fault that their parents were dead in the first place.

Because the first time he'd said that word had been after an argument with his father.

No, he'd said. *No. No. No.*

The next day both of his parents were dead.

His hands shook with the memory, as if reliving it all over again.

"All right, then. So you said yes because you want to settle down? With a woman of Grandfather's choosing?" Bentley chuckled. "The last woman he sent your way had the longest fingernails I'd ever seen." He shuddered. "I had at least three nightmares, all of them including her nails impaling my...well, let's just say I woke up in a cold sweat."

Brock shrugged, and his stomach warmed as the whiskey finally began to take effect. "She wasn't so bad."

"Her name was Pearl."

Brock shifted uncomfortably on his feet while Bentley gave him a pointed stare. "Just march up to him and say 'thanks for the concern, but I nominate Brant as tribute.'"

Smirking, Brock glanced across the room just in time to see Brant press some random woman against the wall and kiss down her neck. "He seems occupied."

"When is he *not* occupied? Though the night is a bit young for him to start his sexual prowl."

"True."

The music got louder, seeming to rise along with Brock's discomfort. "Maybe, one more drink, and then..."

Bentley tried to hand him yet another drink, this time, champagne. Brock refused it. "And then, you and grandfather talk."

"Yes." Brock frowned. "I mean no."

"Grow a pair of balls, brother. Your choice is either man up..." He pointed to the two girls dancing with mindless abandon on the floor. The girl in the black dress bent over, giving them a hellish view of her thong. Both Brock and Bentley shuddered and looked away. "Or it's possible that the vision before you could be your future."

"I'll talk to him," he lied.

"Good man." Bentley sighed. "Now that my single good deed of the year is done, I'm off to find the first woman to catch my eye, one who possesses all her teeth and is of sound mind. I'm not picky; I just need sex."

"Shocking that you get so much ass with that attitude."

"That hurts." Bentley tapped his chest. "Right here." And then he smirked. "But not as much as right here." He grabbed his crotch with a jerk, then laughed and walked off.

Watching Bentley strut across the room like a rooster, Brock tightened his hold on his glass. Both of his brothers were free.

While he lived in a prison of his own making. With gold bars. And a mirror where his grandfather stared back at him

He returned his attention to his grandfather and the group of people who had crowded around him. His vision was starting to blur, but only because of the lights. He could easily hold more alcohol than most.

Then, in a sudden flurry of screaming, a woman was pushed onto the dance floor right into the two crazy women with even crazier lipstick.

A catfight broke out as one of the women ripped at the newcomer's dress almost hard enough to pull the entire thing off and leave her flashing half the club. The girl pressed her hands to her chest while the woman standing on her other side tugged at the girl's hair.

The hell?

How drunk were they?

He started toward the dance floor to pull them apart when suddenly the crowd parted.

The girl glanced up at him with wide eyes.

He stopped walking.

Breathing.

It wasn't her face...her lips...It wasn't the way her body looked poured into her tight black dress.

No, it was her eyes.

As if she was begging for someone to save her.

Protectiveness slammed into him and he shoved his body through the remaining people watching the scene, and picked the girl up into his arms.

CHAPTER FOUR

Jane was pressed so tightly against the wall she would have sworn her body was starting to blend into the wallpaper. Most people didn't give her a second glance. Then again, she wouldn't give herself a second glance either.

Women with fake boobs and injected lips mocked her while rich men in three-piece suits completely ignored her.

She self-consciously tugged at hem of the short black dress. In a last-ditch effort to modernize the dress, or at least add a bit of spice, she'd grabbed her mother's long pearls, wrapped them around her neck twice and called it good.

But the minute they'd arrived at the party she'd wanted to disappear. Her sisters were already semi-drunk, thanks to the vodka they'd had in the car. Against Jane's protests they'd taken shots while she drove. And then she'd paid for parking only to hear them whine that she had parked too far away.

They'd been here for twenty minutes and already she wanted to leave, or at least sit down, but most of the available space was taken by couples talking, eating...kissing.

She was surrounded by the beautiful and rich.

The only reason her sisters had even been invited was because they were complete and total social climbers, and had managed to gain an invitation from a friend who was an heiress to some french fry company.

A waiter passed by with champagne.

She grabbed a glass and downed the entire thing. The alcohol didn't help her nerves, but at least the bubbles semi-calmed her stomach.

Her sweaty feet slid in her too-big red pumps as she pressed harder against the wall to alleviate the ache in her toes.

The music shifted to a loud techno song as the lights went from red to a bright white, and with a gasp she covered her eyes and then blinked a few times to clear her line of vision.

The jumbled sweaty bodies moved aside as the music changed to a slow song. There was just enough of a break for her to see across the room.

"Oh." It was all she could utter, really the only word she was capable of as her breathing picked up. Without thinking, she grabbed another glass of champagne from a passing waiter, suddenly awkward. What was she supposed to do with her hands?

Thick wavy auburn hair fell in disarray over his forehead. It was lush, shiny, perfect. Were guys born with hair like that? Or was his somehow chemically engineered? His full lips pressed together in a secret smile as the equally handsome man next to him said something, then erupted in laughter.

The first man stiffened, then shook his head. His broad shoulders seemed to grow tight as a drum. A slight tic in his jaw was the only clue that he was irritated or maybe outright angry.

And then his shoulders slumped as he was handed another drink and then another.

Nervous. He must be nervous. But what could a man like that possibly have to be nervous about?

He easily towered over most of the men in attendance. Suddenly his posture changed, then he smiled.

Jane felt her mouth drop open in shock.

Dazzling.

He was...like a duke or a lord or a prince from a storybook. Clearly, she read too many romance novels, but his entire presence demanded attention; screamed authority, importance, and sex. Lots and lots of sex.

Yes, his virility was a tangible thing, as if she could reach out and grasp it with her fingertips.

"What are you doing?" Esmeralda yelled in her right ear, interrupting her blatant sexual fantasy about a complete stranger. Great. That's what her life had come to. And sadly? It was the most fun she'd had all night.

Jane turned to Esmeralda, prayed for patience, and answered. "Sorry, I was just thinking."

"You're so boring." Esmeralda rolled her eyes. "No wonder you got dumped."

Another fun fact? Esmeralda was mean when she was drunk.

The reminder of the breakup burned like acid.

It had been a year ago, not that it mattered. It still hurt that the last guy she'd dated had told her that although she was cute, she wasn't really doing it for him anymore.

Right. Doing it.

Maybe that was because she hadn't done anything for him or *with* him, and he found that lacking. But they'd only dated for a few weeks. Did normal girls do that? Put out after a few weeks? Apparently.

She wasn't normal.

But if that was normal, maybe she was better off being strange.

"Jane, are you even listening to me?" Esmeralda whined. "Essence needs you to dance next to her for a bit. I'm tired and tipsy. I want to sit. Plus your dress blends in enough that it won't take attention away from her."

No way. What? What had she just said?

Jane wrapped her arms around her middle. "I'm sorry, what?"

Without warning, Esmeralda grabbed Jane's hand and jerked her toward the dance floor, causing Jane to lose her footing and crash directly into Esmeralda's back. Then, with a ricochet-like effect, she slammed back into Essence.

Jane opened her mouth to shout out an apology, but Esmeralda was already too drunk to listen to reason. With determination in her eyes, she reached for the pearls at Jane's neck but grabbed the fabric of the dress instead.

Her poorly sewn dress ripped instantly, causing the fabric to slink past her strapless bra. A diagonal slit split up her thigh almost all the way to her hip. In an effort to cover herself, she took a step and tripped, thanks to her clunky shoes.

And then she fell to the floor.

Hard.

Her sisters watched in horror—but neither of them offered a hand. They were probably kicking themselves for forcing her to come. Esmeralda leaned over but missed Jane's shoulder by a mile, grabbing her hair and giving it a tug, which only made Jane wince harder.

Both sisters were completely tanked.

And she was less than two minutes away from being trampled by the other sweaty bodies around her.

She glanced up.

And into the eyes of the man she'd just been lusting after.

Oh God, the humiliation was complete.

That one glance told her he'd seen it all. She swallowed back the thickness building in her throat. Of course the only time he'd notice her would be when she'd ripped her dress and nearly took out a few guests on her way down to the dance floor.

The crowd gathered around her.

And the sexy man disappeared—probably off in search of a girl with perfect hair, perfect teeth, perfect clothes.

She *really* should have stayed home.

Tears filled her eyes as a heel pressed into her right hand. With a jerk she tugged her hand free, struggling to get up to stand on her wobbly feet, when suddenly she was pulled to a standing position and then swept up in strong arms.

Jane's eyes were still so blurry from unshed tears she couldn't make out the man's face as he carried her out of the crowd.

He smelled like heaven.

She fought the insane urge to press her face against his chest and just... close her eyes.

Because he felt safe.

Pathetic, when a stranger's arms provided more safety than her own family. And yet he felt... right.

In a world where things for the past ten years had felt so wrong.

He felt right.

Maybe she'd had too much champagne.

"Are you all right?" he whispered in a deep voice with a hint of a southern drawl. He'd brought her into a private room where the music wasn't quite so deafening.

He set her on one of the black leather couches and kicked

the door shut with his foot, muffling the music on the other side.

Blinking, Jane glanced up and gawked, like a starry-eyed teenager. He was the same man she'd seen earlier, the one she'd been captivated by. "Yes."

"Yes?" He looked confused. His amazing eyebrows drew together, and a small line creased the center of his forehead. Even the line was gorgeous, just as gorgeous as the rest of him.

His thickly muscled body screamed power. Her hands slid down the front of his chest. Even his shirt was smooth. She didn't realize she'd been basically petting him until his muscles tensed beneath her palm. Oh crap.

"I mean, yes, I'm fine." She tried to stand then fell back down; her stupid heel was broken. "Or I was fine, until I got trampled."

The line in his forehead deepened. "You're not hurt, are you?"

Jane shook her head then pressed her hand to her chest and gasped out, "My pearls!"

"Wait here." He held out his hands. "I'll get the necklace, I'm sure it's where you fell and—"

"No." Jane slumped, defeated. "They broke off when my sis—" She corrected herself, not wanting to claim the crazies in the other room. "They broke apart when I fell."

The man sighed loudly and ran his fingers through his perfect hair. "I'll talk to the club manager and see if anyone turns them in."

It was on the tip of her tongue to give him all the many reasons why they were irreplaceable, but instead she settled with, "That's really not necessary. It's not your fault I was a victim of the techno craze."

His upper lip curled. "I hate techno."

"Me too."

"Is there something I can do? Anything? You promise you aren't hurt?"

"Careful or you're going to have me believe you got me trampled on purpose in order to trap me in a private room," she joked as a smile tugged at her lips.

"Had I known you were willing, I wouldn't have had to go to such extremes to orchestrate it."

He appeared stunned by his own answer.

Her breath hitched. Was he flirting with her?

His crystal blue eyes twinkled with amusement.

"So..." Her voice was hoarse, like an old woman's. *Great.* "I should probably get back to the party." Why did she need to go back again? All the reasons seemed to disappear as he maneuvered around the couch and popped a bottle of champagne that had been chilling in a nearby crystal bucket.

"Why don't you and I have a drink first?" He peered around the table. "I'll need to send for some shoes. It's the least I can do." His gaze heated. "Shoes are appropriate to purchase for a stranger. A dress, I'm afraid..." The corners of his mouth tilted into a sultry smile as his eyes slowly raked over the scraps of fabric barely covering her breasts. "Not so much."

Did people do that these days? Just send for shoes? Who was this guy? "Really, it's not necessary. I'll just stick to the shadows so I don't scare anyone with my limp and I'll be okay." She sounded more confident than she felt, and her lower lip trembled a bit. Next time she was going to hold her ground, stay home, read a book, and be plain boring Jane. This wasn't her scene. Not by a long shot.

He leaned in close, so close she could smell his aftershave again. "A woman like you doesn't belong in the shadows."

Uncomfortable, she tried to make light of the situation again. "Wow, a hero and good with words. I bet you're just a regular handful, aren't you?"

"Me?" He laughed as if the thought was the funniest thing he'd ever heard. "No, that would be my twin brothers. They're the handfuls. I'm..." He seemed to think about it. "Just Brock."

"Well, Just Brock..." Jane held out her hand. "I'm Just Jane."

His hand completely engulfed hers as their palms pressed against one another. He was so warm. And big.

Huge.

Huge hands. That meant something, right?

Crap, she was still shaking his hand, and he was grinning at her as if it was the funniest thing that had ever happened to him. And he was looking at her. At her eyes, not at the fact that she was half-naked on a couch, with a broken shoe.

With a jerk, she pulled her hand back and nervously reached to tuck a stray piece of hair behind her ear.

"So, Brock." Jane looked down at his shoes. That was safe. Shoes. Nothing sexy about a man's feet, right? Except his were inside shoes that she ventured probably cost more than she'd ever see in a lifetime. "About those shoes."

"Shoes." He repeated the word and then quickly stood. "Right, just wait here."

"But, you don't even know my size!"

His eyes heated as he eyed her up and down. "Would it be too cheesy if I said perfect?"

"Perfect?" she repeated like an idiot. "I don't think I understand."

"The perfect size." His half-lidded gaze was causing her stomach to do flip-flops while she tried to keep a calm demeanor.

With a smile he knelt down and touched her foot.

Touched it.

And then gazed up at her and said, "Eight? Am I close?"

"Eight." She nearly stuttered. "Eight and a half."

With a nod, he stood and disappeared, giving her the breathing room she absolutely needed, only to reappear a few seconds later.

Without shoes.

She frowned; then again, what had she expected? That he'd bang some plastic Barbie over the head with his cell phone, steal her shoes, and then toss them to Jane?

Brock studied her. "Your shoes should be here within the next fifteen minutes. I just sent my degenerate brother across the street. Saks is still open. The night is young."

Saks?

Shoes from *Saks*?

She'd never owned anything from Saks. Ever. But she knew the store; didn't every woman? Still, the most expensive thing she'd ever owned had been the pearls.

"That's really"—she waved her hand in the air and stood—"not necessary. You can tell him that—"

Brock reached for her hand and lightly tugged her back. "Sit. It *is* necessary. And although I typically wait until the third date to buy a woman gifts, I think your nearly getting trampled allows me to break that rule."

Still tense, Jane nodded and took a shaky look around the small, private room.

"To new shoes?" Brock grabbed his drink and lifted it in the air toward her.

She lifted her glass and clinked it against his then took a small sip. The champagne was pink and sweet, with a tart aftertaste. "It's good."

"You sound surprised." Brock's lips lifted in a smile.

She scrunched up her nose. "I'm not much of a drinker, and I typically don't like drinks that are the same color as my underwear."

The minute the words were out of her mouth, she froze, barely managing to suppress the urge to clap a hand over her mouth. She wanted someone to run her over with a car.

With a choke, Brock nearly spit out the sip he'd just taken. Face flushed, he stared her down and then whispered, "You're making me regret my decision to send out for boring black shoes."

"I didn't...I mean, pink is fine." *Stop talking, stop talking.* "Not all of my underwear is pink. I have black, too."

Brock's lips parted with a greedy exhale, and he downed the rest of his drink. "Oh?"

Hell in a handbasket.

Why was she giving him a rundown of her lingerie drawer? As if he were a naughty Santa with a checklist in front of him, putting down little marks on the little boxes that read "red lacy thong"? Check. "Black boyshorts"? Double check.

"I'm more of a boxer brief sort of guy," he said smoothly, bringing her back to the present.

"Huh?"

"Too far?" He chuckled. "I figured if I knew the color of yours...I should at least show you mine." He leaned forward.

Had he said *show*?

Just how drunk was he? Maybe that was the reason his eyes were zeroing in on her mouth. He blinked, and then seemed to sway a bit.

Was he okay? And why was he still staring at her mouth? Did she have something on her face?

Self-consciously, she pressed her fingertips to her lips

only to have him suck in a breath and lift his right hand from his thigh as if wanting to touch the place where her fingers had just been.

"Got the shoes!" a male voice yelled as Jane jerked away from Brock.

What had just happened? And how had enough time passed for someone to find and buy her shoes? "Holy shit, you're hot."

She recognized the man from before. He was about an inch shorter than Brock, but had the same perfect auburn hair. "I'm Bentley, and since this one's about to get married, I feel like it's only fair to let you know that out of the two of us, I'm the single, available one, who's also—lucky for you—been given a higher rating in the sack."

Married?

He was getting married?

And hitting on her?

Or was she hitting on him? After all, she was the one who'd mentioned underwear. Ugh, she wanted to crawl under the table and die.

CHAPTER FIVE

Bentley!" Brock barked and shook his head.

"What?" Bentley shrugged then smoothly walked over to Jane and pulled out a box of black high-heeled pumps in a size eight and a half. "Your foot, milady?"

Brock rolled his eyes. "Give it a rest, Bentley. She can put on her own damn shoes."

Bentley completely ignored him. "I love a woman's foot." He grabbed Jane's broken shoe and tossed it to the side while his hands danced along the arch of her foot. His fingertips danced along her skin. Seduction by foot rub? That was new.

"It's sexy, the arch." He leaned over her, his lips parting just enough to give her the impression he was thinking about kissing her. "The curve of a woman's foot reminds me of her body . . . see? Sexy." He slid the shoe on a very terrified looking Jane and stood. "Perfect fit."

Jane's mouth opened then closed as a rosy flush crept over her face. "Th-thank you."

"I bought you my favorite brand."

Her eyebrows arched. How did he know about Manolo Blahnik? "Oh." And then she nodded and said loudly, "Ohhhh! That makes sense!"

Bentley's eyes narrowed. "Me buying women's shoes?"

"You wearing them," she explained. "That's great. I mean, good for you. I'm sorry I'm so awkward at things like this, but it's good you're...you know..." She bobbed her head and sputtered. "Out and...comfortable with it."

"Out?" Bentley repeated. "I'm confused."

"Of the closet," she said slowly then saw the scowl on Bentley's face. "Or maybe you just like to dress like a woman?" She straightened her shoulders and tried again. "In either case, congratulations on your choice to wear women's clothing!"

Brock about died laughing as Bentley's horrified expression went from stunned to genuine confusion.

"You heard her." Brock held his laughter in check. "Congratulations, brother. I'll take care of the press release: Bachelor Playboy Bentley Wellington and his private women's shoe collection."

Bentley let out a strangled laugh. "Yes, and while we're at it why don't we remind the press that the clock is ticking on that auction of yours? Hmm?"

"Auction?" Jane asked.

"Don't." Brock shook his head. "You don't want to know."

"But she probably already does," Bentley pointed out. "Unless she doesn't read the news...?"

They both stared at her, waiting for an answer.

"I, uh..." She ducked her head, blushing again. "I read books."

"How pure." Bentley smiled and sat down next to her. "And just so we're clear." He leaned in as though he was going to kiss her. "My bat only swings one way...and I can assure you, every time I get thrown a pitch, I hit it out of the park."

"Incredible," Brock muttered. "I've never seen you try so hard—especially with a woman clearly not interested in what you're offering." Brock gripped his brother by the shoulders, aimed him toward the door, and gave a hard shove. "Go."

Bentley cursed Brock the entire way.

Brock turned back to apologize to Jane but she was already trying to sneak past him, both of her hands clutching her dress so it wouldn't fall down.

What the hell?

Logic told him to let her go, but her eyes...damn those eyes, he wanted her to stay. "Enjoy the shoes." He pushed his lips into what he hoped resembled a smile and took a step back. The right thing always won out with Brock. God, he hated himself sometimes. "Jane."

She turned quickly and he had to suppress a groan. Her legs went on for days in those shoes, damn it.

"Thanks again." She smiled self-consciously, but at least it was a real smile. "For the save." She gave him another awkward smile as she pointed behind her. "Out there."

"Any time," he murmured as she disappeared back into the crowded club.

With a sigh, he fell back against the couch and stared up at the ceiling. The best part of his night so far had been spent with a woman who had no clue who he was.

And he'd loved it.

He glanced down at the floor. A small smile spread across his lips.

Jane had left her old shoes.

Curiosity had him picking up the worn shoes. The brand on the inside was worn away from use.

What did he expect to find? Her name and address written inside?

Every cell in his body was telling him he needed to see Jane again. To find out if the connection he'd felt with her was real.

She'd made him laugh.

And engage.

He'd wanted to have an actual conversation that had nothing to do with his money, his brothers, the auction, or his grandfather.

It had been nice.

She had been nice.

And now she was gone.

CHAPTER SIX

Jane!"

Jane pulled her pillow over her face, and for one brief moment wondered if it would be possible to suffocate herself. Not that she was suicidal, but Mondays with her sisters? They always made her violent.

"Jane!" Esmeralda screamed at the top of her lungs. "It's seven! I'm going to be late for work! I'm starving!"

God forbid her sister pour her own coffee.

Grumbling, Jane crawled out of bed, tossed on a ratty sweatshirt, and ran down the stairs just in time to get shoved against the wall as Essence moved breezily past her in a cloud of cloying perfume and cigarette smoke.

Both of her sisters sat at the table expectantly, checking their phones.

"Eggs okay?" Jane asked with fake cheer as she made her way over to the fridge.

Neither of her sisters answered.

Her parents had hated Mondays—and early on had established a family tradition by starting the week with a

home-cooked breakfast. Jane had kept the tradition alive—
long after she suspected that she was the only one who
cared about the tradition.

And then one Monday she'd poured them all cereal,
thinking she was too tired to keep up the tradition no one
else seemed to care about. Her sisters cried.

It was horrible.

Manipulative, yes.

But also horrible.

Everyone mourned in their own way; it didn't matter
that their dad had been gone a few years already, and their
mother longer. It was still hard to be without them. Sometimes it was the only thing Jane thought she had in common
with her sisters—their sadness over the loss of their parents.

Sighing, she quickly made the eggs and fried some turkey
bacon.

"Finally," Essence grumbled, swiping the bacon off the
plate. Her bleached hair was pulled into a knot on top of her
head. "Can you stop off at the dry cleaners and pick up my
clothes?" She slid a receipt across the table.

Jane had to resist the urge to slap her sister's hand with
the spatula.

"You know…" Jane said as she pulled out a chair. It
squeaked across the wood floor, causing both sisters' heads
to bob up. "I've been thinking, about the whole cooking and
errands thing. Why don't we take turns? I'm swamped with
work." Okay, that was a lie; she wasn't exactly swamped.
More like overwhelmed.

Both girls were silent and then Essence reached across
the table and grabbed her hand. "I'm sorry I yelled at you."

Jane's heart clenched.

"Yeah," Esmeralda said. "It's just, you're so good at those
things, and nobody taught us how to cook. We'd probably

starve without you. Besides, you're in that cleaning van all day zipping around town so it's easier for you to run errands. We're stuck in an office building all day."

"True," Jane admitted, "but—"

"Promise we'll think about it." Essence squeezed Jane's hand one last time then pulled away. "But, Jane?"

Oh no.

Essence's eyes filled with tears. "You cook just like Mom used to. And you're so good at it."

The room fell into a tense silence.

The silence made Jane's heart ache with memories of laughter and food fights.

No.

At some point she had to have her own life, away from taking care of her sisters twenty-four seven.

"Yes, but—"

"So it's settled." Essence stood and clapped her hands. "You'll keep helping us around the house! And cooking!" Her lower lip jutted out. "It makes us feel like a family again. Besides, it's what you do for a job anyway. I mean, you own your own cleaning company. How is this different?"

And there it was.

The guilt.

The other reason Jane stayed.

She had sworn to her father that she'd keep the family together at all costs.

"Family," he had said between coughs, *"is all we have in this world. I was never a rich man when it came to material possessions."* Another coughing fit had ensued as Jane tried to hold back the sting of tears. *"But, my Jane, I've always had you."* His eyes were blurred with tears. *"Your sisters don't have your same heart, Jane, and they won't deal with this like you will. I need you to keep them strong. You're the*

youngest but you've always taken care of them. Don't let the family fall apart."

He'd died the next day.

Lung cancer.

Cancer had stolen both of her parents.

Jane stood and started clearing their plates while her sisters chattered endlessly about work.

It was hard to believe that they were both successful lawyers. On the other hand, maybe that was why they were so good at arguing with her, wearing her down, making her feel small.

The front door slammed and Jane looked up.

Would it kill her sisters to say good-bye?

With a sigh, she ate the leftover eggs in three bites, dumped the dishes into the sink, and ran back up the stairs to her room to put on her uniform.

Torn jeans and a white T-shirt.

She never deviated from it. She'd ruined way too many of her favorite shirts because of multiple bleach accidents.

Humming, she opened the curtains to her small room and smiled. Today would be a good one. She wouldn't let the rocky start ruin the rest of the day.

After all, last night had started out terrible. But it had ended on a good note. She touched her lips. Brock hadn't kissed her, but she could imagine what his kiss would feel like all the same. Brock was so out of her league it was laughable, but he'd treated her like an equal, something she wasn't used to even in her own family.

Pushing that depressing thought away, she turned from the window to grab her tennis shoes, only to stumble over a pair of heels that cost more than she made in a week.

They were even prettier in the daylight.

The soft leather glistened.

A small smile formed as she picked up one of the shoes and examined it. These were the kind of shoes that made her feel like she could click the heels together and she'd end up with a different life.

A life where her boyfriend didn't dump her because she was too boring.

A life where her sisters respected her.

A life where she didn't live with the constant nagging guilt of keeping the family together.

A life where men like Brock asked women like her on a date.

She slipped her right foot into the pump and stood on one leg, then slid her left foot in the remaining shoe.

Immediately she was reminded of his smile, his hard muscled body as it pressed against hers.

Jane clicked her heels together and whispered, "I wish..." Her eyes filled with tears. "I want..." She stumbled out of the shoes and stared down at her naked feet.

"I just want more than this," she finished, looking around the room she'd been forced into since both of her sisters had claimed the bigger rooms in the house.

And then her gaze fell on her own reflection in the mirror. Straightening her shoulders, she stared herself down. There were people worse off than she was. She was just being emotional.

Tears blurred her vision—this reaction was so unlike her.

Maybe it was the fact that right above the shoes was a pile of bills that she knew she'd have to pay. Bills that her sisters didn't feel it was their responsibility to help out with.

She kicked one of the heels and crossed her arms—actually, her reaction made perfect sense. Because for one fleeting moment she'd been something more than the Jane who cleaned office buildings and bailed her sisters out of shopping debt.

She'd felt beautiful.

Powerful.

How pathetic, that all it took was a well-dressed man with a gorgeous smile and a pair of shoes, to completely disarm her.

And make her want things that girls like her would never get.

Those shoes were a catalyst.

Those shoes were temptation.

Those shoes were the devil.

CHAPTER SEVEN

Brock woke up with a pounding headache and a shoe in bed with him.

A woman's shoe.

Someone grunted from across the room.

He wasn't alone.

Pasting on a carefully blank expression, he looked around. Shit, had he slept with Cinderella?

God, that smile.

Those hips.

Those legs.

He squeezed the shoe tighter between his hands as lust hit him hard and fast; even with the hangover from hell, he could still see a clear picture of Jane in his head.

"Uhhhhh." The groaning was coming from the bathroom. Slowly, so as not to puke all over the pristine wood floor, he threw the white duvet off his legs and walked to the tune of a jackhammer between his temples...all the way to the bathroom.

A foot poked out through the half-open door.

Definitely not a size eight and a half.

Or feminine.

He kicked at the limb to get the door fully open and the groan turned into cursing. Pushing at the door, he saw Bentley hugging the toilet like a new best friend.

"Rough night?" Brock smirked like the complete bastard he was as Bentley lifted a middle finger in the air and kept it there. He'd tire out, eventually.

Another grunt sounded from somewhere else in the large master bathroom.

Brock stepped around the corner. Brant was sprawled in the bathtub, holding a fluffy white towel close to his chest.

Where was a whistle when Brock needed one? Or a car alarm? Air horn? There had to be an app for that.

Brant opened one eye, then two. "Sleeping Beauty awakes." Shirtless, he stood up on wobbly legs, then stepped out of the claw-foot tub and scratched his naked stomach. "That was a rough one."

"The shots?" Brock guessed, making his way over to the sink to brush his teeth and find some aspirin.

"The hookers," Brant said quickly, causing Brock to inhale an unhealthy amount of toothpaste before nearly choking to death. "Kidding."

Brock choked even harder. "Fuck off."

"Seeing you lose your shit at seven a.m. is one of my favorite things."

"You both smell like shit." And Brock felt like it. "Third drawer down for the unopened toothbrushes." A drawer closed with a thud, and Brock winced. "Stop slamming things!"

Bentley smiled at him in the mirror, and slammed two more drawers before unwrapping a toothbrush. "You know what's sadder than the fact that you can't hold your liquor?"

Brock spat into the sink then wiped his face with his arm. "Twelve shots within ninety minutes is impressive."

Had it been twelve?

Ten?

Did it matter?

After chasing and losing Cinderella in the crowd he'd completely lost his shit, and drank the frustration away. Why the hell hadn't she stayed at the party?

Why did he care?

Bentley completely ignored him and lifted his toothbrush into the air. Light flashed off plastic the color of blood. "This, this is sad, this right here."

Brant moved to Brock's left and splashed his face with water. "Red toothbrushes?"

"Nope." Bentley spread toothpaste across the bristles. "It's sad you don't need these because you have a new woman here every night."

Brock rolled his eyes. Right, because he had time for that.

"What?" Bentley smirked, toothpaste foaming out of his mouth. "You're a sad lonely bastard. No wonder Grandfather thinks he needs to pick out a willing woman and slap the Wellington name across her forehead."

Brant nodded his agreement.

"Remind me why you're both here? You have your own apartments. Nice penthouses full of STDs and whores."

"Aw!" Bentley laughed. "You restocked for us? You're such a good brother."

Patience. Patience. Patience. Brock located a bottle of aspirin and popped two in his mouth then handed it over to Brent, who was already greedily eyeing the white bottle.

"You invited us back here to keep a watchful eye." Bentley used his fingers to make air quotes and then shrugged. "But let's be honest: you were just as tanked after

Cinderella left with no trace as to her name or social security number."

Brock went over to the shower and turned it on. "I wasn't upset. I was just…curious."

All talking ceased.

Brock turned to see his brothers grinning at him like he'd just announced he was going to get a tiger like Mike Tyson and call it Bitch.

"What?" he growled, and then winced when growling set off another jolt of lightning through his brain.

"You cursed last night," Bentley pointed out. "A lot."

"I was drunk," Brock said, irritated to find himself on the defensive.

"Nope." God, he wanted to punch the smug grin from Brant's face. "That's a lie…you curse when you're either really upset or…" He shared a look with Bentley. "When you want something you can't have, which isn't often."

"Bullshit!" Brock yelled. And winced again as blood surged in his head.

Bentley held up his hands. "And we rest our case."

"I'm too tired for this."

Bentley sidestepped Brock then made a beeline for the shower.

"Like hell!" Brock shoved his brother out of the way. "When I'm done showering I want you out of my apartment." He pulled his shirt over his head and dropped it onto the floor as he got into the shower.

"But who's going to make us breakfast?" came Bentley's voice.

"Go!"

Silence ensued and then Brant appeared next to the shower door. He was holding up a black shoe. *Shit*. "So either you have something you want to tell us…or you slept with a woman's shoe last night. Where's the rest of her?"

Groaning, Brock let the hot water singe his back as he leaned against the tile and exhaled roughly. "It's the girl Bentley was talking about... I bought her shoes. Hers broke."

"You do realize that's kind of a weird thing to do for a complete stranger, right? You don't just buy someone expensive shoes after theirs break, especially not a woman. Buying clothes, even in a relationship, usually means commitment."

"How do you know they were expensive?" he asked.

"Weren't they?"

"Eight hundred and fifty," Bentley shouted from the bedroom.

Brant whistled and returned his attention to Brock.

"Go away," Brock grumbled. "Both of you."

"Hmmm." That was Brant's only response, and then there was blessed silence as Brock breathed in the steam from the shower.

She was just a woman. A really pretty, vibrant, girl-next-door, attractive woman.

With seven freckles.

Damn it.

Small straight white teeth.

An overly plump top lip.

"Damn, damn, damn." Brock slammed his hands against the tiled wall.

The reminder of the auction he'd agreed to was like a brick in his stomach, a heavy, horrible brick of guilt.

Today he and Grandfather would go over all of the fine print. A list of potential women and rich families would be compiled based on past donations to Wellington charitable causes.

From that list, Brock knew his grandfather would pick his

favorites, the ones that "made sense," just like Harvard had made sense, and football, and wearing three-piece suits at twenty.

Because at the end of the day that was all that mattered. Keeping his grandfather happy.

The only thing that didn't make sense to Brock was why they even needed this auction. It was a simple question— but one that he was too scared shitless to actually ask. What was the real reason behind the auction? Did they really need good press that desperately?

When he turned off the shower, he stepped over the shoe—the elephant in the room.

A giant elephant, reminding him he needed to start living life for himself.

He stared back down at the shoe, and a smile lifted the corners of his mouth. The girl from last night...he knew her name, and that was a start. How hard would it be to find out who she really was? Maybe he'd luck out and she'd be from one of the wealthy families donating to the cause.

Right. And maybe he'd get struck by lightning.

But if she wasn't part of the auction what would be the point?

Because even as his heart thumped *yes, yes, yes* when he thought about pursuing her—logic screamed no.

Maybe if he was to just randomly bump into her, joke about having her old shoes?

Good pick-up line.

Solid.

She'd be eating out of the palm of his hand.

With another groan he quickly got ready to go to the office. Images of a woman with brown eyes and plump lips invaded his thoughts the entire time.

CHAPTER EIGHT

A sense of dread washed over Brock as he entered his grandfather's office.

And it wasn't because his grandfather was waiting to seal his fate without a word of argument from Brock.

No, hell had started the minute he got out of his car and made his way into the lobby of the Wellington building, and was fucking mauled by enough reporters to cover a presidential nomination. Democratic *and* Republican.

"Shit." There had been no sidestepping, no avoiding. So he did what he always did, what he'd been trained to do.

What he hated.

He smiled, shook hands, and made his way through the crowd with the excuse of being late for an important meeting with his grandfather.

"Is it true?" One reporter asked, shoving a microphone in his face.

"Is what true?" he asked through clenched teeth. And why the hell was he even engaging?

The reporter wore red lipstick and a tight black pantsuit.

She grinned widely as more microphones were thrust into his face.

"The marriage."

Two words.

"Marriage?" He spat the word. "There will be no marriage."

The reporter gave him a confused look. "So it's not true that your grandfather has agreed to choose a suitable wife for the Wellington Dynasty from one of the many women who attempt to purchase you at the auction?"

That was a rumor the press had started buzzing about ever since they'd learned of the auction. There was no way in hell his grandfather would take it that far.

"No more questions," he barked, jabbing the elevator button harder than necessary. Thank God the doors opened and closed on the waiting crowd just in time for him to have a full-fledged panic attack as the elevator surged to the top floor.

Marriage.

No.

He wouldn't.

His grandfather wasn't that insane.

Was he?

Talk about fucking with Brock's life. That would be—a prickling sensation ran down his neck and arms.

That would be exactly like something his grandfather would do.

The elevator doors opened.

"Hi, Brock. I'll just tell him you're here," Mrs. Everly began, but the smile dropped from her face the moment she got a good look at Brock.

"No need. I'm going in." He slammed his hands against the large wood doors as he pushed into his grandfather's office.

As usual, Grandfather was sitting behind his desk, a newspaper propped up in front of him.

Grandfather was a creature of habit.

Brock's stomach clenched with anger.

If he wasn't careful, his future was staring right at him.

And it looked bleak.

Lonely.

Hell, it looked like marriage to a woman of his grandfather's choosing.

"Brock!" Grandfather placed his weathered hand on the mahogany desk and stood on shaky knees. "Sit, sit!"

"I think I'll stand," he said through clenched teeth.

"Suit yourself." Grandfather shrugged.

"No."

"Pardon?" Grandfather's eyebrows furrowed as he moved around the desk and crossed his arms. "What was that, son?"

"I. Won't. Do. It." Brock's body shook. With rage. With dread. He knew the ramifications of saying no, but he couldn't control the words coming out of his mouth.

His grandfather held out his hands as if to tell Brock to settle down. "Brock, you seem upset—"

"I'm beyond upset!" Brock took a step backward. "Find someone else. Though God knows why you think this is good publicity. We get enough attention from the twins, who seem to land themselves in every newspaper and magazine in the country."

Grandfather suddenly went pale; his hand went to his chest and then with a strangled gasp, he collapsed.

*　*　*

Three hours after Brock thought he'd nearly killed his grandfather by actually standing up for himself he was still in the office.

The EMTs were long gone.

Grandfather was going to be fine.

An anxiety attack.

From stress.

"What were you discussing when he collapsed?" the first EMT asked.

Brock had felt too sick to answer; he just shook his head and asked in a strangled voice. "Is he going to make it?"

"His heart's just fine." The other EMT was giving Grandfather oxygen, or at least trying to. Grandfather was fighting him every step of the way, saying he had just felt a tightening in his chest and then hot all over.

And now they were back to square one.

What should have been a brief meeting had turned into one of the scariest moments of Brock's life.

"How are you feeling?" he asked.

"I'm fine, Brock," his grandfather lied.

His grandfather coughed and sputtered into a handkerchief, then stuffed it in the pocket of his three-piece suit. The sound of his leather seat giving way filled the office, as Grandfather leaned back in the cushions and placed his hands in front of his face, tapping his fingers against one another, signaling he was deep in thought.

Brock tugged at his suddenly too-tight tie.

"Shall we...go over the plans for the auction?" Grandfather asked with hopeful eyes. And just like that.

He got his way.

Again.

"Sure."

"Oh"—Grandfather thumbed through a folder on his desk and waved him off—"I guess that can wait for later. First I want to discuss the ranch. I'm preparing it for your new family."

His new family.

As in…

One he chose? Or his grandfather? He was afraid to ask. Afraid he'd yell again and really kill the old man this time.

"Oh?"

"Yes." Grandfather thumbed through a few papers before his eyes lit up when he found what he was looking for. "Once you're married, I'll sign over the deed." He slid a paper forward. "This is a list of all employees currently on payroll. They take care of the horses, chickens." Since when did they have chickens? "Goats, the cock, and the mean old ass that Bentley won in a bet."

"Bentley won an ass?"

Grandfather let out a heavy sigh. "He bet his brother, his version of an ass, and the other party bet an actual animal. Simple misunderstanding."

"How did I not know about this?"

"You rarely come to my parties," Grandfather said with a twinkle in his eyes.

"Parties? What parties?"

What alternate universe had he just stepped into?

Grandfather ignored him. "It's good for these old bones to jump and jive every once in a while."

Jump and jive? The hell?

"You've been busy," Grandfather interrupted. Brock shifted uncomfortably in his chair. "You've been working yourself into the ground. I want you to take an official vacation until the press dies down a bit over this whole auction business." A guilty look flashed across his face. "I assume they're still downstairs."

"Let me get this straight." Anger started pulsating through Brock's body once more. "First, you force me to participate in the auction in order to get us publicity and gain the trust of the board, and now you want me gone?"

His grandfather wasn't making any sense. None of it made sense. "What's really going on?"

His grandfather fidgeted in his seat. He never fidgeted. "The publicity team thinks the hype of you disappearing out of the limelight will keep Wellington Inc. in the press until we auction you off at the ball."

Brock pressed the backs of his palms against his eyes and bit back a string of curses. "I can't just leave."

Not after what had just happened with his grandfather.

"It's what I want." His grandfather stared him down. "It's what's best for you. For the company." His eyes lingered on a piece of paper on his desk. "The shareholders..." Tears filled his eyes. "They don't trust you boys to take over the company. Brant and Bentley sleep with anything that walks, and you're guilty by association." His smile was apologetic but all it did was burn like acid in Brock's stomach. "The auction...it re-establishes our control. Reminds the shareholders that we're the face of the company and that this company"—he jabbed his finger onto the desk—"needs the Wellington men!"

Oh hell.

And now it all made sense.

Grandfather began to sweat and patted his handkerchief across his forehead and sighed. "Titus Enterprises has also agreed to participate in the auction as a way to show good relations between our two companies." He shrugged. "The shareholders have been itching to mend the relationship between us and the Titus family and I've kept my promise that I would do everything in my power to do that. The point is, I promised them Titus, the auction, and you, and in return our name stays glued to this company." He looked down and then back up at Brock with an unreadable expression. "Things are shaky with Titus Enterprises at best. One little snag and they'll pull out."

"I don't suppose you'll tell me why."

"It's not your concern. I've got it handled." Grandfather shrugged. "A nice little vacation is just what you need. Besides, what could possibly be keeping you here? Let me run the company—*my* company—for a few weeks to get the faith of the shareholders back in our court. They'll see that you're being the dutiful grandson by agreeing to be auctioned off and we'll let the press do what they do best."

"Destroy lives?" Brock offered.

"Don't be so dramatic." Grandfather pulled the papers into a neat pile and leaned forward. "Now, was there anything else?"

He was officially being dismissed.

Brock stood and nodded his head. "I don't like being kept in the dark."

"If I worry about you, you'll worry about me, which in turn makes me worry about you more."

Brock jerked back as if he'd just been slapped. "You worry about me?"

"Ever since that day when I watched the light fade from your eyes. The same day the responsibility for you boys came to rest on my shoulders. Do this for me, Brock. I'm not telling, I'm asking."

He wanted nothing more than to push back. To turn and walk away from this conversation, from this life. To yell *no* over and over again until his voice was hoarse, but he was caught.

Memories of his parents' deaths flooded his brain. The shock, the tears, the twins waiting for them to come home, the knowledge they never would.

And he knew his thoughts were written all over his face, because his grandfather stared at him with pity-filled eyes, as if to say, *"We can talk about it."*

But he didn't want to talk about it. He wanted to push the whole horrible situation to the furthest recesses of his mind and put it on lockdown, where he didn't have to deal with it—any of it.

Because once he dealt with it, healed, and got over the trauma, there was this lingering fear that he'd forget them.

"Yes," he whispered and closed his eyes. "The answer is yes."

"Good." Grandfather's smile was strained; he looked like he was about to say more, but didn't.

God, it was always the same with them.

So much was always left unsaid.

A fake smile replaced Grandfather's worried one.

And there it was.

His mind immediately went to all the freedom he'd lose.

And the girl with pretty lips and wide eyes that he'd probably never see again.

"The list," he found himself saying, "from the launch party last night, do you have it?"

"The list?" Grandfather's eyes narrowed. "Why?"

"I need it."

"You need it?"

"Stop repeating everything I'm saying and just e-mail me the damn list."

He could have sworn Grandfather's lips twitched at the corners. "I'm merely curious what you could possibly want with a list of names—though maybe the idea of settling down with one of the bidders is starting to sound like a good idea?"

It wasn't a list of names he wanted. It was one name.

A name attached to a beautiful woman who'd taken over his every waking thought.

Brock stiffened. "Well, I should at least do some homework if you want me to be part of the auction. Weren't a majority of the people at the launch event the same ones that are planning on donating?"

"Yes, that's true." Grandfather tapped his chin. "I'll send you the list. I'm just glad that you're taking this seriously. This company is important to us; it's your future."

Brock suddenly wanted to run.

And then punch his fist through a wall.

His future.

Right.

"The auction is set for three weeks from tomorrow. The night will start off with the ball, but you don't need to concern yourself with that. I have marketing and publicity working on the details. All you have to do is show up with a smile on your face."

"Okay."

Grandfather tilted his head to the side. "Was there something else you wanted to say to me?"

Yes. There were a million things he wanted to say. All of which started with "I'm sorry I can't do this" and "I'm sorry they died." "I'm sorry it's my fault." "I'm sorry that you lost your son and daughter-in-law."

Because he was.

So fucking sorry.

"Are you sure?" Grandfather prodded further. "You know you can talk to me about anything, Brock."

No, he really couldn't. Because clearly bad things always happened when he said no, and his grandfather was the glue that held the family together.

And he was being selfish for wanting more for himself when his grandfather had sacrificed everything to raise three hellion boys who'd lost their parents.

"No." Brock shot to his feet. "No, there's nothing else."

Grandfather sighed. "That's too bad."

"What was that?" It was hard to miss the hopeful look in his grandfather's eyes. What could he possibly expect Brock to ask?

"The weather." Grandfather nodded. "It's supposed to get bad. Try not to leave too late on your trip to the ranch house."

The ranch house.

Chills ran up and down Brock's arms.

The last time he'd been there he'd been a broken child searching for answers.

Funny how some things change, and some things don't.

Because somehow he still felt broken.

CHAPTER NINE

Cinderella Cleaning, you make the mess, and we'll clean it up before you can utter 'bibbidi bobbidy boo.'" Jane seriously needed to consider changing her company's motto. Yawning, she put a hand over her mouth to stifle the sound and scrunched her nose at the scent.

Lemon Pine-Sol was her perfume these days. She loathed every part of her job—except the way things looked once she was finished. That, she appreciated. But Cinderella Cleaning had been her father's business. And it had helped get her through college. And it made sense.

Like everything else in her boring life. It made sense to take over his business, as if it was somehow keeping his memory alive. She'd even kept his surfboard key chain.

Thumbing the little board, she yawned again as the person on the other end of the line coughed and sputtered.

"Sorry." The man sounded old. Real old. Great. A while

ago she'd discovered that her phone number was nearly identical to one that belonged to a massage service that she was pretty sure offered happy endings. "This old cold has me down."

"It's okay." Jane let out a sigh and turned off the engine. She had just pulled in to Starbucks, in need of a giant pick-me-up. "What can I help you with?"

"I have pipes that need cleaning, among other things."

"Oh um, well." She made a face and then cringed at her reflection in the rearview mirror. Mascara from last night streaked down her cheeks. Crap! She'd forgotten to wash it off. "I don't...I think the number you're looking for has an eight instead of a seven at the end. This is Cinderella Cleaning Company."

A long pause and then, "I know. I need things cleaned."

"Look, sir, I clean houses and offices."

"Fantastic!" He seemed overjoyed at the idea. Was he drunk? "I have a very old house that needs a bit of attention. I won't be in residence, but there will be someone there to help you out. I'm afraid I would need you round the clock for an extended amount of time."

"I'm not really a live-in maid," she said, as visions of being locked in the attic Jane Eyre–style filled her head.

"It's only for a few days. I'll pay handsomely." The man started coughing again. "Five thousand a week."

"Dollars?" she shouted, dropping the phone into her lap and staring at it in shock before picking it up again.

He chuckled on the other end. "I didn't think you'd be interested in alternate forms of payment. Although I do have some chickens. Doubt I could get more than one good egg out of 'em, though. Five thousand? Good night, they'd probably explode. Ah, but then again, chickens need love, too. I believe mine simply enjoy the act of love-making more than the production of eggs. That's all there is to it."

Jane stared at the phone then put it back near her ear. Was he talking about chicken sex?

"At any rate..." he sighed. "I'd like to hire you, if you don't mind. We can go over specifics tomorrow when I send a car for you."

"I haven't said yes yet."

"You will."

"Why?" She drew out the word slowly.

"Because you need an adventure," he said so quietly she almost didn't hear him.

"Who the hell is this?" Her skin prickled with awareness as she nervously glanced out the window. Was he watching her? How creepy!

"Eh, think of me as your fairy godfather."

"Thanks, but no thanks."

"Fifteen thousand dollars a week."

"Good-bye."

She hung up the phone with shaking hands.

Within a minute, it started ringing again.

She let it go to voice mail.

This was crazy. Right?

He could be a homicidal maniac. Luring maids or house cleaners into his home with the promise of money.

But still.

She couldn't deny she was tempted by the idea of an adventure. Or that she could use a break from the hamster wheel that was life with her sisters.

Especially after this morning.

Her phone beeped, alerting her to his message.

She should just delete the message, but coffee first. Coffee always first. With a sigh, she got out of the large cleaning van and made her way into Starbucks, walking purposefully toward the counter, only to be cut in front of the minute she got close enough to order.

And like an idiot she allowed it.

Just like she allowed her sisters to walk all over her.

With a grimace she stared down at her phone and nearly threw it against the wall when a text from Essence popped up on her screen.

We're going to be home late! Drinks after work! Save food for us?

Irritated, she didn't answer.

They didn't have money for drinks after work—every night of the week! It was bad enough that her sisters were probably going to stay until happy hour was over—but they always bought drinks for their friends, too.

With a groan, she tossed her phone back into her purse.

Jane ordered a large black coffee and headed back to the van. But the minute she turned the key in the ignition she knew something was terribly, horribly wrong.

The van shuddered, made a crazy choking sound, and puffed out enough black smoke to kill a person.

"No, no, no," she said aloud. She'd just taken it into the shop and the mechanic had warned her if she didn't fix a few things the engine would die. But the few things had turned into close to five thousand dollars' worth of work. She didn't have that kind of money.

Tears stung her eyes.

Her van wasn't a want—it was a necessity for her to actually run the business.

She jerked the keys out of the ignition and picked up her phone, chewing her lower lip before pressing play on her voice mail and putting the phone on speaker.

"We seem to have gotten off on the wrong foot, Miss

Cinderella Cleaning." The man had another coughing fit. "If you do this job for me, I will pay you thirty grand, final offer. I won't be at the estate while you are in residence. In fact, you'll probably be bored out of your mind. We have state-of-the-art security, and I believe the only concern you'll have is when the ass gets loose, which I'm sorry to report happens quite often, if my ranch hand is to be believed. Then again, he's old, so maybe he's imagining it." Another long sputter. "Call me back, we'll make arrangements. You'll open the house, keep it clean, and prepare it for its new tenants, all the while taking breaks out by the pool. How hard could it be?"

Jane chewed her lower lip.

How hard indeed?

CHAPTER TEN

Jane!" Esmeralda shrieked so loudly that Jane winced beneath the warmth of her old blanket. "Jane!" Another loud yell was followed by stomping up the creaky wood stairs.

The wool blanket was jerked away and tossed onto the floor.

Esmeralda towered over the bed, arms crossed. "It's seven."

"I know," Jane said in a small voice. "It's also Tuesday. You go into work at nine on Tuesdays."

Esmeralda's eyes narrowed into tiny slits. "But I still need to eat, and Essence wants to get in early, so hurry the hell up. God, I don't know why we put up with you."

They'd been fighting with Jane ever since Monday night, when she had gotten into it again with them about staying out late and spending money that they didn't have. It didn't help that Esmeralda didn't get the promotion she'd thought she was up for, which meant no pay raise. Essence had said as much when she got home last night. Her face was pale when she'd mentioned that Esmeralda had been counting on the money.

Jane didn't want to know.

Didn't ask.

Because she had a sinking feeling her sister had done something stupid. And they couldn't afford to bail her out again.

Jane waited until the door slammed after her sister then allowed the tears to fall freely. She'd been having the best dream.

About Brock.

Because naturally a man that good-looking just had to invade her dreams, as well as every time she thought about shoes, or dark hair, or men with kind smiles. He'd been so nice.

So. Nice.

Typically, she just cleaned offices, moving through the day while people passed her by, not giving the cleaning lady a second glance. She was okay with that; she'd always been okay with that.

Until now.

Until someone... had stopped.

Until someone beautiful... had smiled.

Gah!

She pounded her fists into the mattress as her name was screamed up into the rafters yet again, this time by Essence.

She grabbed her sweatshirt like she did every other day, threw it over her head, and slowly ambled down the stairs.

Both girls were seated in their spots at the table, and Jane got a sudden vision of her future.

She'd be eighty and still cleaning up their messes.

In the same ratty sweatshirt.

In the same sad pathetic flip-flops.

Frowning, she grabbed one of the skillets and tossed in some bacon. She'd promised her father, but what if, by keeping her promise...she lost her soul? Her will to live?

"Damn." Essence let out a long whistle. "I wouldn't kick him out of bed."

"Let me see!" Esmeralda snatched the paper from Essence's hands. "Please. He didn't even look at you the other night."

"He would have," Essence grumbled, "if Jane hadn't fallen and caused such a commotion."

"I wish we had the money to bid on him," Esmeralda whined, and then both girls fell silent.

Prickles of awareness shivered down Jane's spine.

"Jane, dear?" Essence said first. "Didn't Daddy leave you some money?"

"No," she said quickly, irritated by the knowledge that if she had an inheritance they'd expect her to fork it over just so they could bid on chance to marry a millionaire. She didn't have to turn around and read the newspaper to know they were talking about Brock. She'd looked him up after the party.

He was rich.

But it wasn't just that he was loaded—he was famous.

Famous for being brilliant.

Famous for being nice.

Famous for being a terror in the boardroom, which he clearly made up for by doing good deeds during the holiday season.

He spent every Christmas at the freaking homeless shelter serving turkey dinners. He was an actual saint.

So should it surprise her that he'd bought her shoes?

No.

He'd do it for anyone.

She was nobody special.

And a few hundred dollars for shoes? Meant nothing to a man like him—meanwhile meaning the world to her.

"Jane?" Essence wrapped her arms around Jane's waist then pressed her head against her shoulder the way she had when they were younger. "Come on, we just want a little bit. It says in the article that any girl that bids over two hundred grand automatically makes it to the ball."

Jane shrugged away from her grasp and choked out a laugh. "Two hundred grand? Are you serious? Do you think I would still be a cleaning lady if I had that much money?"

Essence shrugged. "Who knows? You were always Daddy's favorite. Hell, he probably gave you more than that, and you're just too selfish to share it with us."

Esmeralda tensed, looking between both of them, and then a slow nod from Essence had her jumping right in. "You always were selfish—first with Daddy's love and now with whatever he left us. Figures you would keep it all to yourself."

With a sigh, Jane plopped the bacon onto a plate and placed her hands on her hips. "If I had money, you guys would know about it. All I have is the business, and I highly doubt it's worth more than a hundred grand, if that." She frowned. "What's this really about?"

The girls both fell silent and then they shared another one of the looks they were famous for. One where Jane was left out.

It was awkward. Tense.

Finally Esmeralda stood. "I should go to work. Thanks for breakfast." She glared down at the bacon then purposefully walked by it, her heels clicking on the floor.

"Wait!" Jane called after her. "Are you wearing my

shoes?" She pointed to the new shoes on Esmeralda's feet. The exact ones that Brock had bought her two nights ago.

Essence breezed past them. "Let's go!"

"Esmeralda!" Jane yelled after her sister, but her only response was the slam of the front door. Typical.

And typically infuriating.

It hadn't always been this bad.

Jane remembered times when they'd watch movies together, do each other's hair. But that hadn't happened in years.

What had happened to her family? And why did it seem she was the only one who cared?

Her phone burned in her pocket.

Three weeks away from her sisters.

Three weeks away from this.

Enough money to fix the van.

And a much-needed break from whatever her sisters were conspiring to do.

She pulled her phone from her back pocket.

"Hello?" the old man answered on the first ring.

"I'll do it." The words rushed out before she could stop them.

"Wonderful decision, my dear. How soon can you make arrangements?"

Jane smiled. "Give me a day."

CHAPTER ELEVEN

Thunder rumbled loudly as the sky lit up with a flash of lightning. The weather had gone from bad to worse since he'd left his house, and the drive to the ranch had taken twice as long as it should have.

He was irritated.

The rain wasn't helping.

Jane's name hadn't been on the guest list he'd gotten from Grandfather. Maybe it was the universe's way of telling him to just leave her alone—what good would it do anyway? Ask her on a date and then end the date by saying, "oh and by the way I'm going to have to put you on a time-out while I go drink wine with that rich supermodel who bid on me"?

Thunder rumbled louder as rain pelted against the windshield.

Brock had always hated thunderstorms. Their loud, majestic power was yet another reminder that he was a very small part of a very big universe. Something that normally would humble a man made him feel weak, reminded him that he didn't have the power to do anything, really.

His body chilled, he turned up the heated seat and focused on the rest of the drive down the three-mile-long, tree-lined dirt road that led up to the main house. He hadn't been back since he was a child.

The place held too many painful memories.

Memories that he'd always wanted to keep locked down, until now.

"Twirls me, twirls me, Daddy!" Brock giggled as his father twirled him around and around. "Higher, higher, Daddy!"

His dad suddenly stopped and set Brock back onto his feet. Out of breath, he'd mumbled, "You're getting so big!"

"I four."

"I'm four," his father repeated with a laugh as he messed with Brock's dark hair and then leaned in with arms open wide. "Now give your dad a hug. It's time to go in for dinner."

Brock hung his head. "I not hungry."

"I'm not hungry." His dad said the sentence again, correcting it for Brock. He'd had a speech problem as a child, was unable to say most of his R's, and had been blind as a bat before glasses, and later, contacts.

Brock took a deep breath and repeated. "I'm not hungry, Dad."

"But your mother worked very hard on this meal, so even though you aren't hungry, we need to still be respectful of the time she put into making the food so you grow big and strong, yes?"

Brock nodded his head.

"Now, how about that hug?" His dad's arms opened wide.

Brock ran into them and his dad twirled him around on the grass one last time.

It was impossible to see the actual patch of grass that they'd so often played on, but Brock knew it was there, fifteenth tree in, to the left.

Brock briefly closed his eyes and slowed the car to a stop. With shaking hands, he put the car into park and sat there listening to the rain. He still had a mile or so to get to the house but he needed a minute. Just one goddamn minute to get his head on straight.

Finally, Brock sucked in a long soothing breath, put the car back in drive, and pressed down on the accelerator. Only to have the tires squeal in protest.

"What the hell?" He tried again but got the same response. Muttering a curse, he slammed his hand against the leather steering wheel.

Brock grabbed his coat and stepped out into the cold, wet rain. Lightning sizzled across the sky followed by the bellow of thunder as he made his way to the back of the Audi and inspected the damage. The tire was caught in the mud, which would have been fine if he'd had someone who could hit the accelerator while he pushed.

"Damn it." He was going to have to walk.

CHAPTER TWELVE

Jane giddily walked around the property, her shirt attaching itself to her body like a second skin. Rain slid down her cheeks, thunder rolled, and she was deliriously happy.

She'd left her sisters a note.

A freaking note.

She laughed out loud again at the freedom she felt. They were going to be so mad, but it was only three weeks. She imagined their clothes would be pink from their trying to figure out how to do the laundry, and they'd probably lose weight because they didn't even know how to pour milk into a bowl for cereal.

Arms spread wide, she twirled, over and over again, then nearly ran smack-dab into one of the large oak trees that had been planted on the property.

The owner must like trees, because there were hundreds lining the long driveway and a forest behind the ranch, with trails leading around the thirty acres.

In all reality, the house was a dream.

Her dream.

Judging by what she was getting paid to get the place ready for the new tenants, she assumed the man who'd called her had money, but the house didn't shout money. Sure, the kitchen was gourmet and immaculate, but every single wall had pictures of a family that she'd suddenly, very desperately wanted to meet.

Three little boys.

Two smiling parents.

And a grandfather in a cowboy hat.

They were lucky, that family.

Lightning streaked across the sky. She should probably go inside. After all, she had to meet the elderly ranch hand first thing in the morning, and she was tired.

Escaping prison did that to a person.

With another giggle, she started making her way back to the house.

* * *

He'd walked more than a mile before Brock finally made it to where he could actually see the house.

He was soaked.

Pissed.

Exhausted.

Damn it, he'd do anything for a whiskey.

And a nice crackling fire.

Maybe he'd steal one of his grandfather's cigars like he had that time when he was a kid. Only, that adventure had ended with him puking hits guts out on the back porch while Grandfather made him smoke the rest of the stash to teach him a lesson.

He smiled at the memory and picked up his pace.

The porch light was on. *Hunh.* Well, Grandfather did say that George, the ranch hand, would have things ready for him. He hoped that included a hot meal by the fire.

When he finally reached the porch, he sighed in relief, took one step, then felt the barrel of a shotgun shoved up against his back.

"What the hell?" he hissed, waving his arms in the air.

The gun bobbled back and then a gunshot rang out, hitting the porch light and blanketing him and the intruder in darkness.

"St-stay where you are." The feminine voice was shaky, uncertain. "I have a gun."

"No shit." She'd nearly taken off his head with it!

"Don't talk!"

"Fine."

"I said"—she shoved the barrel of the gun harder into his spine—"no talking. Now..." Her breathing was ragged. "I want you to take two steps backward and turn around. And go back to wherever you came from. This isn't your house!"

"Actually—" He coughed, trying to clear his throat. "It is."

"Crap!" The gun fell to the ground in a clatter then went off, sending dirt and pieces of rock all over his feet.

"Fuck!"

"George!" the woman yelled. "I'm so sorry! You poor thing!" Warm hands wrapped around his shoulders. "Oh no, and you're so old."

What the hell? "I'm not—" He barely got the two words out before she started babbling again.

"Old. No, of course not, how rude of me to say that. Come on, up you go." As soon as he'd picked up the gun and straightened to his full height she scooted around him and made her way up the front steps.

"I mean, of course you'd want to greet me and make sure I got settled in!" She laughed nervously as she pushed open the door and stepped into the shadowy foyer. He put the safety back on the gun and set it on the entryway table.

"Stay here, and I'll just..." Her pert ass moved back and forth as she jogged in the general direction of the kitchen. He'd just managed to find a lamp—that flooded the room with light when he turned it on, thank God—when she came back with a large ugly black purse and dug through it, finally pulling out a bottle of pills.

"So..." She took a few steps toward him. "I just need to grab you water and—"

With a gasp, she dropped the pills as she uttered a dumbstruck "You?"

His mouth dropped open. "Just Jane?"

"Just Brock." A smile formed around her sensual mouth. "Clearly not pushing seventy."

"God, I hope not," he joked. "Though it feels like it. My car got stuck in the mud. Then I got stuck in the mud. I left my pride about a mile back, highly doubt I'm going to get it back now."

She made a face as she eyed the mud he was dripping all over the floor.

"What are you doing here?" Jane's features softened. "Were you the old man who called me about this job?"

"I'd really like it if you could stop leading every sentence with the word 'old.'" He gave a half-shrug. "You know, pride and all."

A flush broke out across her neck. "Sorry."

"An old man called you?" He sat in the nearest chair and tried not to laugh at Jane's wince over his obvious destruction of said chair. "Why don't you start at the beginning? Why are you here?"

Her mouth formed an O as she crossed her arms, un-crossed them, then placed them on her hips. It was damn near impossible not to stare at her breasts as they were perkily directing all their attention at him. Never had he been so thankful for wet white T-shirts.

"Well, this old..."

Brock sighed.

"Sorry, this *man* called and asked for my services—"

Brock's eyebrows shot up.

"No, no, no." Her blush deepened. "Not those types of services. That is, I clean houses and offices. I own a business. Cinderella Cleaning Company. He, um, he needed someone to serve as a maid for the house for the next few weeks, get it ready for the tenants, and honestly it's not my normal job but..." She swallowed and looked down. "Let's just say I needed to get away."

"Mafia?" he said in a deadpan voice.

A giggle escaped her lips. "Close." Her eyes met his. "Sisters."

"Ah, well. I have twin brothers. Pain in my ass, both of them."

"I, uh"—she tucked a piece of wet hair behind her ear—remember."

"Old man, you say?" His eyes narrowed. "And I imagine he's paying you handsomely?"

She broke eye contact and then nodded.

"If I were a betting man I'd say my grandfather called you. So I guess, just a happy coincidence that Cinderella left her shoe at the dance club and now she's here...in my house." He frowned. How the hell had his grandfather been able to find her when Brock hadn't even seen her on the guest list?

"Your grandfather," she said slowly. "Your house..." Her eyes narrowed. "New tenant?"

He stood, towering over her small frame, and her lips parted as she took a step backward, away from him.

What the hell was his grandfather up to? And how the hell was he supposed to survive being in the same house as the one woman he wanted—but couldn't have? Goddamn his grandfather!

Brock took one look around the room—at the dozens of pictures of his once-happy family—*of his parents*—lining the walls, and dead center was a picture of his grandfather.

His vision tunneled to black as the meaning of his presence at the house settled fully on his shoulders.

Another man would be able to raise his hand and brush away the streak of mud from her cheek. He'd kiss the frown from her face and ask her how it was possible that she'd gone so many years without knowing how devastating an effect she had on the male population.

On him.

But his reality had never been more clear.

"It's my house," he said finally. Needing to say the words out loud so that she understood and maybe so he would, too.

"Okay."

They stood in tense silence. He wasn't sure what else there was to say so he defaulted—to the familiar.

"You probably have things to clean." Apparently being a jackass was how he was the most comfortable. He inwardly cursed himself as he saw her hurt expression.

"Yes." She nodded, breaking eye contact. "Yes, um, of course. Yes sir." Was it his imagination or was she shaking?

"I'm going upstairs to take a shower." He called over his shoulder and stomped off.

Leaving the ghosts of his family behind.

Leaving Jane.

CHAPTER THIRTEEN

Jane let out a loud exhale once she was sure that Brock was out of hearing distance. He seemed bigger than before, more masculine, if that were even possible. At the club he'd done nothing but give her the impression that he was a kind, generous man. But here...here they were on his turf. And it was glaringly obvious they were from vastly different worlds.

This was *his* house. And she was *cleaning* it.

She'd physically flinched, as if he'd punched her in the stomach when he'd basically told her to clean up after him.

Stupid. She was so stupid to think he would be interested

Just because he'd done a nice thing for her at the party did not mean he wanted to sleep with the help.

A laugh built up inside her chest, threatening to escape. But of course she'd be attracted to someone like him, someone who embodied security, beauty, family, everything she'd always wanted wrapped up into one shiny package. Prince Charming he was not.

Sighing, she moved down the hall and into her bedroom. Thinking she'd be the only one staying at the house, she'd taken the master. Embarrassed, she managed to stuff most of her belongings back into her suitcase and roll it down the hall to the next available room. If Brock was going to stay here, she had no business being in the master suite, although she'd been dreaming of taking a bath in that tub— heck, more like swimming in it. But she'd be fine; all of the guest rooms were beautiful.

With a shrug, she pushed open the door to the room she'd chosen and wheeled her suitcase in, then pulled out some of her clothes and started putting them in the dresser drawers. The room was quaint, around two hundred square feet, with floor-to-ceiling windows on the east wall, and an attached bathroom. It was perfect for her.

Jane located a bulky sweatshirt and hurriedly peeled off her wet T-shirt, flinching at the sucking sound it made when she pulled the fabric over her head.

"What the hell are you doing?" Brock's voice came from behind her just as the shirt got caught on one of her earrings.

Panicked, she twisted as she tried to pull the shirt back down, but it wouldn't budge.

"Um..." Realizing she was almost facing him now, Jane turned away from the direction of his voice. "I was changing my clothes. Why are you in my room?"

"*Your* room?" His voice rose. "And here I thought it was my house."

Well, that was an asinine thing to say! "So why aren't you in the master bedroom?"

"I don't stay there," he barked.

How was she supposed to know that?

"It's the bigger room, and since you're moving in, I just assumed—"

"Is this part of the deal? You clean my house and strip for me after hours?"

Tears threatened. What a complete jackass! "I'm sort of—stuck."

"Stuck?"

"Are you just going to repeat everything I say?"

He didn't respond.

Whatever.

He was clearly still there. She could feel his presence, watching her. Thank God she was wearing her good bra.

She gave another tug and was able to get part of the shirt back down, but the other half was still stuck on her earring and over her head.

"I would help but..." Brock's voice was closer. Her body buzzed with awareness. "I think I like watching you struggle a hell of a lot more."

"I've got it," she snapped, trying to put some distance between them.

"Yes." His voice held mild amusement as she tugged harder. At this rate, she was going to pull her ear off. "I can see that."

"Damn it!" She stomped her foot and he sucked in a breath. "Brock?"

"Yes, Just Jane."

"I think...I need help."

"You think?"

"You don't have to be a jackass."

"I know I don't *have* to be..."

This night needed to be over already. Jane's right arm was cramping, and she'd been flashing poor Brock for the past five minutes.

"Here." Brock's breath was warm on her neck. "Allow me."

Within seconds he'd located the part of the shirt attached to her earring and with a soft tug, the shirt came over her head.

"Hey!" She turned to yell at him for making her more naked when she was trying for less, but she let out a little moan instead.

He grinned. "Problem?"

"You." Her tongue stuck to the roof of her mouth as she took in his shirtless state, and the unbuttoned pants he wore.

His body was...not of this world.

There was no way.

Without thinking, she found herself touching him, pressing her fingertips against his chest, just to check that he wasn't a figment of her imagination.

Hard. So *hard*.

The planes of thick bulging muscle were in direct defiance to the smooth-talking man that had bought her shoes. When she'd seen him last, he'd been large, intimidating, and very much the businessman. Now? Now she could clearly see every muscle ripple, and felt her body react to him as she tried to keep her composure.

She could handle the single, rich bachelor who was kind.

What she couldn't handle? A man. A man who was all man, through and through, who had a body to match all that dominance and masculine goodness.

"Jane?" Brock whispered her name.

She jerked her hand away then took two steps backward, nearly colliding with her suitcase as she folded her arms across her breasts. "Thanks."

"If I'd known that getting eye-fucked was going to be my thank you, I would have come to your rescue a lot sooner."

Her eyes narrowed while he fluidly moved past her into what she assumed was a bathroom.

Before shutting the door he turned and barked, "Take the master."

CHAPTER FOURTEEN

Take the master." Could he be more of a dick? What the hell was wrong with him, ordering her around like she was a servant?

Damn it.

All he'd wanted was to be away from her—her and the memories of this once-happy home.

And then she'd gone and touched him, and all his wants—every single one of them—had suddenly shifted into dangerous territory, one he knew wouldn't be fair to either of them.

He would be auctioned off to the highest bidder in a few weeks.

He was *basically* in a committed relationship.

With a complete stranger he hadn't even met yet.

And lusting after another.

He swore as his mind rewound images of her pert breasts, rosy peaks straining behind nearly sheer lace, and her rain-slickened skin. He'd wanted to run his tongue down the side of her neck. Just a taste, just one, maybe two, three. Hell, he'd been five seconds away from tugging her onto the bed and helping her out of the rest of her clothes.

He cursed as his body tightened painfully, and then he flipped the hot water to the frigid cold he needed to get himself under control.

These were going to be his last few weeks of peace before his grandfather decided yet another element of his future.

He wasn't going to waste them wanting something he couldn't have.

If there was anything he'd learned in his life, it was that the minute you got something you wanted, or cared for, it hurt that much more when it was ripped out of your hands.

He knew that firsthand.

Because everything he'd ever cared about had been taken from him in this very house.

The master bedroom.

He hadn't set foot in that room since his parents' deaths.

His grandfather had preferred a smaller room—leaving the larger to his parents—and God, it felt like their ghosts were still there.

If he had it his way, he'd redo the entire west wing of the house and bulldoze the shit out of the walls in an effort to get rid of the memories.

Sighing, he grabbed one of the towels and dried off, then quickly dressed. Maybe being here was a good thing. Maybe he could battle his demons once and for all.

*   *   *

Somehow he managed to make it out of the shower without jacking off to the vision of a shirtless Jane.

"Fuck." He pulled a clean T-shirt over his head and ran

his fingers through his hair. So she was going to be cleaning the house; it wasn't like he would see her every second of every day.

And it wasn't even that dirty—his grandfather scarcely used it.

Maybe she would finish early?

Besides, she was an employee.

Which meant she would be making herself scarce.

That was what he should want.

He slammed his fists against the bathroom counter and glared at his reflection in the mirror. A man of thirty five stared back at him, but he didn't see the man. He saw the exterior, the shell, but on the inside, he knew what he felt like.

What this fucking house made him feel like.

A lonely boy.

A terrified lonely boy whose only plan in life was to please everyone but himself.

With a growl he ran his hands over his face. Amazing that all it had taken was walking in the door, and his emotions were all over the place.

Jane's presence wouldn't help matters either.

Having her clean things, rifle through his family's stuff— it wasn't just uncomfortable, it was—well he wasn't sure what it was, but he didn't like it.

With a sigh, he picked up his phone and called his grandfather.

Of course, the old man answered on the first ring.

"Brock! I take it you've made it? How's the ass?"

Brock paused, then rolled his eyes. "I haven't had the opportunity to greet the animals."

"A shame."

"Yes," he said in a dry voice. "My thoughts exactly. Then

again I've been a bit distracted. You wouldn't know anything about that, now would you?"

"Hmm?"

"Grandfather—"

"Don't take that tone with me. I taught you that tone, boy," Grandfather grumbled. "She's only there helping air out the property and clean the rooms, unless you'd rather tend to those things while you're there?"

"It hardly needs a deep clean."

"Of course it does, especially after the chickens got loose in the hall."

Brock frowned. "Since when did the chickens get loose?"

"New Year's." Grandfather chuckled. "To be fair, we weren't actually betting on the cocks, but you know how parties tend to get out of control."

Hunh?

"Anyway." He cleared his throat. "She'll stay mostly out of the way, and I hardly think she'll be a distraction, all things considered. I mean, you're practically family!"

Brock froze, gripping the phone with his hand so tightly he was afraid it was going to break in half. "Come again?"

"Family," Grandfather said in a painfully slow voice. "God knows she could be."

"What!" Brock seriously hoped this was another of his grandfather's more senile moments.

Grandfather burst out laughing. "I recognized her last name when I was looking to hire out a cleaning company and did some digging. I knew her grandmother—gorgeous lady, just like her granddaughter. At any rate, she'd been left a widow in her prime and we had several one-night stands. Glorious one-night stands. All before your grandmother, of course, rest her soul."

"All right then." Brock tried to stop the flow of information from his grandfather but the old man wouldn't stop talking.

"The things she could do with that body of hers," Grandfather sighed longingly. "Such a shame, such a shame."

"I hope you're done traumatizing me now."

Grandfather coughed. "Never."

"Didn't think so."

"The point I'm trying to make is, she shouldn't be a temptation. I'm sure she's a pretty girl, but like her grandmother, quite completely out of our league."

"I think you mean we're out of her league," Brock corrected him.

"No." Grandfather sighed. "I said it correctly. Now, make sure the cock stays in the barn and the ass has enough food and water."

Brock groaned. "That's what the ranch hand is for—"

"Oh, I sent him on vacation; didn't I tell you?"

Brock froze and then wheezed out a choked cough. "What?"

"You need to get used to taking care of the animals. After all, it's your house, or will be soon. If you can't manage a few cocks in the henhouse, you truly have no business getting married in the first place, am I right?"

"Please stop saying 'cock.'"

Grandfather made a weird clicking noise with his tongue, sneezed, then uttered a curse before mumbling. "Cock."

"Are you day drinking again?" Brock asked.

"Of course not." Grandfather sounded offended. "Though I may still be drunk from last night. Bentley had another one of his parties and what type of guardian would I be if I didn't attend and keep my eye on him?"

"The normal kind," Brock said with an irritated edge.

"Don't tell me I'm going to have to keep your ass out of the newspapers now as well."

Grandfather laughed out loud. "Silly boy, when have you ever needed to watch out for me?"

Groaning, Brock had a brief vision of slamming his cell phone against the nearest wall and following it with his fist, then his head.

"Now then, make sure to check in on those animals. It would be a shame if they died because you were too busy flirting with Jane. Remember, out of your league."

With that, the conversation ended. Brock was met with silence as a stab of irritation hit him square in the chest.

"Did he just hang up on me?" Brock stared at his cell then glared at himself in the mirror.

Could it really be a coincidence that his grandfather had just happened to hire Jane and her company? It had to be. There was no damn name on the list when he'd checked. He let out a frustrated sigh.

Regardless. It didn't matter.

He walked into the living room and nearly groaned aloud when the grandfather clock chimed nine at night—just another reminder that he was literally his own ticking time bomb. He opened his mouth to say something to Jane—anything that would put them back on even ground rather than the shaky-as-hell situation that had him ready to ram his fist through a wall.

What he'd expected to find was a woman doing her job.

What he found instead?

A woman on her hands and knees cleaning the very same floor that his mother used to clean. In the exact same position. Only there was nothing familial about Jane.

Raw lust pounded through his system as she moved her hands back and forth over the wood. And then, his gaze lifted to the side table where a few vases and pictures lined the wall.

One of the vases was missing.

There were always three.

Always.

And then he noticed a piece of crystal on the ground. "What happened here?"

Jane's hands jerked on the rag she was using for the floor. "Sorry, I bumped into the table."

"Sorry doesn't bring back the vase," he heard himself saying.

"I can replace it." She looked up at him with wide eyes. "It was an accident. I was moving some of the pictures."

That, of course, made him look at the pictures, then back at Jane. "It's not replaceable. Just how long have you been cleaning?" Great, now he was questioning her. And from the angry look in her eyes he knew he'd pushed her too far.

"Four years," she said through clenched teeth.

"Four years what?" He shook his head, clearing the memories of his mother arranging and rearranging those vases. One for each of her sons.

"You asked how long I'd been cleaning." She stood to her full height. She wasn't very tall but she somehow still managed to make herself look menacing as she jutted out her finger. "Did you want to see my references, Mr. Wellington?"

Hell. He didn't have the energy to fight with her and the longer he stayed inside the more he felt choked by the memories—the louder they screamed, begging to be dealt with.

"I'll be outside," he snapped, turning on his heel. "Try not to break anything else, or I'll be forced to take it out of your paycheck."

He heard her sharp intake of breath as the screen door slammed behind him. She was probably plotting his murder right now, and he'd deserve it. But she was the one moving things.

Cleaning out ghosts.

Even though she didn't realize it.

And his reaction was instinctive—even if it was wrong.

A cool breeze picked up, and now, thanks to his grandfather, he had animals to find.

A cock, to be exact.

CHAPTER FIFTEEN

He smelled like pine soap.

Not Pine-Sol, but pine soap, the kind that reminds a person of cozy nights sipping wine by the fire.

Not that she'd ever really had any nights like that—at least not recently—but still, he reminded her of *warmth*.

Oh heck, it wasn't even warmth; that word made him sound boring, like he was temperate—rather than hot, sizzling to the touch.

Jane shivered as the memory of his hands pounded through her body. It was as if he was touching her all over again, pulling her shirt from her body and gazing at her like she possessed something he wanted.

Too bad he'd turned into a complete tool.

"Are you okay?" Brock's voice interrupted her scrubbing.

Jane stood too fast, nearly knocking over the bucket of soapy water, and pressed a wet hand and rag to her face, causing dirty water to run down her chin. "I was just... scrubbing." Great, was he going to accuse her of doing that wrong, too? It was bad enough that she'd apparently broken a family heirloom.

"Scrubbing." He wiped his face with his hands and let out a frustrated sigh. He might be beautiful to look at but tension rolled off him in waves. And when he opened that gorgeous mouth, at least since this morning, all he'd had to offer were angry biting words.

With a curse, he seemed to force a smile that looked more irritated than amused. It was a smile that reminded her yet again she didn't really belong in his world, let alone his house.

He didn't want her here any more than she wanted to be here.

With him.

Trapped.

She took a few steps back and nodded. "I'm almost done cleaning the mud off these floors and then I'll go back to my room—your room." She frowned. "Well, my room now and…" She nodded again. Why? Why was she suddenly afflicted with one ability? Nodding in his direction and embarrassing herself.

"Why?" He barked out gruffly.

"Hmm?" She blinked up at his face, trying to keep herself from staring at the way his T-shirt molded to each and every one of his muscles.

"Why are you going to your room?" He said it more slowly this time, drawing out the sentence as if she was stupid, which grated on her nerves. It wasn't like people had never talked down to her before; she just didn't expect *him* to.

Not the man who'd bought her shoes.

And made her feel like a real-life Cinderella.

Better that the dream got shattered before she started the

hero worship, she decided. He was just like every other man out there.

Embarrassment washed over her as she croaked out, "It's been a long night."

"It has," he agreed.

The staredown that followed had her suddenly wishing she was wearing a sweater she could pull across her body. Brock apparently wasn't the type of man who stared; he looked through people with a laser-like intensity that had a way of making her feel naked and way too hot.

With a gulp, she bent down to retrieve the bucket of soapy water and begged her legs to move faster as she scurried past him and dumped the water into the sink.

Ignore him.

She could ignore him, right?

After all, it wasn't like he was going to be following her around, offering his help or advice on how best to get stains out of the carpet.

That idea was laughable.

He probably didn't even know how to iron a shirt.

"Something funny?" came a raspy voice behind her, causing her to jump a foot and let out a little squeak.

"Just…" She gulped. "Nope. Nothing at all."

A large masculine hand moved into her line of vision and turned off the faucet. "Just Jane, I think we should talk."

She fought to keep her shoulders from slumping. After all, she knew that tone of voice, so well in fact that she had these types of speeches memorized by heart.

Every human voice in existence sounded just this way when relaying bad news. The doctors had when her father was diagnosed with cancer and there was nothing they could do; so had her boyfriends who'd gotten bored; even past employers, when upset with her work, had this type of voice.

She should be used to it.

But coming from a man like him? A man that a few days ago had been like a dream, a dream she could rely on to take her away from the monotony of her life... well, it affected her more than it should.

He affected her more than a stranger should.

"Okay." She managed to turn around and keep her face impassive.

His crystal blue eyes searched hers briefly before he crossed his arms over his bulky chest. "Three weeks."

She frowned. "Yes..." Her head tilted just slightly as she tried to digest his meaning. "It's going to be three weeks of cleaning?"

"Are you asking or telling?"

"Telling." She winced at her airy tone. "Is that what you wanted to discuss? The amount of time I'll be here?"

His eyes stayed glued to her face and then, as if she'd scared him, he took a large step backward and shook his head. "You know what? I'm tired, too. We'll talk in the morning. Just try to stay out of my way, and I'll stay out of yours."

"Don't worry." She held her head high. "I'm very good at being invisible."

He opened his mouth, then shut it.

Nothing.

Her prince didn't offer up any excuse for why he was being mean and she supposed he didn't have to.

He was Brock Wellington, one of the most sought-after bachelors in the country.

And she was a maid.

CHAPTER SIXTEEN

What did a man do when he knew he was being a jackass? He drank, of course.

So that was what Brock did.

Until two a.m.

It didn't help.

He even moved from the bedroom to the living room in hopes the couch wouldn't trigger the memories he'd tried so hard to lock down.

It should have helped.

But the whiskey seemed to bring alive every single memory that he'd worked so hard to keep trapped inside this house. He hadn't realized how messed up his head still was until he saw Jane leaning over the sink, smiling.

His mom had loved that sink because it was so deep. She'd joked that she used to wash Brock in it when he was a baby because it was easier than the tub.

Seeing Jane there had been absolute hell.

And telling her that she reminded him of his mother

seemed like the worst idea in history. So he'd done the only thing he knew how to do.

He'd pushed her away.

So he'd had a shitty start to what he was beginning to realize was a haunting vacation.

Too many ghosts.

Too many memories.

He managed to fall asleep around three in the morning, only to toss and turn with an ache in his groin that refused to go away. Finally in a moment of desperation he gripped himself and in a drugged sleep envisioned Jane's sweet mouth.

It was over in seconds.

As he spilled into his hand, in a drunken stupor he imagined what the next three weeks might be like if he could live them for himself.

His sight blurred as the idea washed over him.

Three weeks where his grandfather wasn't watching his every move.

Three weeks where he wasn't Brock Wellington, millionaire, but Brock Wellington, ranch hand.

Three weeks...

* * *

Sunlight heated Brock's chest and then a loud animalistic bellow sent him flying off the couch and onto the floor.

He rubbed his head and blinked his eyes as a giant donkey stared at him from the middle of the floor.

The donkey made another ear-splitting noise and glared.

It was too early.

Way too early for a donkey in the middle of the room.

How the hell had it gotten into the house?

"Coffee?" Brock asked aloud. "Can't I at least have coffee first?"

"Are you talking to a donkey?" came Jane's silky voice from behind him.

Brock's headache gripped his head like a vise. "Well, it seemed the other option was to ignore him and I wasn't sure if that would just piss the damn thing off more."

"Fred's harmless." She breezed past him and moved into the kitchen while the donkey continued staring at Brock like he was the one who didn't belong here.

"Wait. Did you call him Fred?" Brock stood slowly, eyeing the donkey for any sudden moves.

"Yup," came her reply. "All the animals have names. The ranch hand said it makes them feel more like pets. He left a list on the fridge."

"Donkeys aren't pets."

Jane's eyes twinkled. "Oh?"

"No," Brock argued.

Jane pointed. "He seems to think differently."

The donkey was directly behind him; the damn thing had followed him into the kitchen.

"Out!" Brock clapped his hands, which of course made the donkey neigh or whatever the hell they did—louder, until the ear-splitting sound was deafening.

"You didn't use his name," Jane teased.

Brock glared. "Did you let him in? Is this punishment for my being rude last night?"

She snorted. "The idea does have merit, but no, I didn't sic Fred on you. I'd like to think I'm more creative than that."

Fred nudged Brock to the side then slowly moved into the kitchen and stopped in front of Jane.

"I think he's hungry," Jane whispered, patting Fred on the head.

A slight twinge of jealousy had Brock ready to drop kick the donkey and push him out of the way. Her hands roamed over the donkey's head.

"Lucky bastard," Brock said under his breath.

"Hmm?" Jane looked up.

Brock swore.

"Can you make coffee already?" he barked at a startled Jane, whose face managed to say everything she didn't as it crumpled before him.

"Of course. Anything else, sir?" she asked in a dead voice. *Shit.*

What the hell was wrong with him?

A nagging voice in his head blamed her—but she was just the unlucky target and it didn't help that every time he locked eyes with her he thought of her soft mouth—of trailing kisses down her neck.

Or just pinning her against the wall.

But in a sick twist of fate, the only woman who'd managed to spike his interest in years was off limits. At least to someone like him. Someone who didn't get to choose his own path.

Repression. That's what was happening. He'd spent so many years being a yes man that he was finally cracking, saying things he didn't mean, snapping, and then dreaming about kissing the scowl from her lips.

She'd probably slap the shit out of him.

And he'd deserve it.

"No." He finally found his voice. "Actually"—he smirked—"Why don't you make breakfast and coffee while I kick the ass out of the house and make sure he's the only animal that escaped during the storm?"

Jane grabbed a skillet and slammed it onto the stovetop. When he cursed she offered a polite smile. "Headache?"

He glared.

Smile still in place, she lifted her chin. "How do you like your eggs?"

He frowned.

And then frowned harder.

"I have no damn clue."

"Well," she said, making her way to the fridge, "that's helpful. Are you going to fire me if I guess wrong?"

"And if I do?" he challenged, suddenly realizing he liked the way her eyes lit up when she was angry. "What then? Will you leave?"

"No."

"Didn't think so."

"Why are you being difficult?"

"Because I finished a fifth of whiskey by myself last night, because this damn house has living breathing ghosts, but mainly because you look too damn good, and I'm suddenly discovering that this house has a way of shredding every ounce of self-control I possess. So unless you want to find yourself naked and in my bed, I suggest you do your job and stay the hell away."

With that, he stomped out of the house. Luckily for him, the ass trotted after him as if they were playing a version of Follow the Leader.

That had gone well.

He let out a frustrated curse.

Great. Now Jane probably thought he was going to jump her in the night. Her shocked expression hit him in the gut, twisting like a knife.

At least he'd been honest with her about how attracted to her he was.

Hopefully she'd stay far away. How hard could it be to just do her job and ignore him?

Furthermore. Why. Was. She. Here?

His grandfather had been vague.

For some reason he still felt puppet strings digging into his skin, and he couldn't shake the suspicion that Jane was just another way his grandfather was manipulating him.

Desperation filled him.

A desperation to be free.

And to not let his grandfather win.

And yet...

Where would that leave him?

Another funeral?

Another obituary?

Another ghost.

The donkey made a strangled noise and kicked dirt into the air once they reached the barn. Brock let out a frustrated sigh.

The door to the barn was completely open. A horse neighed and then trotted out toward him.

"Buttercup!" He smiled. "Come here, girl."

The horse stopped, swished her tail, then turned away and trotted off.

"Well, at least I have you, Fred."

There was no response.

He turned around.

"Fred?" Where the hell had the ass gone?

A gaggle of geese walked by, followed by a few chicks. Just then, he heard the cock.

Like in some horrible Western movie, the rooster stared him down from the other side of the barn, where light filtered in from the hole in the roof like a spotlight on the scene.

"Just you and me, eh?" Brock wondered if the fact that he was talking to the cock meant he was just as insane as his grandfather.

The cock kicked the dirt.

Brock did the same.

And then, the damn thing charged him.

Unsure of what to do, Brock stood his ground, until it started flapping up in his face.

He swatted it away and when it still wouldn't stop attacking him, he ran back to the house to get a gun. He'd just come barreling through the kitchen door when he slammed into Jane, sending the skillet and eggs she'd scrambled all over the floor.

"Son of a bitch!" Brock yelled.

The rooster crowed.

Jane's eyes widened as they locked on to what he assumed was the cock behind him. "The door's open."

"I'm going to kill it." Brock jerked the screen door shut just before the rooster slammed into it, throwing a fit.

A few feathers went flying.

"Question." Brock turned to Jane, who was brandishing the frying pan like a weapon. "Can you eat cock?"

The words were out before he could take them back.

"Are you asking about me, personally? Or people in general? Because I'm sure, given your reputation, you already know the answer to that question," Jane said in a cheerful voice.

Brock looked heavenward and then turned around. "I meant the rooster."

"Did you, though?" she asked coyly. A silent taunt rose out of those eyes, and then she pressed her lips together in a way that had him hard in seconds.

The rooster started flapping again.

"Still got that gun?" he asked.

"You aren't shooting the cock."

He grinned. "Cock?"

"I mean rooster." She blushed bright red.

"Did you, though?"

"Very funny."

She grabbed some paper towels and started cleaning the eggs off the floor.

"Let me help." He knelt beside her but she jerked away from him.

"I've got it. After all, you told me I needed to do my damn job, right?"

Brock opened his mouth to speak, but she didn't let him get a word in edgewise.

"I'm going to be cleaning the upstairs bathrooms along with the two extra guest rooms on the far end of the hall. If you need me, you know where to find me."

He didn't want her to leave.

But what could he do to get her to stay?

Nothing.

Because her job was not to entertain him or save him from farm animals.

But then she turned and gave him a half-shy smile, and he knew self-preservation was all that mattered.

Push her away.

He pasted an arrogant grin on his face. "But what about breakfast?"

"That wasn't part of the job description," she said slowly. "Your grandfather said—"

"I just talked with him last night. He said you're here to help get the house ready for the new tenants, right?" God, he was a jackass.

She gave him a weak nod.

"And since I'm the new tenant, don't you think that probably extends to cooking? You're already cleaning, and it is part of your service, you know."

"*Service?*" There was that fiery glint again. Perhaps this wasn't his best idea. But he just couldn't seem to stop himself from being an ass.

"It says Cinderella Cleaning and Housekeeping on your nice shiny van." He'd seen it on his way out to the barn and done a double take over the silly tiara on the side. Maid service. Didn't that mean she cooked, too? "If you don't cook that's false advertising. At least, that's what I'll say when I give you a review on Yelp."

Her eyes widened. "Are you threatening me?" Her chest heaved. He tried to look away. Tried and failed.

"That depends. Will you cook?"

Her hands balled into tight fists. "You know you could have asked nicely and I might have said yes. You don't have to be an ass. We already have Fred."

"Oh, I'm aware." He took a step toward her. "But if I'm nice, I miss out on the opportunity to see this." He was pushing her too far. He was taking everything too far, but the minute her cheeks flushed red with anger he wanted to touch her. Wanted to make those cheeks flush for other reasons.

He cupped her face with his right hand and leaned in, his lips lingering near her ear. "You're pretty when you're angry."

"I'm not *just* angry," she whispered in a wobbly voice.

"Oh?" He pulled back. "What else are you?"

She stared down at the floor then swept her gaze back up and regarded him with big brown eyes. "Disappointed."

Jane jerked away from his embrace. He reached for her again, so she shoved against his rock-hard chest, slapped him on the cheek, and stormed out of the room.

CHAPTER SEVENTEEN

Jane wiped the sweat from her forehead and braced her rubber-gloved hands against the toilet. She hadn't meant to lose her temper with Brock earlier. She wasn't the type to lose her temper—ever.

She'd lived with two of the brattiest women in the world for her entire life and managed to make it through the day with a smile pasted on her face and at least one good thing to say about them, for the most part.

But with Brock?

Things were different.

He brought out the worst in her.

And she didn't even know him! With an irritated grunt, she scrubbed the inside of the toilet harder. How dare he demand that she make breakfast? On top of cleaning? He hadn't even hired her!

The more she thought about his arrogant attitude the harder she scrubbed, until the entire bathroom was completely spotless.

It was a shame that the house had only been used for occasional visits and parties.

The bathrooms alone probably cost a fortune to build, with heated tile floors and huge hotel-like walk-in showers—they reminded her of a spa, not that she'd ever been to a spa. But she'd seen them on TV and read about them in books, and this was what she imagined they looked like.

Flawless, sparkling, immaculate.

"Is my grandfather paying you to stare in the mirrors all day?" Brock's smooth voice broke the silence.

Jane gulped and clenched her rubber gloves together before she turned and arched her eyebrows. "I was just admiring my work."

He stared at her for a good minute before scowling.

"I don't want you cleaning the room next door."

The only thing she knew about the room was that the door had pieces of white paper stuck to it, like stickers had been ripped off it. Red designs drawn in marker circled the doorknob—she assumed it had been a child's room.

"Your grandfather's instructions were specific. He said to clean every room and bathroom in the house. So yes, I am going to clean that room, because as stupid as it may sound I do take pride in what I do."

That seemed to give him pause; his arrogant mask slipped, revealing something she didn't really want to acknowledge.

Respect.

But as soon as she saw it, he stiffened. "I'll talk to him."

"But—"

"If he agrees with me, you stay out of the room."

"What? Do you have bodies hidden in it?"

His face went pale. "You should probably move on to the

next bathroom if you want to finish before dinner. After all, it won't cook itself."

Tears stung in the backs of her eyes.

What happened to the man at the club? The one who had rescued her? Bought her shoes, picked her up off the floor and flirted with her?

Suddenly Brock cursed under his breath. "Don't move," he whispered. Which was weird. But weirder still was the look on his face as he stared at the ceiling above her head.

Jane froze, but driven by curiosity, she slowly craned her neck to see what he was giving the death stare.

"I said," Brock ground through clenched teeth, "don't. Move."

"But—"

"For fuck's sake just stop arguing!"

Her shoulders slumped. Was it necessary to yell at her?

"Two mice." His eyes narrowed. "And by the looks of them they've either eaten their young or been feeding off the donkey for the past few months."

"Not the cock?" she mumbled.

Brock's eyes heated, dipping down to her mouth before flashing with anger. "Clearly you don't clean as well as you think."

She refused to let the insult sting. "It's a ranch house. They probably snuck in through a crack on the wall. I'll shoo them away and you can start fixing things up, handyman."

"Me?" He snorted. "No, no, I think that falls under the hired help category. Sorry, sweetheart."

"Hunh."

"What?" He frowned. "What's that look?"

"I just should have expected someone like you to be like this. I bet you get manicures, too...and since you probably don't want to get a sliver, I guess I'll have to step up. Where's your hammer?"

"Let's leave my hammer out of this."

"The real hammer, not the sexual one you're envisioning in your mind in order to distract me from the fact that you're a spoiled, silver spoon–fed city boy with the brain of a gnat."

He burst out laughing. "You think you know all about me, hunh?"

"Not much to know," she challenged, crossing her arms. "At least from this vantage point." She made sure to lower her eyes and smirk. "Nothing at all."

He took a step toward her but she backed away. "I'll be back. It seems I have a rat to deal with."

"They're mice," he called after her.

"Wasn't talking about them!" she yelled back, making her way down the stairs and out the screen door. It slammed behind her.

The hot Arizona sun burned down on her skin.

The bastard!

She took a few deep breaths and glanced back at the house. Could he be more insulting?

Okay, she sighed. If I was a mousetrap where would I hide?

After a few minutes rummaging in the barn, where the ass was currently watching her with terrifying intensity, she found some rat poison and two mousetraps.

She walked back into the house, grabbed some peanut butter for the traps, then carefully walked up the stairs.

Brock hadn't moved from his spot. Instead, he was staring into the bathroom as if he'd just seen a ghost.

"Move." She pushed by him.

"Maybe we should just shut the door," he offered in a quiet voice.

She jerked away from his body. "Shut the door? And what? Let the mice just spread throughout the house?"

He seemed unsure, and then with a nod stepped away from her as she made her way back into the bathroom.

Both mice were huddled in the corner, as if people didn't bother them one bit.

Were they pets or something?

They looked at her, then at each other, then back at her, and slowly approached like she was holding out treats.

"I can't do it." She stood and slowly backed out of the room.

"What the hell do you mean you can't do it?" Brock roared. "They're mice. They carry diseases."

"They have kind eyes!" She lowered the traps. "And I can't be responsible for their deaths."

"You're serious?"

She nodded and shoved the traps into his hands. In hindsight, she could have done it more slowly, possibly more gently, but the minute the traps snapped she knew it was too late.

With a loud roar, Brock stumbled backward, one trap clinging to his fingers, the other hanging from his T-shirt from what looked like part of his nipple.

He was still yelling in rage.

Jane covered her face with her hands.

When he was done swearing, she jerked the trap from his chest, harder perhaps than necessary.

His glare said it all. "It's not funny."

She bit down on her bottom lip and grabbed the other trap from his right hand.

"There." She couldn't stop laughing. "You're as good as new."

Nostrils flaring, he brushed up against her, setting her body instantly on fire. "You did that on purpose."

"Had I done it on purpose I would have aimed lower," she said sweetly, blinking her eyes in innocence while trying to get out of the too-small bathroom with the large man in it. Regardless of how many times he acted like a jerk, he intrigued her way more than she cared to admit. Because she couldn't forget how kind he'd been at the party. And that guy had to be in there, too, right?

He shook out his right hand and placed both hands on his narrow hips, which only drew her attention once again to his body.

"Just stay out of the room next door." He brushed past her and went straight down the stairs, leaving her alone with the mice, the traps, and the distinct impression that if he had a choice between her and the traps...

He'd probably choose the traps.

CHAPTER EIGHTEEN

Women asked too many questions.

Stupid questions.

Brock held the ice pack against his sore chest and winced as the memory of his last encounter with Jane played back in his head.

Something inside of him was snapping.

It was this damn house.

The fucking living room with all of the pictures.

The way that he couldn't even look at the stairway without thinking about his father making them a slide down the stairs.

Or the Legos that used to be scattered in every single corner until his father tripped on one of Brock's latest inventions, only to fall down the stairs and sprain his ankle.

Everywhere he looked, he saw happiness.

Until the memory shifted and he was that same little boy, playing with the same toys—alone. The blinds drawn, the laughter gone.

"Hell." He wiped his face with his hands and cursed. It wasn't her fault she was here.

But she was an easy target.

Because she made him feel things.

She was a tangible reminder of all he'd lost, all he'd never have. She was doing exactly what his mother had done in this house—cooking, cleaning, laughing, smiling—and it was fucking killing him.

Logically, he knew it made no sense at all.

Keep the old man happy, keep him alive.

But trauma had a way of stealing all logic and replacing it with survival.

He realized, as he blinked down at his phone, that's all he'd been doing.

Surviving.

Not living.

Two missed calls from Bentley.

And three missed calls from his grandfather. For the first time in his life, he didn't call back right away. Instead, he stared at the locked screen and waited.

For the apocalypse? For the sky to fall? For something.

His answer came five minutes later, when he dialed Bentley's number only to hear the familiar Jay Z ring tone flood the hall.

"Does this mean I'm the prodigal son?" Bentley's cocky-as-hell voice said. "Since I stepped over the threshold first."

There was a loud thump, followed by cursing and laughter.

Brock stood and walked around the corner.

The twins were on the floor.

And they were drunk.

"What the hell are you both doing here?" Better yet, how did they get here if they were drunk off their asses? Brock's thoughts suddenly turned dark and thunderous as he remembered who was upstairs. In a few minutes they'd be trying to seduce her into their beds. That's what they did. And sometimes, they shared.

No chance in hell.

She was his.

His torture? Was that it?

"Admit it." Bentley flashed him a smug grin. "You missed us!"

"Yes," Brock said in a dry tone. "That's why I kept ignoring your calls. It hurt too much to hear your voices."

"You look like hell." Brant sidestepped Bentley and eyed Brock with more clarity than felt comfortable. "How is it possible you look older and it's only been a day?"

Brock groaned. "Seriously, why are you both here? Did you miss the part where this is my last vacation before I get tossed into a pit of rich women with fake tits and trust funds?"

"Commitment." Bentley winced. "I'll move to Canada before that becomes my fate."

"He'll find you anywhere," Brant said in an annoyed tone. "Believe me. One time I was taking a piss in Costa Rica, and naturally Grandfather walks in with a prostitute and—"

Brock held up his hand. "I don't think I need to hear the rest of that story."

"Yeah, man, not in front of Sheldon," Bentley snapped.

"Who the ever-loving hell is Sheldon?" Brock glanced around the room until his eyes settled on the open door, where the donkey he'd been calling Fred was hanging out casually in front of it. "Something's not right with that donkey."

"Sheldon!" Bentley charged the poor ass and started patting its head. Sheldon, clearly confused that he was a donkey and not a dog, cuddled closer to Bentley. "How are you, old boy?"

The donkey made a noise.

Brock's mouth dropped open. "It talks?"

Bentley shrugged. "Sheldon used to be a magician's assistant—he was part of the disappearing act. He can basically escape or break into anything. But he was too old to keep doing tricks. I won him."

"Yes, Grandfather mentioned."

"He's very valuable. You have no idea how expensive it is to train a donkey." He nodded seriously. "Hunh, Sheldon? What's that, boy? You want to fetch?"

"Donkeys don't fetch." Brant sighed. "Though I wager ten bucks Sheldon has his own Frisbee."

"Go home." Brock opened the screen door. "Both of you, damn it."

Bentley's eyes narrowed. "Cursing a lot, I see. Under some stress?"

"He has bloodshot eyes," Brant added in a cool, calculating tone.

"Out," Brock repeated himself. "Seriously, go torture someone else."

"Grandfather wants to introduce Brant to a woman. He said I was next. I had both our asses packed before he micromanaged yet another one of us." He smiled widely.

"The point is this." Bentley pushed against Brock's chest, moving him from the screen door and farther into the house. "We need to lay low for a while, and what better place to have some family bonding than here?"

"I can name at least ten." Brock clenched his teeth, his hangover suddenly coming back with a vengeance. "Twenty. Hell, go out of the country!"

"Brock." Jane's voice carried through the house. "Brock!"

Bentley and Brant both stared.

"Are you hiding a woman?" Bentley shoved Brock aside

and headed toward the sound of Jane's voice. Brant followed.

He stomped after them, ready to use any means necessary to get them the hell out of the house.

He knew he was fucked when Bentley opened his mouth.

"Look who we have here," Bentley said in a husky voice. "Shoe girl...I'd recognize that arch anywhere." His challenging glare to Brock said it all. It wasn't playful and it sure as hell wasn't welcome.

Bentley loved a challenge.

He loved taking what wasn't his.

And Jane.

Jane was *his*.

Well, under his roof.

Damn it.

"What are you doing here?" Bentley continued his assault, moving casually around her, his eyes lingering on her ass before he finally locked eyes with her and smiled.

"Well..." Jane blinked over at Brock, then stared back at the floor. "Your grandfather hired me to clean the house and get it ready for—" her eyes flashed—"for Brock, so I'm just going through all the rooms."

Brant whistled then offered her a wink. "That's a huge job. Do you want us to help you?"

The twins didn't even know how to do their own laundry, let alone clean a toilet.

"Bentley," Brock snapped. "A word?"

His brother's response was a grin. "Go ahead; I'm waiting."

"Alone."

"Anything you say to me in private can be said in front of Jane. After all, she's your friend, right?"

Brock had never hated a word more in his life. "Yes," he

managed to choke out as he took in her nearly see-through white T-shirt and ass-hugging jeans. "Friends."

"You look frustrated," Brant muttered aloud. "I wonder if it's the pressure of running the company, the auction, no sex..."

"I knew he would crack one day," Bentley added. "Good thing we came when we did, right, Brock?"

"A good intervention is hard to accomplish, but we'll do what we can." Brant smirked and then offered a wink in Jane's direction.

They needed to go.

Both of them.

He rubbed a hand over his injured chest, which had gone from a stinging pain to a dull, roaring throb.

Jane eyed his hand, then her eyes narrowed as a sly smile spread across her mouth. "How's your damaged nipple, Brock? I hope the clamp didn't tear it completely off."

Bentley's eyes widened with shock while Brant started to slowly clap.

"It's not what it sounds like," Brock said defensively.

"Isn't it, though?" Jane flashed him a giant, fake bright smile. "After all, you were the one who said to take care of the situation. I was just doing my job, right?"

"We should have come sooner," mumbled Bentley.

"There was a mouse," Brock said, not taking his eyes off Jane.

"The mouse tore your nipple off?" Brant winced.

"No, the clamp did that," Jane said helpfully.

"So you were dressed up as mice?" Bentley blinked.

"Why don't I go make dinner?" Jane interrupted. "And you can explain to your brothers why half of your nipple is most likely gone, and how you're going to start being nice so the hired help isn't tempted to set up traps in your bed while you sleep."

With that she flounced off, leaving a whiff of vanilla and sugar behind her.

"I like her," Bentley said in a low, lust-filled voice. "Any woman who threatens me is welcome on top"—he eyed Brock and kept talking—"or bottom. As long as I'm inside, I don't give a fuck."

Brock slammed him against the nearest wall. "Touch her and I swear I'll kill you in your sleep."

Bentley held up his hands and smirked. "I knew it."

Brock released him. "Knew what?"

"You like the maid."

"She's..." What? Not a maid? But she was. Not that it mattered. She was Just Jane—sweet, spicy, beautiful Just Jane, and that was the real problem.

"She's sexy." Brant peered around the corner. "So what if she's the help? She's a person. A pretty, right-in-front-of-you person. According to the press you'll be marching toward an arranged marriage in three weeks. Why not enjoy her now?"

"Good idea. I'll just screw the maid and then marry someone else; why hadn't I thought of that?" The temptation to run over both of his brothers with a car had never been so strong. What the hell were they thinking? Were they always this insensitive?

A feminine cough interrupted their fight. "I just, um, was wondering if you guys wanted to eat indoors or outdoors."

"Indoors," Bentley answered, and he had the decency to look ashamed at being caught talking about her like she was a piece of meat. "Thanks, Jane."

Her smile was forced as she nodded and turned on her heel and left.

CHAPTER NINETEEN

Jane pounded the chicken with the mallet over and over again, picturing Brock's face with each whack.

Why was she so upset?

It wasn't like he was wrong. She was the maid. It was her job, it was what she did, but he'd made her feel…low, dirty, like her job didn't mean anything. Like by sleeping with her he'd be doing her a favor.

The arrogant prick!

Slam.

Pieces of chicken went flying.

Slam.

How dare he joke about sleeping with the maid?

Slam.

"Jane." A warm hand cupped her shoulder. "You're scaring Sheldon."

She glanced up into Bentley's emerald green eyes. "We have another dinner guest?"

"No, the donkey."

"Fred?" She frowned.

Bentley's expression mirrored her own. "Did you re-name my pet ass?"

"The list said his name was Fred."

"What list?"

"The one on the fridge with all the names of the animals." Jane pointed over her shoulder. "At least that's what I as-sumed it was. Next to each animal is a name. Why else would it be there?"

Bentley pulled down the laminated piece of paper and burst out laughing. "My parents put these together." He chuckled harder. "They're approved-of words to say instead of swearing. So if you want to say ass you say, 'don't be a Fred.'" He grinned. "Instead of saying suck my..." He grinned shamelessly. "You can say suck Mr. Feathers."

Jane read the rest of the names—really read them. The list was like a kid's glossary for saying naughty words.

"It all started when Brock learned the word 'shit,'" Bent-ley said with amusement. "And things quickly went down-hill from there. We turned it into a game, and well, now you know."

Jane tried to keep herself from smiling at the thought of a young Brock strutting around the house screaming "shit" at the top of his lungs.

"He's not always an ass, you know," Bentley said in a gentle voice, his hand covering hers on the countertop.

"No?" Jane swallowed against a lump in her throat. "Just most of the time, then?"

"He bought you shoes," Bentley reminded her. "Really nice shoes."

"Actually, you bought me shoes."

"After he made me." Bentley removed his hand and offered a wicked grin. "But hey, if you want to switch broth-ers I'm all for it."

"Excuse me?" Jane sidestepped him to grab the butter out of the fridge.

Bentley laughed. "I'm kidding."

Jane rolled her eyes.

"Sort of." He shrugged. "Okay, so maybe like ten percent kidding? But apparently you only have eyes for the ass."

"Fred?"

"Brock."

"You understand how I'd be confused, though, right?" She teased while Bentley flashed her another one of those grins, the ones she was one hundred percent sure he practiced in front of the mirror.

"Need any help in here?" Something about the way Brant walked into the room was calculating, like every step he made was for a purpose he already had in mind, a plan. His smile was as charming and dangerous as his twin's. "I thought I heard the words 'ass' and 'shit,' so I figured either we were talking about Brock or we were talking about Brock." His grin widened. "It's one of my favorite things in the world—brother shaming."

Bentley flipped him off.

"Not you." Brant rolled his eyes.

Jane again tried to focus on the dinner. It was nearly impossible to have a solid thought in her brain when she had the twins talking and flirting with her.

She'd have to be either dead or insane not to notice how devastatingly handsome the men were. Charisma rolled off them in waves, but they weren't intimidating.

Not like Brock.

His mere presence nearly stilled her breath and had her wishing for more time to look at him and just study his features—which sounded so lame in her head that she wanted to slam her palm against her own cheek.

He was a jackass.

A privileged jackass.

"What's going on in here?" Brock's low voice rumbled through the kitchen.

His dark wavy hair looked like he'd just spent the last five minutes running his hands through it: mussed and sexy. She had to avert her eyes before her thoughts went into dangerous territory.

"Look." Bentley snatched the sheet from the fridge and handed it to Brock. "She found your swear sheet!"

"That's a load of hairy ants and you know it!" Bentley yelled. "How dare you goat my cock!"

Jane giggled behind her hand.

"That isn't even on this sheet," Brock said in a strangled voice as he ran his fingers through his hair again. The simple action was so sexy she had to look away.

"Made it up just now. Sounds dirty, right? Goat my cock." Bentley shrugged and maneuvered his way over to Jane, sliding his arm around her body. "What do you think, Jane? What would a lady's response be to that question? Hmm?" He leaned in too close, his eyes focused on her lips. "Would you goat my cock?"

Uncomfortable, she ducked away from him and returned to preparing dinner while Brock leveled his brother with a glare that would have left her trembling, though she wasn't sure if it would be from fear or excitement. Maybe both. "All right, no more talk of cocks or asses. I'm trying to make dinner. Why don't you guys go set the table or something?"

Everyone froze.

She glanced at each of their panicked expressions, finally landing on a thunderous Brock. His fists clenched and unclenched as a muscle twitched in his jaw.

"Sure thing." Bentley and Brant quickly exited the room while Brock stayed.

He wasn't saying anything, just staring her down like she was able to read minds.

Finally, she set down her knife and sighed. "What? What did I do this time?"

Brock's eyes narrowed. "There won't be any setting of the table. We'll eat in the living room."

"Fine." Jane was too tired to argue and needed him to leave. Just being in the same room as him made her want to launch across the floor and beat him with her fists, and kiss him senseless. Something was seriously wrong with her. "We'll eat in the living room."

Bentley poked his head around the corner. "Are we using the china or—"

With a growl Brock turned on his heel and barked out. "Don't set the table."

"But—"

"I said"—Brock pounded his hand against the nearest wall—"we aren't setting the fucking table."

The next twenty minutes went by painfully slowly.

The twins helped her serve the food, but the meal was deathly silent except for the sounds of forks scraping against plates.

Brock was the first to finish.

He stood with his plate and stomped into the kitchen. The sound of running water filled the air, then the garbage disposal, then nothing.

"I'm going to bed," he announced once he was back in the living room. He headed down the hall and then a door slammed.

Twice.

"He's always been dramatic." Bentley yawned, visibly relaxing as he set down his plate and leaned back in his chair. "Sorry, Jane."

"Don't be." She hid her own yawn behind her hand. "He's not my problem, nor my responsibility."

"Hah." Brant's eyebrows shot up. "Brock has never been anyone's responsibility."

Jane frowned. "What do you mean?"

The twins shared a look before Bentley spoke. "He takes care of people; they don't take care of him. Hell, the last time someone took care of him"—he lowered his head—"was when our parents were alive. He'd skinned his knee after falling off his bike, and our dad helped patch him up. It was the last time I saw Brock cry or show any sort of emotion other than irritation and anger."

What? How could that be true? He'd smiled at the club when they'd been in the private room, when he'd given her the shoes. Her thoughts jumbled together as she pressed a hand against her chest. "You," Bentley said softly. "He smiled with you."

CHAPTER TWENTY

He was literally going to get a medal for being an asshole. It wasn't her fault, but she was the easiest target. Projecting every damn feeling of insecurity and loss onto her just seemed...easier, easier then dealing with it. Seeing her in the kitchen had been a fucking nightmare.

She was pounding the hell out of chicken, for shit's sake.

Just like his mom.

She looked nothing like his mom—nothing.

And yet, seeing her there made his chest ache and his stomach drop to his knees. And with his brothers home, the house was full again.

It was all too familiar.

With a curse, Brock tossed off the giant comforter, pulled on a pair of sweats, and walked out of the room. He needed whiskey if he was going to have any hope of sleep.

Lots of whiskey.

He'd always prided himself on his control.

Until her.

And the house.

Both of them were grating his very last nerve. Set the table? Seriously? Like his brothers both weren't completely aware that the last meal they'd had as a family had been shared at that very table.

With a shudder, he quietly pulled the whiskey from the pantry and poured a heavy dose into a coffee cup, then made his way to the living room. Maybe he'd sleep on the couch again.

Maybe he'd get drunk again.

And just maybe, he'd forget all about how good Jane smelled and how beautiful she looked—while cleaning a damn toilet.

Yeah, he was so screwed.

Brock surveyed the room as he took a sip of whiskey. The leather couches were the only new thing in the entire house. Everything else was exactly how he remembered it, from the woodsy smell to the way the wood floors creaked when you walked into the living room.

Another slow sip and he was sinking down onto the couch.

A little squeak erupted from where he tried to sit, and he jumped back up.

"Hey!" Jane's quick movements were almost impossible to make out in the dark, but her voice? It was clear, smooth, and it sent really irrational feelings straight to his heart. Every muscle in his body tensed.

Because that was what happened when you treated people like shit—people who didn't deserve it.

His body, aware that things were about to get uncomfortable, braced for impact, while his brain scurried to come up with the right words that would form nice-sounding sentences, sentences that would make things better without going as far as an apology.

Dumbstruck, the only thing he could utter was, "Sorry, didn't see you there."

"You didn't even look." She tucked her legs under the large afghan and yawned behind her hand. Her dark hair was pulled into a long braid that draped over her right shoulder. A white tank top was visible beneath part of the blanket.

Her expression was tired.

As the fog cleared from his head he managed to sit across from her in his own chair. Buying time, he sipped more whiskey from his coffee cup. "Why are you out here?"

A long pause descended over them like a hot itchy blanket before she answered. "I couldn't sleep."

"You know, you can always switch to another room if it's the bed."

"It's not the bed," she answered in a whisper.

"Or . . ." He licked his suddenly dry lips. "I think I can find you some NyQuil or something to help."

She smiled. He could see the white of her teeth as her nose scrunched up in a cute little expression that he really needed to not stare at too long—lest his body take it as an invitation and suddenly launch itself over to the couch.

"Actually," she said, adjusting herself on the couch again. "It's more like I keep getting texts from my evil sisters."

"Turn off your phone."

"I finally did, but there were things said before the phone went off, things that made it so I couldn't sleep."

He wanted to help her—and for some reason, thinking about her problems was a hell of a lot more welcome than thinking about the ghosts floating around the room, staring at him, begging to be dealt with. "Here." He thrust his mug of whiskey in her direction.

With a frown, she leaned forward, her hands coming into contact with his as they wrapped around the cup. He released the cup into her care, his hands tingling from the sensation of her skin against his.

"What is this?" She sniffed, then made a face.

"Whiskey. Believe me, it helps."

She sighed. "If you say so." One small sip and she was coughing, her eyes tearing up as she got off the couch and handed the mug back to him.

His eyes moved from her sock-clad feet up her danger-ously long legs, to short black shorts that nearly gave him a view of perfect ass cheeks. Licking his lips, he grabbed the mug and met her pointed gaze. "You didn't have to get up."

"Well, you look exhausted. I don't want you to make any extra effort on my behalf, only to blame me tomorrow for being more tired than you already are."

He winced. "I deserved that."

"Totally." And there was that shy smile again.

Locking eyes on her, Brock sipped from the mug exactly where her lips had been, his tongue swiping across the ce-ramic mug unnecessarily. Yup. Losing his mind. Or maybe just that desperate for her.

Jane's eyes hooded before she took a cautious step back and finally grabbed the blanket, resuming her place on the couch. A safe place.

A safe distance away from him.

He wasn't so sure he liked it.

"Did it help?"

She nodded warily.

"Good."

Another pause followed. He knew he should say some-thing, possibly apologize, but he wasn't even sure where to start, or how to go about doing it without laying all of his cards on the table.

So he said nothing.

He was good at that.

Saying nothing when he should say something.

"The blinds," he finally blurted. "I think I hate the blinds the most."

"The blinds," she repeated in a curious tone. "Can I ask why?"

He snorted. "They always used to be open." He flashed her a smile. "The sunlight streams all the way into the kitchen, and my mom—" His voice cracked, damn it. "She loved getting up early to make coffee and cinnamon rolls. She said that she saw heaven in this room—knew without a shadow of a doubt that it existed, because of the light."

"That's beautiful," Jane whispered.

"She was beautiful." He glared hard at the stupid wooden blinds. They were objects, stupid objects, but they still held power, made him feel weak. "They were closed the day they died. And they've stayed that way ever since. I hate them. They remind me that things are different. They remind me of the day my life changed forever."

Jane didn't move.

Nor did she say anything.

He kept talking. "It was an accident." He stared down at his hands. "Fuck, I hate the word 'accident,' like that makes the death part easier. A thunderstorm, followed by a plane crash. The twins were little, so Grandfather told me first. He walked into this room and shattered the perfect world I lived in."

He swallowed and glanced back up at the blinds. "They were closed that day. I knew something was different because they were closed and my mom, she always had them open. Funny, how such a small thing can stay with you."

They sat in companionable silence for a few minutes before Jane cleared her throat. "My sisters hate me."

"That can't be true." He shifted in his chair so he could see her better. "Why would they hate you?"

"I was born?" She offered with a forced laugh. "I don't know; they always make comments about how my dad favored me, but I think he just saw a lot of himself in me. I actually cared about what he cared about, and our relationship was different because I was the youngest." Her voice broke. "Anyway, I may have taken this job without fully telling them where I'd be and how long I'd be gone."

"So they're worried about you?"

Jane slumped forward. "No, it's more like they're pissed that nobody's home to do all of their laundry and cooking. The last text I got called me a selfish bitch for refusing to think about their needs."

Brock frowned so hard his face hurt. "How old are they?"

"Twenty-seven and twenty-five."

Brock burst out laughing. "Why don't they just order takeout?"

"Thank you!" Jane threw her hands into the air. "That's exactly what I said, but apparently looking up the restaurants in their tiny little phones after getting their nails done is, and I quote, 'super-duper hard.' Then they started freaking out about having a delivery guy at the door who was probably a college dropout and looking to rob them."

Brock shook his head. "They sound like a real...treat."

"You have no idea."

Guilt slammed into his chest. "Am I right when I say this was supposed to be more like a working vacation?"

She gave him a silent nod.

"Where the tenant wouldn't be a jackass like your sisters?"

Another nod.

"Shit."

"It's not my fault, you know."

"What isn't?"

"The blinds."

He blinked, and then blinked again. "I'm not blaming you for the blinds."

"You are." A sad smile spread across her lips. "I don't know you well enough to know anything about your personality except you're angry. And whether you're angry at yourself, me, the house, the blinds, the only person it's hurting is you." She shrugged. "It wouldn't hurt to stop trying to control the memories. Maybe in order to get through the grief, you need to face them."

"Sometimes it's easier to offer advice than it is to take it."

Jane visibly tensed. "It's getting late. I think I'll head to bed."

"Jane, wait. I'm so—"

"No you're not. You're not sorry. Don't pretend to know my story, and I won't pretend to know yours. It wasn't my place. I apologize."

The blanket slid off her body into a pool on the floor. She left him alone, staring at the blinds.

They stared back at him.

And he wondered if the blinds were just that: a symbol of the day he'd decided to let his grandfather control his life solely based on the fear of a twelve-year-old boy who'd felt he had no other choice but to hold on to the man who promised him everything would be okay.

The blinds still stared.

And he stared right back, challenging them—wondering if he pulled them open, what exactly would happen?

Would the sky fall?

Would Grandfather die?

Or would his life be exactly the same?

He stood and walked over to the blinds, lifting a shaky hand to the string that held them closed, and then jerked his hand away.

Some memories were best left buried.

CHAPTER TWENTY-ONE

Jane woke up with a knot in her neck and a dizzying feeling of anticipation. Talking with Brock hadn't been a wise idea, mainly because she was reminded that underneath all that fear—the very fear she saw in his eyes when he spoke of the past—was a decent guy.

He was in there next to all the yelling and insults.

Well, she'd always loved a good project; finding a new home for a rescue dog, walking an old lady across the road, bringing food to the homeless. Helping a man she was insanely attracted to get over the death of his parents...

She clenched her fists.

No. She refused to help him.

He didn't deserve it! And what would come of it if she did? She'd help him see past his demons, he'd become the man he was supposed to be, and they'd ride off into the sunset together?

More like, he'd thank her, give her a hug—that was, if it actually worked and he didn't strangle her first—and he'd ride off into the sunset with Barbie's twin. They'd have beautiful children, who in turn would have beautiful children, and people like her would watch from the sidelines.

She swallowed the giant lump forming in her throat.

Something needed to change in her life—and it started now.

With trembling hands she turned on her phone again and gasped as texts flooded her inbox.

All of them from her sisters.

It seemed like they'd gone from angry to understanding in an instant.

Esmeralda: *Jane I'm so sorry, just come home. We miss you!*
Essence: *HUGS!*
Esmeralda: *Best sister ever!*

Jane groaned into her hands and continued reading the messages. After five or six kind messages they started turning threatening and manipulative again.

Esmeralda: *You can't just leave like this. You're our family. What would dad have said? It's so selfish!*

Guilt spread through her body. In a way, it *was* selfish of her to leave them, but she was going crazy! They were choking the life out of her and they didn't even seem to care how they were hurting her.

She was just ready to text back when another message popped up.

It was a picture of Essence.

And she was wearing Jane's pearls.

The ones that had broken all over the nightclub floor. But how? She'd just assumed they were done for. It had been dark in the club and bodies had been everywhere.

Essence: *This just got delivered, but since you're gone…*

Jane texted furiously.

Jane: *My pearls! Who sent them? How?*

Essence: *Oh, so NOW you respond? When there's something you want?*

Tears blurred her eyes as she typed back.

Jane: *No! I had my phone off. Please! I'll be home in a few weeks! Just keep them safe.*

Essence: *No promises.*

Emotion clogged Jane's throat as she touched the screen to her phone. It wasn't the fact that they were expensive—it was the fact that the pearls had been her mother's.

Given to her.

The next text was a picture of Esmeralda wearing Jane's shoes, the ones Brock had gotten for her.

Esmeralda: *They look better on me.*

She knew it. She'd just known that Esmeralda had taken the shoes that day, but she'd been too weak to fight her on it; she didn't want to start a fight she knew she couldn't win or finish.

But now. She turned the phone back off and let the reality of her situation with her sisters hit her full force.

Brock hadn't realized it, but he was right, and she had been talking about herself as much as she was talking about him. She needed to face her demons, her ghosts, and deal with them once and for all.

It was amazing how easy it was to see how her sisters manipulated her, now that she was away from them. It was as if a fog had cleared, and she could see that the only reason they kept her around…

Was for them.

Her father wouldn't want her to live that way.

It was a revelation she'd never had before, and it was the

first time in the last five years that even though her body was sore, her heart felt light.

She was getting paid thirty grand.

That was more than enough for her to be able to either bribe them to move out, or sell the house and move out herself. The only problem would be getting her sisters' approval to sell it.

Her shoulders slumped. It would never work. She adored that house—she'd grown up in that house. To just let them have it—trash it?

The thought made her shudder.

She quickly pulled her hair back into a bun and tossed on a pair of ripped jeans, a gray tank top, and white Converse sneakers, her cleaning uniform for the day.

Except.

Brock.

No matter how hard she tried she couldn't get his defeated expression out of her mind, or the way he looked at her, noticed her, even when he seemed annoyed with himself for being that transparent.

He wasn't a reason to put on makeup.

After all, he seemed angry whenever she drew his attention and the last thing she needed was more anger from him.

She shook her head and glanced one last time in the mirror. Large brown eyes with matching brown hair, a strong jaw, black eyelashes.

Makeup would help.

She moved past the mirror, stopped, started walking again. "This is ridiculous," she muttered, finally swiping on some pink lipstick from the nearby dresser and rubbing her lips together.

The lipstick was for her.

Not him.

Never him.

It made her feel confident. Like she'd just put on a suit of armor.

She walked into the living room and paused. The blanket from the night before was still draped across the floor and part of the couch.

Last night he'd looked at her...really looked at her. Maybe it had been her imagination but his lips seemed to linger over the ceramic cup when they locked eyes.

She shivered and wrapped her arms around her chest. The dark room was suddenly too small, too depressing. She glanced around for the light, but the minute she flipped the switch, the blinds seemed to come alive, begging to be pulled.

Well, he couldn't get any more angry with her. His conflicted expression flashed in her mind. A minute ago she was trying not to make him angry and now she was going to poke the bear.

With a sigh, she grabbed each of the strings to the blinds and pulled them completely up.

Light immediately flooded the room, opening it up, making it feel bigger—massive, actually. And just like Brock had said, the light flooded all the way into the kitchen, creating a beautiful streak of sunlight as if heaven really was looking down and smiling.

With a grin, she skipped over to the kitchen, doing a few twirls in her Converses on the way.

"She used to do that," came a rough voice. "Dance in the sunlight."

Nearly tripping into the wall, Jane recovered and turned around. A sleepy Bentley was making his way into the room. "I don't remember much, but I do remember that."

"I'm sorry." Jane felt horrible.

Bentley frowned. "Why would you feel sorry for dancing in streams of sunlight?" His face transformed into a grin before he grabbed her body and pulled it against his, twirling her around the room.

"You know the quick step?" She let out a breathless laugh.

"Grandfather raised me right." He winked, tugging her body across the floor directly into the sunlight.

A burst of laughter escaped her as he bent her down and his lips hovered near her neck.

"Careful," he warned, eyes locking with hers. "You'll make me think you want me more than Brock, and I would hate getting strangled to death." He leaned in toward her mouth. "Then again, it may be worth it."

"What. The. Hell." Brock's voice was deafening. "Is happening in here?"

Bentley pulled her to her feet and turned. "Dancing. You know, where you move your feet and hold a woman close enough to feel the tips of her breasts press against your chest and—"

"Bentley, I swear I really will kill you if you finish that sentence," Brock barked, his eyes thunderous as he looked between the two.

Suddenly feeling guilty, Jane backed slowly away from the testosterone and went into the kitchen.

She knew exactly what she was going to make.

Luckily, she'd gotten a few groceries from the store, including a few frozen treats.

Twenty minutes later the smell of cinnamon filled the house.

The timer went off. She grabbed the oven mitts and pulled the tray of cinnamon rolls out, then slowly began to drizzle icing across them.

"Are those"—Brock was suddenly behind her, and she could feel the heat of every warm masculine inch of him—"what I think they are?"

She gulped. He was going to yell. She just knew it.

Tensing, she gave him a jerky nod.

"And was it you who opened the blinds?"

"Y-yes," she stammered.

His hands moved to her shoulders and then slid down her arms. With a sharp inhale he whispered gruffly, "Thank you."

And then he was gone.

Her arms, however, kept the memory of the way his hands had caressed her body.

It took a few minutes for her to regain her composure, and by then all three men were in and out of the kitchen as they grabbed coffee. Each of them tried to swipe icing off the rolls as they passed by.

"Let them cool!" she yelled when Brock came in for the second time.

He held his hands in the air. "I was just going to ask when they would be ready."

"They're ready when they're ready!" She shoved him out of the kitchen.

"Heartless wench!" Bentley yelled. "Give us food!"

"Man hungry," Brant growled, slamming his hand against the table. "Man need food!"

She shook her head and tried to keep the laugh in, but when they all started arguing she knew it was useless; they were walking, talking chaos.

Finally, she grabbed a few plates and piled the cinnamon rolls high, then deposited them in the middle of the table.

Hands went surging forward.

Within minutes, all of the cinnamon rolls were gone.

Even the icing was all but licked from the plate.

"So, I have a completely nonsexual proposition for you." Brant leaned back and patted his stomach. "Live with me, bake for me, I'll make you a very happy woman. Cars." He spread his hands wide. "Money. Furs."

Bentley nodded encouragingly. "You'll be our kept woman. But you have to bake every day. Don't worry, we'll give you a safe word, just in case things get too crazy."

"Who needs a safe word for cooking?" Brant asked, licking his finger while he winked at Jane.

"Food's erotic." Bentley blinked. "You're almost as clueless as Brock."

Brock groaned slowly and started banging his head against the table.

Both men ignored him and continued to argue about what Jane's safe word should be.

"Potato!" Bentley snapped his fingers.

"There's nothing liberating about a damn potato!" Brant argued. "How about 'cherry'?" He smirked. "Get it? Cherry?"

Brock stood abruptly and started grabbing all of the plates, making more noise than necessary as he fumbled with the forks and left the dining area.

"Better go help him, Cherry." Bentley winked. "Fuck me, I love sexy nicknames."

She knew he was kidding but she was still embarrassed. With a weak wave of her hand she went into the kitchen, only to find Brock doing the dishes.

For someone who had been doing nothing but cleaning up after other people her entire life, it was like watching porn.

His denim shirt was rolled up to his elbows; tanned forearms flexed as he dipped a dish into the water and began to wipe.

A whimper escaped her lips before she could stop it.

He looked up at the sound and a smile spread across his face. "Imagine what would happen if I had a larger...plate," he teased.

Her face probably did look like a cherry.

Clearing her throat, she grabbed one of the wet dishes and started drying it, only to have him pull the towel from her hands and jerk the plate away from her.

Great, he was mad again. Just when she'd gotten him to smile.

His large body loomed over hers, his blue eyes flashed, and then his mouth slammed against hers.

She wasn't ready for it.

Then again, she imagined as his tongue slid past her lips, a woman could never be prepared for a kiss like this.

It was as if he was claiming her, consuming her, and the very last thing she wanted to scream out was "Cherry."

His body pressed so hard against hers she could feel his arousal strain against his jeans. Jane gripped his shirt, bunching it in her hands as he deepened the kiss with a growl, only to abruptly pull away.

Chest heaving, he whispered a hoarse "thank you" before walking out of the kitchen.

She didn't move.

She couldn't.

"Everything okay in here?" Bentley poked his head around the corner then grinned. "Oh, never mind, I can see things went just fine. Need to go take a cold shower?"

Jane glared.

"Don't deny it. I can practically smell sexual arousal when it hits the air. Just remember to use protection; I'm too young to be an uncle."

"Don't you have a job?" Her voice was stupidly weak.

"Yup." He nodded. "And I'm so good at it and so rich that I rarely need to be in the office. Lucky you."

"Yes, just what I was thinking. Lucky me."

He smirked. "Do you want help with the rest of the dishes? I can dry while you overanalyze the panty-melting kiss he just gave you."

Searing heat blazed her cheeks, and she turned around and shoved her hands into the soapy water.

Bentley grabbed a plate and started drying. "Did he use tongue?"

Water sloshed over the edge of the sink.

Bentley tilted his head and nodded. "That slick bastard. He dark-horsed me, didn't he?"

"Hunh?" She blinked over at him and dipped a plate into the hot soapy water.

"Brock's the Dark Horse. He just staked his claim and ran like the ass he is, but it's good to see him actually do something for himself for once." He was quiet. "Damn, must have been some kiss if you're still thinking about it."

"You're really, really aggravating." She ignored the question just like she ignored the tightening in her stomach. Brock's kiss had been...everything.

Ugh, she was in so much trouble.

She had over two weeks of suffering, knowing what his lips felt like on hers? What his body was capable of?

"You're about to break that dish." Bentley pried it from her hands and started wiping. "Why don't you go fix your lipstick, since half of it is currently sitting nice on my brother's mouth, while the other half is smeared just here." He pointed to her cheek. "Not that I'm not a huge fan of a sexed-up woman; I just want you to be aware that men are attracted to that look, the one you still have, so if you don't want Brock to attack you again, you may want to"—he lifted a shoulder—"fix it."

"Th-thanks." She backed away slowly, tucking her hair behind her ear. How had it come out of its bun? When had that even happened?

Bentley's smile was slow, dangerous. "You know, once you go Brock you never go back."

She sighed. "It would be bad enough if there were only one of you, but there's two. Literally."

"Ain't it great?" He winked.

"I'll just go deal with...this." She pointed to her head.

"Good. Oh, and Jane?"

She stopped and turned back around. "Hmm?"

"Brock likes ponytails."

CHAPTER TWENTY-TWO

Brock kicked the side of the barn over and over and over again. The cock clearly thought it was being threatened and came barreling toward him, wings raised, beak out.

"Hell," he rasped, jumping over the stall wall and joining Buttercup.

Right. He'd just kissed the shit out of a woman that he had no business messing with and now he was in a horse stall hiding from a cock.

As if sensing his distress, Buttercup neighed and nudged his shoulder with her soft nose.

"Sorry, girl." He patted her head. The last time he'd ridden her had been years ago, but whoever had been taking care of the ranch was doing a good job. The barn was still a bit run-down but it was clean, the horses clearly fat and happy with plenty of roaming room and the best oats money could buy.

But still.

He felt guilty.

Damn it, he was so tired of the constant guilt.

Guilt made him say yes when he wanted to say no.

Guilt had him turning into a complete madman when it came to Jane. Hell, he'd mauled her and then run away.

She'd made those cinnamon buns for him. He knew that. He just didn't know why—especially after he'd been such an ass to her. Blaming her for things that weren't her fault.

With a sigh, he patted Buttercup's nose again and ran his hands down the side of her belly. "Wanna go for a ride, girl?"

Maybe it would distract him from marching back into the house, stripping Jane naked, and having his way with her next to the cinnamon roll crumbs.

His blood heated at the thought.

Buttercup kicked her hoof as if excited to get out and run. There was more thrill than hesitation on his part as he gently placed a saddle pad on her back then positioned the saddle before tightening the first cinch. When he was finished he put the bit into her mouth and ran his hand down the side of her nose.

"You ready, girl?" Fear slid into his chest, warning him against riding a horse he hadn't ridden since the week of his parents' accident. She'd been young then, so young that he'd probably had no business getting on her in the first place. And now she was old enough that it was a miracle she still looked so good.

He glanced back at the house, then at the horse. What other choice did he have? Going back into the house only meant temptation, and if he didn't move away from the cock it was going to attack the shit out of him. He opened the gate and hopped onto Buttercup.

And everything clicked into place.

Memories of riding her.

The trails they used to take.

Being on the back of his horse made Brock feel the most

centered he had in a while, especially after kissing a girl who made him want a life he would never have. Was that what it was about Jane? The fact that when he was with her he was tempted to want more and actually believed he could have it? Somehow, kissing her had made him feel more alive than he had in months—years. It felt freeing. *She* was freeing.

Buttercup let out a little snort as she started to gallop across the field, to where his grandfather used to train his old horses back when the ranch was active with horse breeding.

"Good girl." He patted the sweaty horseflesh and breathed in deep.

"Thought I might find you out here," a male voice called.

Frowning, Brock turned around and burst into laughter.

The twins were both attempting to ride one of the shortest horses in the barn. Its girth made up for whatever it lacked in height, but the idea that they were both able to stay on it without the horse biting them was impressive.

"What the hell is that?" He pointed to the scruffy bay horse with short legs.

"Oh, this bad-ass thing?" Bentley rubbed the horse's neck. "Don't listen to him, Frodo, he's just pissed because his dick isn't balls deep in—"

"Finish that sentence, I dare you."

"In his hand?" Brant said with a laugh. "By the way you look really sexy out here, your hair blowing in the wind. I almost orgasmed twice."

Brock rolled his eyes. "Why are you guys following me?"

"Oh, that." Bentley kicked Frodo's sides and the poor horse trotted forward, its eyes wide. "We came to tell you what a jackass you are."

Brock groaned out loud. "Is this about Jane?"

"It's sure as hell isn't about us." Brant shrugged. "You're

lucky Bentley's off his game or he'd swoop in and steal her before you could make up your mind if you're man enough to even go after her."

"What the hell!" Brock yelled. "She isn't some prize to be won, and she sure as hell isn't up for grabs! Not by either of you."

Brant narrowed his eyes at Brock. "Are you actually going to grow a pair of balls and go after her?"

Brock growled. "Back the fuck off. I mean it. She isn't like the girls you normally date." He cleared his throat. "She's better than that." The idea that they would even contemplate actually doing more than hitting on her made Brock want to punch something.

"She seemed embarrassed that you just took off after making out with her. Probably isn't used to all the attention only to have the guy who just kissed her run out of the house like she has Ebola," Bentley said softly. "And stop looking at me like I've grown another head. I'm a manwhore, not heartless."

"I didn't," Brock said defensively. "I just needed to think."

"We know." Brant's eyes flashed. "But we grew up with you so we know how you deal with shit. She, however, doesn't."

"I never thought I'd see the day where you two are the ones lecturing me." Brock shifted uncomfortably in the saddle. They were right. And he hated it.

"So." Bentley rubbed his hands together. "Who's going after the girl? First man back to the house wins?"

"First man to the house, my ass." Brock leaned over the horse's neck as they glided across the pasture and made it back to the barn in record time. He made sure Buttercup had fresh water and gave her a handful of oats before putting her in her stall, promising to take the saddle off once he made sure Jane was okay.

Buttercup seemed too immersed in the oats to care.

Long strides took him up the stairs and into the house.

The kitchen was spotless.

No Jane.

"Jane?" he yelled.

Nothing.

He took the stairs two at a time and swore as he spotted her, bent over in front of him, washing the floor with a rag.

He gulped. "No mops?"

Her ass was pointed straight at him, and so help him God he wanted to take a bite out of it. He gripped the wall with one hand and let out a rough exhale.

"This hard wood deserves more attention than a simple mop. I want to get in all the crevices." She didn't stop moving her hands back and forth.

His dick ached with each movement, as if she was stroking him instead of the wood. What the hell was it about this woman? This small, intimidating woman with her silky brown hair and chocolate eyes?

She let out a little grunt, turning on her hands and knees to get the section directly in front of his feet, and slowly she raised her head, cheeks flushed.

His breathing slowed as she moved one hand back and forth across the wood, and the smell of lemon soap and water filled his nostrils as he watched her work. Pieces of hair poked out of her bun, kissing her neck and shoulders. Her hand moved a bit faster.

He clenched his free hand into a fist.

She was stunning.

From her freckles to her toes.

Damn it.

"You're really good at that." Brock wanted to slap himself in the face, or run headfirst into the wall. Did he really just say that out loud?

She smiled. "Cleaning hardwood?"

Hardwood. Yeah, his wood was definitely hard. Fuck. If he kept watching, he was going to explode on the spot, like a teenage boy.

"Cleaning," he said with a rasp.

"I love it." She smiled down at the floor, her body visibly relaxing. "I know some people think it's demeaning, but there's nothing better than removing the dust and grime and seeing what's beneath a dirty surface. There's always something, you know? Something beautiful. No matter how it starts, it ends beautifully. I think objects deserve that, just..." She sighed. "Just like people."

"You're a fixer." He almost groaned. Was *he* her next project?

"I like to think of myself as a helper. After all, you can't fix others, only yourself."

"And me?" He just had to ask as he leaned down to her level. "Am I worth cleaning up, you think?" He hated how vulnerable he sounded, how weak the question made him, and how hungry he was for her response.

"Obviously." She stopped moving her hand and glanced up at him. "Or you wouldn't be brave enough to even ask."

He leaned forward, cupping her face with his hand.

Her mouth trembled.

"Brock..."

"Don't say no."

"But—"

"Please?"

He lowered his head just as something bit him in the ass. Or pecked him. He fell against the couch with a curse.

"Forget to close the front door?" Jane asked in an amused voice.

He kicked toward the cock. "Go away!"

His volume seemed to only encourage the rooster as it made an ear-splitting noise and flapped toward him with a fury that would only be matched by Satan himself. Feathers puffed into the air with each angry flap.

"Son of a bitch!" Brock grabbed Jane's hand and tried to run, but the floor was too wet. He went down, and took Jane with him.

The cock flew at them both.

A loud whistle stopped it from killing them, and then another whistle had the cock turning around and flapping toward the stairway.

"Saved your life," Bentley said in a bored tone. "But what can I say, I'm good with my cock." He winked at Jane.

Brock offered Jane his hand but she was wincing as if she was in pain.

"Are you okay?" he asked.

She nodded, but then pointed to her foot. "I think I may have twisted my ankle sometime between the cock rising into the air for the final kill and running to escape whatever swift death he had planned."

"If I had a dollar..." Bentley joked, moving toward them over the slippery floor. He touched Jane's ankle, giving Brock the sudden urge to growl and punch his brother in the face. "It's starting to swell."

"No!" Jane shoved him away. "I swear it's fine. I can still work." She tried to stand. "See? No problem!" Tears welled in her eyes.

Despite her claim, Brock lifted her into his arms and carried her into the master bedroom. "Bentley, get me some Advil and ice."

"On it." Bentley was immediately gone.

"Please." Jane's lower lip trembled. "I really want to stay and work. Please?"

Brock sighed. "Jane, you can't work with a sprained ankle."

"I can!" Her nostrils flared. "It's just a stupid ankle. I'll be fine."

Brock pulled off her socks and made a face when he saw the purple and blue bruising that had already moved past her swollen ankle up to her calf. "Yeah, I'm going to have to say no."

"But—"

"You need to stay off your feet."

She sighed. "Fine. If you just help me pack my things, I can be gone this afternoon."

He blinked in confusion. "To the hospital? I don't think that's necessary."

"No." She groaned, lying back against the pillows. "Home! I can't do my job, therefore I can't stay."

"The hell you can't," Brock fired back. "I'm sure it will only take a few days to heal, which leaves you plenty of time to clean later, right?"

She worried her lower lip. "I guess. It's just, it's a really big house."

"I think we can figure something out. After all, the twins are bored; why not let them help me clean while you heal up?"

Jane froze then licked her lips. "You? Clean?"

Brock tried not to be offended. "Of course I can clean! What do you think, I have a maid or something?"

She arched her eyebrows.

"Okay fine, I have maids, but how hard can it be?"

She glared.

"Shit, I didn't mean it like that. I just meant, I can figure it out, it's not rocket science." He swore. "I'm not helping my case at all, am I?"

Jane shook her head and smiled.

"I respect what you do and I will try my hardest to be just as good when I rub out the wood."

Jane giggled. "Rub out the wood?"

"Oh hell." Brock groaned. "I meant scrub, clean." His throat tightened as he swallowed and tried to get the vision of her on her hands and knees out of his mind.

"Sure you did."

"Bentley!" Brock yelled. "Where are we with that ice?"

"Need to cool off?" Jane teased in a breathless voice. Her eyes were on his mouth. Maybe she was reliving the kiss just like he was—or anticipating more.

Brock eyed her up and down then swore. "You have no idea."

CHAPTER TWENTY-THREE

Jane smiled when Brock fussed over her ankle, making sure to put a towel between her skin and the ice pack. Truthfully, it hurt bad. Enough that every time she tried to stand to prove to them she was fine, a shot of pain would run up her leg, stealing her breath away.

All because of an out-of-control cock.

"I think he's jealous of me," Brock announced when he walked back into the room with a tray of food. "The cock, I mean."

Jane grinned. "How do you figure?"

"Every time he gets really aggressive, it's when I'm with you."

"Has the cock always lived here?"

"Older than dirt, that cock." Brock smirked. "My grand-father bought it to protect the hens, but it refused to stay in the henhouse. The damn thing used to strut around the ranch like he owned it. I honestly thought it would be dead by now, but apparently he's as stubborn as Grandfather. You know how they say dogs resemble their owners? Clearly they've never met Diablo."

"Diablo?" Jane asked. "You named the cock Diablo?"

"Satan sounded too tame and Beelzebub wasn't quite strong enough, so Diablo it is. I figured if he had a name we could stop using the word 'cock.'"

"You should make him a collar."

"He'd be impossible to live with." Brock's smile was wide, and his dimples were wreaking havoc on her already weakened body. "Now, do you want cream and sugar in your coffee? Or black?"

"Black," she rasped, reaching for the cup at the same time as Brock. Their fingers brushed, and she jerked back. "Sorry."

"I'm not going to toss it in your face if that's what you're worried about."

She went with it; better she let him assume she was still afraid he hated her than admit that she was so attracted to him she wasn't sure how to breathe sometimes when he looked at her the way he was now. Like she existed, like she was important. "Sorry; old habits."

He made a face and sipped some of his own coffee. "Do you want to..." He licked his full lips and ran his fingers through his long hair. "Shit."

"Do I want to shit?" She giggled.

His face actually reddened a bit. "That's not what I meant."

"I know."

"Someone's feeling better."

"Advil," she lied. It was the company. Again, he didn't need to know that.

"Yeah well, don't put it past Bentley to try to sneak muscle relaxers into your food, or Molly."

"Molly? You're kidding."

"Grandfather still claims the reason he went to the hospital was dehydration, not the drug; never mind that the drug causes dehydration."

"Wait, wait, wait." Jane held up her hand. "Your grandfather? The one pushing eighty-two? Was taking Molly?"

Brock shrugged. "He was at a rave. I've learned not to ask questions."

"But he's old."

"Doesn't stop him from doing whatever the hell he wants, believe me." Brock stared down into his coffee as if lost in his thoughts.

Jane wasn't sure what to say. Bringing up the auction seemed like a bad idea. She didn't want a reminder that he was going to be with someone else, and that someone else wasn't her. The last thing she wanted was for Brock to be thinking about it, too.

Because for a few brief moments today, she'd imagined what it would be like to share more kisses in the kitchen. She'd even get chased by Diablo every day if it meant she could be with someone like him.

She pushed the thought away, because that was all it was—a fleeting thought that could so easily turn into a dream, which meant that when it didn't come true, it would hurt.

She shivered.

"Are you cold?" Brock quickly stood and walked over to the chair, grabbing a large blanket and tucking it around her body.

"You don't have to stay, you know." She kept her voice even. "I know you probably want to relax and…" She lifted a shoulder into the air, not finishing her thought.

"Diablo's blocking the door," Brock said. "And the twins

are making dinner. Actually, Bentley's eating the dinner Brant's trying to make. The point is, I have all the time in the world."

And he was spending it with her.

She chewed her bottom lip as his gaze lowered.

"Checkers?" she blurted.

Brock's expression relaxed. "Sure. Just don't get mad when I kick your ass."

"Hmm. What do I get if I win?"

"Oh, she likes to gamble." He flashed her a tempting smile that she felt all the way down to her toes. "If you win I'll give you one favor. You can ask for anything but money."

"I would never ask for money." She said in a horrified voice.

Brock studied her with an intensity that had her nearly squirming in her own skin. "I know."

She broke eye contact. "And if you win, I'll give you a favor. Clearly you can't ask for money because I don't have any."

"I would never take money from a woman anyway."

"You're making me want to bet money now." She snorted.

"Don't get your panties in a bunch." He winked. "All right, let's play."

She nodded and rubbed her hands together. "Prepare to have your world rocked."

Jane could have sworn she heard him whisper under his breath. "Too late."

CHAPTER TWENTY-FOUR

He's going to lose," Bentley announced, tossing more money into the pot. He and Brant had started betting once they heard that Brock and Jane were playing checkers, and now they were sitting on Jane's bedroom floor being annoying as usual.

They had gone from making a simple five-dollar bet to five hundred dollars.

Which, all things considering, was pretty tame for his brothers, given the last thing that Bentley had won was an ass.

"Shh, you just take your time," Brant coached Jane. "In and out, there you go, deep breaths, make your decision then stick with it, stick it to him hard." He gave Brock a wicked smirk and mouthed *fuck you.*

"Don't listen to Brant, Brock. Just focus."

Jane moved her black checker forward. It was a bad move; he could easily jump it, so clearly he was missing something. He glanced around the board. Impossible. She'd just given him the game!

And this was their tie-breaking game.

The first she'd won.

The second he'd won.

"You've just lost." Brock smiled arrogantly.

Her poker face stayed completely unreadable as she gave him a noncommittal shrug and glanced down at the board. "Then move."

He moved his red checker, hopping over the black and stealing it. "The way I see it, you have two left. I have three."

"Mmm-hmmm." She smiled sweetly and then, very quickly, jumped one of her other black checkers, one he hadn't noticed because he'd been so focused on that damned stupid move she'd just made. All in all he lost two checkers. Leaving him with a lingering thought that he'd completely underestimated her ability at board games. "What was that? About losing?"

"Son of a bitch!" Bentley yelled. "The hell, man! I told you to focus!"

"You mean you saw that?" Brock roared.

Bentley held up his hands. "Rules are rules, no audience participation."

"Thank you." Brant grabbed the pot of money on the floor and threw it in the air. "Hey, if we have dollar bills I bet the cock will dance for us."

Brock rolled his eyes. "And Grandfather wonders how you guys end up in every newspaper in the country."

Bentley shrugged. "We're hot and rich. Two plus two, man; two plus two."

"It's good that humility runs in the family." Jane nodded while Brant gave her a kiss on the head and a pat on the back, like she'd just won him a freaking car or something.

"How's the ankle?" Bentley moved to her side. There were entirely too many people in this room. Brock wanted to shove everyone out but that would look bad. Him forcing his brothers to leave so he could do what? Kiss her again? Stare at her? Watch her kissable lips pout?

"It's good." Jane yawned behind her hand. "Sorry, all the excitement must have worn me out."

"Checkers. Almost like running a marathon with your hands." Bentley winked. "Lay down; it's dudes' night to clean up."

Brock had no choice but to stand.

And follow his brothers out of the room, shutting the door quietly behind him.

But the minute he turned from the door, both Brant and Bentley gave him dumbfounded looks.

"What?" He crossed his arms. "Why are you both looking at me like that?"

"You're an idiot." Brant shook his head slowly. "Did you really just...leave?"

Brock glanced back at the door then back at them. "She said she was tired! She yawned!"

"That doesn't mean you leave!" Bentley slapped a hand to his forehead. "You're such an idiot."

Brant just continued shaking his head in disappointment.

Brock lifted his hands into the air. "What the hell was I supposed to do? Fluff her damn pillow?"

"*Yes!*" They both yelled in unison.

"Offer a massage," said Bentley.

"'Do you need a glass of water?'" offered Brant.

"'More blankets?'" added Bentley.

"How about a fucking bedtime story?"

"What's that? You want me to stay with you until you fall asleep, get naked under the covers? What? You want me to touch your sweaty naked body and—" Bentley had always been the storyteller in the family.

Brant coughed.

"Sorry." Bentley exhaled. "I got carried away." He pointed in Brock's direction. "Stupidity does that to me."

Brock ran his hands through his hair and turned to re-open the door.

"No!" Brant shoved him back. "It's too late. Now you seem creepy and unsure."

Bentley nodded his head in agreement. "Completely wasted opportunity. I've never been so disappointed in a brother, and I live next door to this asshat."

"Thanks, man." Brant nodded.

"Anytime." Bentley flashed a smile. "Brock, go to bed. Think about all the bad choices made in just the past ten minutes and for fuck's sake fix them. Do you really want to spend the next seventeen days without seeing her naked?"

"It's not about that," Brock said defensively.

"Even better." Brant suddenly grew serious. "Even better."

"What the hell is that supposed to mean?" Brock clenched his fists.

"It means"—Bentley stood between them, pressing a hand against Brock's chest—"that it's about damn time you do something for you. Not for us. Not for our dead parents and sure as hell not for Grandfather, but for you. And that girl in that room? She's for you."

Stunned, Brock could only gape at Bentley as if his brother had grown two heads.

"There's always tomorrow," Brant encouraged. "'Night, guys."

"There isn't," Brock said under his breath. "We aren't promised tomorrow."

Bentley paused in the hall, his expression pained. "Then why the hell are you allowing someone else to control your life? If you died tomorrow, what would people remember about you? How easygoing you were? How controlled? How rich? Is that what you want, *boring Brock*?"

The old nickname was a solid hit to his chest. His brothers hadn't called him that since college.

"Well?" Bentley's eyebrows shot up. "Boring Brock would walk away, but I don't think that's what you want anymore."

"It's all I know. It's for him. For them."

"Never for you." Bentley sighed. "Look, man, I get it, believe me. I get the pressure, but do you ever wonder who put it there in the first place? Because the way I see it, it sure wasn't Grandfather. It was a scared twelve-year-old boy who took the baggage and cheerfully carried it out the door, refusing to let anyone help him along the way. And for what? Did anyone throw you a parade? Did anyone notice how hard it was? No, just you."

"When the fuck did you get so wise?"

Bentley laughed. "Let's not let that get around. If Grandfather ever found out he'd auction me off next. God help the poor woman saddled with me for the rest of her life."

"Nothing wrong with commitment."

Bentley paled. "We all have our demons."

"Goodnight, Bentley."

"Night... Boring Brock."

Brock smiled the entire way back to his room.

Tomorrow, after all, was a new day.

CHAPTER TWENTY-FIVE

Lying awake in bed, staring up at the ceiling and wishing she'd packed some sort of sleep aid—not that it would work, because for the most part she knew the reason behind the no sleep—was becoming a new habit for Jane.

Brock.

If only she could walk. Maybe sleeping on the couch would help, or maybe she'd just raid Brock's whiskey closet.

After another hour of tossing and turning, she finally made the decision to hobble downstairs. So what if it took an hour? At least the slow journey would exhaust her.

Once she sat up in bed she was careful not to put any weight on her foot. Rather, she hobbled, loudly, toward the door. Her tank top and shorts didn't really hide anything but it was dark and everyone else would be sleeping.

She hoped.

Or did she?

Rejecting the thought of Brock sitting in the living room,

waiting for her, she opened the door and glanced down the hall to the right and to the left.

All clear.

With a wince, she hobbled a few feet then lost her balance, nearly face planting against the wall and knocking out a tooth.

"Need help?" asked an amused voice to her left.

Slowly she turned. Brock's smile was easy, wide.

"I'm fine. I was just..." She searched for a better excuse than *I couldn't sleep* but she had nothing. "I'm having trouble sleeping."

His eyes twinkled. "Me too."

She was quiet. What was she supposed to say?

"Whiskey?" He offered his arm.

She stared down at it then back up at him. Decision made, she slid her hand through. He started walking them down the rest of the hallway, then with a heave she was in his arms as he carried her down the stairs.

She'd always thought of herself as curvy, not light as a feather, but Brock carried her like she weighed nothing more than a cup of rice. She remembered how strong he'd felt when he'd picked her up at the party—how good he smelled. Memories of their first meeting surfaced as his body flexed around hers.

He deposited her on the couch, went into the kitchen, and returned with two mugs of whiskey.

"Thanks." Her voice was rough, edged with the tension already coiling in her belly at Brock's proximity and her own sudden change of heart. Maybe it would be best if he was still angry with her, projecting all his feelings onto the help. At least then she wouldn't fall for him, right?

"I see why you couldn't sleep." His light southern drawl

wrapped around her like liquid heat. "If you stare any harder at the wall it's going to crack."

Jane immediately looked down into her mug and took a slow slip, careful not to cough and spew whiskey all over him. "Just a lot on my mind."

"Want to talk about it?"

No. Because talking meant bonding, bonding meant hurt later on down the road. And she didn't want to focus on the future, a future where she wouldn't be able to sit in the world's most perfect ranch house with the world's most beautiful man and sip whiskey out of a nice brown mug.

"Tell me about the auction."

That did it. His smile fell and a cold expression chilled his features. He sat back and took a giant swig of whiskey that seemed to go on forever. He finally set his empty cup down and made a face. "It's for charity."

She almost laughed out loud at his disgusted expression. "And you hate being charitable?"

"Hardly." He snorted. "I'd much rather throw millions of dollars at a charity by hosting a dinner; even the ball that the old man's throwing is a good idea. Ten thousand dollars a head is a good way to bring in money to the foundation. It's the whole auction part that's..." He cursed. "Are you sure you don't want to talk about you?"

"You're much more interesting." He'd brought up a blanket and she tried pulling it over her ankle, but before she could do it herself Brock was at her side. He pulled the blanket over her and within the same breath he lifted her foot, sat down next to her, and placed her leg over his lap.

Jane's breath hitched as he ran his fingers over her ankle in a smooth caress before locking eyes with her. "Is this okay?"

She gave him a jerky nod, mentally groaning at how eager she must look for his touch, his proximity.

Oh, this was bad.

So bad.

His hand started to move up her calf. Oh, this was good, so very good.

"You were saying." Somehow, miraculously, she found her voice as he continued to lightly knead the muscles in her calf.

"The auction is stupid. Plain and simple."

She frowned. "Then why did you say yes?"

His hand froze and he went completely still. "Saying no wasn't an option."

"But…" Her eyes narrowed. "You always have a choice."

"It would seem that way. I believe that's how life is supposed to work—you're in control of your own destiny, you always have a choice, but what people never admit is that although you can say no to something, there might be horrible consequences. Which basically means it's not really a choice. The word 'choice' is just there so that it seems fair, so that it looks good, so the situation looks balanced, when it's never been balanced, not for a long time."

Jane wasn't sure if they were still talking about the auction or something else.

"So, what do you think about the auction? Don't lie and say you have no opinion about it, either."

A smile teased the corners of her mouth. "Clearly you know me well."

"All women have an opinion."

"And all men are led by their stomachs." She winked.

He licked his lips. "Among other things, yes."

"I, uh…" She twisted her hands in her lap, suddenly nervous. "I think that it's nice that you're willing to put your future in the hands of a grandfather with a desire to go to raves at the age of eighty-two."

Brock groaned as his head fell back against the couch. "Ugh, tell me about it."

"It's...cute," she said, trying to make him feel better.

"Cute," he repeated, still not looking at her. "Cute."

He said it a few more times before glancing at her.

"What?" She rubbed her lips together.

"A man my age doesn't want to be cute."

"Your age?"

"Hey, you're the one that called me old."

"You're thirty-five."

"I know my age, thank you."

"So maybe according to my twenty-two years you seem old. That's all I meant." She smiled as his face paled.

"T-twenty two?" He stared at her. Hard. "You're twenty-two?"

"You say it like I'm diseased."

His mouth dropped open and closed. "I suddenly feel like a cradle robber."

"Because I'm a child?" She pulled the blanket closer, needing the protection, thinking that if she could just bury her body into it, he wouldn't see how his words affected her.

"Shit." He took one look at her expression and leaned across the couch and cupped her face. "I didn't mean that. I just...it took me by surprise, that's all."

Tears welled in her eyes. "I'm sorry; maybe I'm more tired than I thought. I should probably go back to bed."

"I'll join you," Brock added then stumbled over his words. "I mean, I'll take you. Damn it, sorry. Clearly we're both tired."

She didn't have a chance to say anything more before he picked her up and carried her slowly up the stairs, careful not to bang her ankle on the wall. Once they were back in her bedroom he placed her on the bed and pulled the covers over her, his eyes searching, yearning, as raw emotion raged like a war across his dark features.

Did he want something more from her? Did he feel the electric pull between them, too? So many times it seemed like he had more to say, like he wanted to pull her into his arms and devour her. Just the thought had a shiver running down her spine.

God knew, she wanted him.

Even though she knew she would end up without him in the end, it didn't make her feelings toward him go away, though she wished they would.

"I'm sorry, Jane," he whispered, tucking her hair behind her ear over and over again, as if he couldn't stop touching her. "Like I said, I was surprised, and apparently I turn into an ass when I'm caught off guard."

"Most old people do," she joked in a deadpan voice. "I think they're afraid of heart failure. Either that or their hearing is already going so they get defensive."

His eyes darkened. "Very funny."

She laughed into the blankets. "I thought so."

"Keep making fun of me and I'll throw you over my knee."

She stilled.

His smile froze and then turned very dangerous, so dangerous she could feel the impact of it all over her body.

"I should go," he whispered, still not moving.

"Probably." Her throat worked hard to swallow as he leaned over the bed and pressed a kiss to her forehead. His lips slid down to her temple and then her cheek. An inch from her mouth he waited, hesitated.

Her body burned for more of his kisses, more of his touch.

But she didn't know what to do. The last man who had

kissed her had told her she was frigid because she wouldn't sleep with him.

Would Brock be the same?

He was used to women giving him whatever he wanted— she'd fall short.

Finally, she sank back into the pillows. "Goodnight, Brock."

He let out a heavy sigh and pulled back. "Goodnight, Just Jane."

When he was almost to the door, she called out, "Don't forget to remove the dentures!"

With a curse, Brock stumbled into the door and then turned around and glared. "What did I say about teasing me?"

Feeling braver now that he was farther away, she arched her brow. "Maybe I like being punished."

He gripped the doorway with his large hands and swore. "Now she tells me."

"I figured you were already leaving so I was safe."

"I could always sprint back toward that bed."

"But you won't."

He sighed. "Not tonight. But Jane?"

"Yes?" Was that her voice? All husky and desperate?

"Tomorrow is a new day, isn't it?"

"Yes," she croaked, "it is."

"Sweet dreams."

"You too."

"If you think I can leave your room and actually sleep…" He shook his head, then gave her a sad smile. "Cheers to a night of tossing and turning."

CHAPTER TWENTY-SIX

The next morning, Brock yawned over his scrambled eggs and toast, then yawned again as he took a long draw of coffee, and one last time as he stabbed his sausage with a fork.

"Long night?" Bentley said with a grin. "Dreaming about all the possibilities that didn't actually happen? Dancing like little erotic ballerinas in your head? Ones who rhyme with shame? Lame? Game?"

Brock let out a grunt and flipped off his brother just as Brant helped Jane to the table. Brock nearly jumped to his feet, knocking his chair backward against the floor. "You're up?"

Jane thanked Brant by kissing him on the cheek, and sat in the chair across from Brock. *The rutting bastard*, thought Brock. "Yes, sorry I slept in."

Damn, if that's what sleeping in looks like, sign me up. From her bright chocolate eyes to the pink spreading across her cheekbones, she looked stunning.

He gripped his fork so damn hard he was surprised it didn't bend in half.

"Pity, it's such nice silverware, too. Some might say an antique." Bentley grinned at Brock's hand while Jane gave them both a confused look.

"You clearly slept well, my beautiful, sexy, sweet—" Bentley stopped talking the minute Brock slid a knife toward him and glared. "Jane?"

"It's too early for violence," Brant muttered.

"Um, I slept okay." Jane stared down at her empty plate, a smile curving her lips like she was keeping a secret.

Brock found himself grinning at her, like he had a right to, like he'd spent the night in her arms, when really he'd taken a cold shower and slept with half a bottle of whiskey. Hence the hangover currently pounding on both sides of his head.

"Glad to hear it," Bentley sighed. "I was worried you'd be all hot and bothered." He paused, sharing a look with Brock. "You know, because of all the blankets I'm sure this jackass piled on top of you before abandoning you."

"Oh, Brock didn't abandon me." Jane shrugged. "We shared a midnight drink last night."

"No," Brant said in a dry tone. "That's a shock. What did he do? Pound down your door and demand you pour whiskey into his cup because he lacks the intelligence to do it himself?"

Brock groaned. "I don't know why I put up with either of you."

"Family sticks together," Bentley pointed out. "Just ask Grandfather."

The room fell silent and tense.

"Jane." Suddenly desperate to spend more time with her away from his brothers—even though he knew nothing could come of it—he stood. "Why don't you eat a few more bites and I'll start the cleaning."

Bentley choked on his coffee while Brant hid a laugh behind his hand.

"What?" Brock shrugged. "I'm going to help her. What are you jackasses going to do? Take a selfie and post it on Instagram?"

Brant removed his hand from his mouth. "Did you just say selfie?"

"Does he even know what Instagram is?" Bentley added. "Jane, do me a solid; check the window and see if one of the pigs is flying."

Brock clenched his teeth. "I know about Instagram. I just choose not to take pictures of myself with the world's longest selfie stick!"

"Known as my penis." Bentley grinned then raised his hand for a high five. Brant hit it and gave Brock an apologetic look while Jane burst out laughing.

Great; he was back to being Boring Brock, getting offended and uncomfortable while his brothers laughed at his expense.

"Why don't you start with the game room?" Jane said, completely ignoring his brothers. "And I'll have one of the guys help me up."

The hell they would.

Brock sat. "I'll wait."

"'Course he will." Brant sighed. "Have you even fed the animals yet today?"

Brock gave them a blank stare.

"Fine." Bentley stood. "We'll do it. We'll start with the pigs. But if you hear screaming you better come running. I've heard they eat humans, and I can't promise I won't accidentally push Brant into the mud for a photo op."

"It may be worth all the comments." Brant nodded thoughtfully. "Think of all the sex I would get. I'd be a hero."

"Yes." Bentley blinked in confusion. "A hero for surviving a pig attack. God, I can see the headlines now! Millionaire falls into pigpen, gets up, and walks right out! MIRACLE!"

Brant slapped him on the back of the head as they both made their way slowly out of the kitchen and out of the house. The screen door slammed behind them.

Jane was still staring after them when Brock piled food high onto her plate. "Eat."

"Am I eating for five people?"

He felt himself tense. "No, I just... You're small, you need..." Why was he so bad with the words? Why? "Fat."

"I need fat," she replied.

He winced. "Something like that."

"Okay." She pressed her lips together as though she was trying to suppress a smile. "Then fat it is." Poking her fork into a grease-laden sausage, she devoured half her plate before finally announcing she was done and that he might need his brothers' help getting her upstairs.

"I'm sure I can handle it."

Jane made a face. "Are you sure? Because I just ate enough for three people. I really didn't mean to take you up on the whole fat-eating but the food was incredible!" Jane seemed giddy; her face lit up like she'd just been taken to the most expensive restaurant in the world. "It's just, nobody ever cooks for me. The last person to make me breakfast was my—"

As if he'd just been sucker-punched, Brock's breath stilled. "Your boyfriend?"

After a pause where he prayed to God he was wrong, she answered.

"Mother." Jane licked her lips, a nervous habit he was coming to despise since it reminded him of kissing her. "She was big into waffles every Monday morning, and during the week she made sausage and pancakes. French toast was always my favorite." She straightened her shoulders and then wiped underneath her eyes. "Her name was Rosie. She died...from cancer. It was a long time ago but a girl always wants her mother, you know?"

Of course he knew.

He knew because a boy needed his father.

He thought that might be why he'd latched onto his grandfather so completely.

"I'm sorry," he whispered.

"Like I said, it was a long time ago. I just..." Her sadness shifted to a smile. "I have a soft spot for waffles."

Brock stored that information for later.

Damn it, he'd cook for her every day if he got that reaction. Maybe he didn't need to be a poet or a wordsmith around Jane; maybe relating to Jane, getting her to like him, had more to do with action.

Action he could do.

After all, his brothers were the talkers.

He'd always been the doer.

His thoughts jumbled as he realized he was no longer flirting with the idea of pursuing her, but actively conjuring up a way to seduce her.

CHAPTER TWENTY-SEVEN

Jane tried to calm her jittery stomach while Brock put on HGTV without her even asking, and then wrapped a blanket around her while he grabbed her cleaning supplies and got to work.

He stared down at the supplies like he wasn't sure which to use first and then glanced over his shoulder and winked at her. His expression changed as he took two steps toward her and then pulled the blanket over her feet making sure they were completely covered—as if she could catch a chill with a man like him paying attention to her.

"Are you comfortable enough?" His eyebrows drew together as he leaned over her, his massive frame dwarfing hers. "Do you have everything you need?" He seemed genuinely concerned as he reached for her ankle but then pulled back and looked away.

"I'm...perfect," she whispered. "And thanks to you, wrapped up like a burrito."

The corners of his mouth lifted into a smile as he backed off and went back to the cleaning supplies.

Sure, her favorite channel was on.

But Brock was cleaning.

And she was supervising.

Muscles flexed beneath his black T-shirt as he moved around the room, first vacuuming—sending her apologetic looks every time he got close to her and the TV—and next, grabbing Windex and starting in on the windows.

The room was so dusty he'd need to vacuum twice.

But she didn't want to tell him that. In fact, it would have been smarter for him to vacuum last, but again, interrupting the dream currently taking place in front of her very eyes seemed like a stupid idea.

He didn't move fast.

He wasn't graceful.

But he moved with a purpose, like he'd been given an important job and he was going to see it through. Her entire body clenched as his large hands moved across the glass, muscles still flexing. She almost wondered if the windows were going to crack under the pressure; it wasn't as if he had a light touch.

Though she knew him capable of one.

Shivering, she pulled the blanket closer.

Why was he even helping her?

Was it out of pity? Or because he really did want her company? Maybe even blamed himself for the rooster attack?

"So." Brock made his way back over to her after cleaning the last window. "There's still dust. How is there still dust?"

She grinned. "You need to dust to make the dust go away."

"I knew that."

"I know."

"I was just checking." He didn't move, his smile growing. "And where would I find the...duster?"

"Close."

"Damn it," he mumbled.

She would not laugh. Not when he looked that embarrassed and miserable. "You know, why don't I dust the coffee table and show you?" She leaned over. "It's right in front of me so it won't be hard."

He swallowed, his eyes shuttering closed before he let out a raspy breath. "All right."

Frowning, she waited for him to grab her cleaning bucket and bring it over. Once it was settled in front of her, she grabbed the Pledge and one of the dusting rags and went to work.

The wood was beautiful beneath all that dust, except for some tiny marks on the edge of the table. It looked like some kid had taken a knife to it in order to keep tally marks for some sort of game.

"So you just spray it?" Brock asked. "And then..." He made a motion with his hand. "Rub?"

"Yes, that's about as complicated as it gets."

"Is it hot in here? Should I turn on the AC?" He stood abruptly, nearly stumbling into the table.

"Actually, I was kind of cold," she said honestly, pulling the blanket tighter around herself again. "But if you're hot I'll just cover up more."

"No!" he shouted. "I mean, no, it's not a big deal." His eyes flickered to her chest and then back up; he was clearly embarrassed. "I'll just finish up the table."

"Great." She leaned over again, and his eyes flickered closed as he mumbled a curse. "Brock, are you okay?"

"Hmm?" His gaze locked on hers. "Yup. Fantastic."

"Okay." She leaned over again and sprayed the Pledge on

the remaining dusty parts of the table, only to have him bite out another curse.

"Hey, Jane?"

"Yes?"

"Don't take this wrong."

"Okay..." Her guard shot straight up.

"But every time you lean over the table I can literally see straight down your shirt, and as much as you joked last night about me being old, I'm still a hot-blooded male. And the sight of two perfectly rounded breasts keeps taking my attention away from the task at hand, so if you could just..." He gently reached for her and pushed her back against the couch. "Stay. Right here. Then I can finish up before I lose my fucking mind."

She was stunned, and her mouth dropped open. Then she looked down. V-neck. Duh, she hadn't even thought about it.

Brock followed her gaze, his eyes heating.

"Jane." It was a whisper, it was a question, and then his mouth was on hers—harsh, forceful, but so inviting she whimpered at the contact—and when his hands reached for her breasts, she leaned even more into him, begging him with her body to take what she couldn't voice aloud.

It was a bad idea.

He was a bad idea.

Taken.

Ready to be married off.

But in the game room, on the couch, he was hers.

So she kissed him back with as much passion as she possessed, her hands digging into the front of his shirt while his teeth nipped at her bottom lip; his hips ground against hers until with a groan he pressed her back against the couch.

His hands slid beneath her shirt, unhooking her bra with ease as he nudged her thighs apart.

"You feel so soft," he murmured against her mouth. "Perfect." Another plundering kiss, his tongue flicking hers before his lips slid down her neck and sucked. "So damn good."

With a moan, she pressed as close as she could against him, nearly riding his leg in an effort to get more of him.

"That's it," he encouraged while she clawed at him.

"Brock!" Bentley's voice pierced the air. "Did you need help?"

Brock froze above her, his face filled with irritation. "Open that door, Bentley, and I'm selling every car you own and replacing it with a Honda!"

Silence.

"You don't mean it." The knob turned.

Jane's eyes widened in alarm as Brock quickly moved away from her and tossed the blanket…over her head. Right, like that was going to look normal. She pulled the blanket off her face and tried in vain to find her bra while frantically pulling her hair back into a ponytail.

Bentley entered, took one look at both of them and smiled. "Clearly things were dirtier than we thought?" He tilted his head at Jane. "Or maybe not dirty enough?"

"Out!" Brock barked.

"But—"

"Go!"

"Fine," Bentley grumbled. "I'm leaving. I just thought you should know that Grandfather called and wanted to know how the maid was working out. I told him that you've been helping her since the cock attacked and she sprained her ankle. He was concerned about her finishing the job."

"What did you say?" Brock grabbed Bentley by the shirt and gave a little shake.

Bentley held up his hands. "Chill. I told him that while she'd hurt her ankle she would make a full recovery, that she refused to sue, and that you were taking care of the situation. Because that's all you're doing, right, Brock? Taking care of the situation..." He peered around Brock at Jane.

Feeling suddenly more naked than she actually was, she covered herself up with the blanket.

What had she been thinking?

It was daylight!

And his brothers were both within shouting distance!

The last thing she needed was to be seen sprawled naked across Brock's chest.

It was beyond unprofessional.

Tears burned the backs of her eyes.

She was being stupid.

And paranoid.

"Thanks, Bent." Brock sighed, running his hands through his already mussed hair.

Bentley saluted him then added quietly. "For the record, any girl that can get Boring Brock to bend the rules is a keeper."

Brock bit back a curse as Bentley shut the door.

"Boring Brock?" Jane asked.

"It's about as bad as it sounds."

"Well, I'm Plain Jane, so...I understand."

He turned. "You've never been plain a day in your life."

"I think you've already learned that you don't need to give me pretty compliments to get me to kiss you."

"You have seven freckles. You press your lips together to keep yourself from saying things you shouldn't. You hum when you clean, and though I'm not sure what the tune is, it's familiar. When you eat, you watch people rather than your own food, and I'm just going to come out and say it:

you eat sausage like an animal, the most erotic thing I've ever seen."

Jane covered her face with her hands. "It was flattering until you said that last part."

Brock laughed. "Seeing a woman dig into her food like she hasn't eaten in weeks? It's one of the most erotic visions I've ever had."

Emotion flashed across his face as he made his way over to her and kissed her again, pulling away with her name on his lips. "Jane, I want you."

"Thought I was just the help." The walls around her heart started to slip; she felt it in the way her body rose against him. Already he'd noticed things about her nobody ever had, and he'd fed her, and he was helping her, and he was beautiful. Was it so wrong to want that? For herself? Once in her life?

"You're more than that, and you know it." His eyes locked on to hers as his deep voice washed over her.

"You're getting auctioned off in two weeks and you know it."

He paused, his expression going completely ice-cold before he looked away and then back at her. "And if I wasn't? What then?"

"Then..." She bit down on her bottom lip. "I'd ask you to kiss me again."

CHAPTER TWENTY-EIGHT

Brock paced back and forth in the barn, keeping a wary eye on the cock, who was circling him and flapping his wings.

Finally, he dialed his grandfather's number.

"Brock?" Grandfather answered on the fourth ring. "How's my favorite grandson?"

"Brant was your favorite last time I checked. Don't tell me you're switching sides now?"

Grandfather coughed loudly then sniffed. "Well, I think it best to always keep you guys guessing. I find it keeps the twins in line."

Brock snorted.

"What was that?"

"Nothing."

"So, what can I do you for? I have a meeting in a few minutes, and before you start asking what it's about, it's just to tie up minor details for the ball. I've ordered your tux. You'll be in all black, of course. A matching set, you and I."

"And the twins?" Brock tried to keep the irritation out of his voice.

"They can wear whatever they want as long as they aren't naked."

And there it was. Brock, of course, needed to match his grandfather because he was a carbon copy. But the twins? They could do whatever the hell they wanted! Granted, a part of him knew his wasn't a fair assessment; his grandfather just didn't want to deal with the twins.

"Is something wrong? You're more quiet than usual," Grandfather asked with another sniff.

Brock sighed. "Nothing, I just...I was thinking. The auction is a great idea, for charity, but you were kidding about me actually marrying one of those women...right? I mean I know that the press took that idea and ran with it but..." *Please laugh, please laugh.*

Grandfather laughed.

Brock exhaled loudly.

"I thought you understood how this was going to work," Grandfather said quickly.

The sense of dread was back. "I assumed from the notes last week that the auction is going to take place halfway through the dinner at the ball. You'll pick from one of the five women who bids the most. I go out on a date with them, take pictures, and..." He gulped. "We get good publicity. The shareholders get to see us as a united front, the press goes wild, and everyone wins. I didn't think, I mean...marriage..."

"Of course you won't have to marry right away! But you never know. You may fall for one of the girls. The media is having a field day about where you've gotten off to, so everything is working according to plan." Grandfather lowered his voice. "Brock, I'm not trying to upset you, but things could get bad..."

Brock gulped and closed his eyes. "How bad?"

"If I die—"

Brock inhaled sharply. "Are you sick?"

"Not now." Grandfather sighed heavily. "But if I die and you and your brothers aren't cemented within the company, the shareholders will push you out. Right now the only thing keeping them satisfied is the publicity the auction is bringing in and the idea that Wellington Incorporated and Titus Enterprises could one day merge."

Brock wasn't so sure how he felt about any potential merger with a company that up until now had always been a complete pain in the ass. Grandfather kept on talking. "The auction is a show of goodwill. Besides, you aren't seeing anyone. You have to marry someone eventually."

Brock rolled his eyes. "I'm a person. With feelings. I want to marry a person I have actual feelings for."

Grandfather gasped. "I've never heard you admit to such a thing. What is this really about?"

Brock stared back at the house then kicked at the dirt. "A kiss."

With a curse, his grandfather spoke clearly into the phone. "Well, best push that kiss and any others out of your head. A kiss is a kiss, and what you do with your time until the ball is fine, as long as it doesn't affect our company's image. This is front-page news. The last thing we need is for the media to catch wind that you're kissing the maid. That type of news is not what the shareholders need to see. Do you understand?"

History was repeating itself.

The way it tended to do.

The "no" was on the tip of his tongue, ready to slide forward, but at the last minute Brock retracted and uttered the dreaded, "Yes sir."

Only this time. It was a total lie.

He understood, all right. He understood that no matter what he said, he wouldn't win, and the fear of saying no still made him want to puke, so he said yes.

But he didn't mean it.

"Good boy. You always were the serious one, the one who understood how important our reputation is to the company. My father started this company with his bare hands! I can't"—his breath hitched—"I can't imagine it going into anyone else's hands but yours. I know I'm hard on you, but it's because I see so much of myself in you."

"Right." The more his grandfather talked, the sicker he felt. It was such a backhanded compliment, because all he'd ever wanted was his grandfather's happiness. It had almost always been at the expense of his, but he knew in his heart that his grandfather only wanted the best for him. The problem was, they had very different definitions of "best." "I need to go."

"Me too. See you in two weeks!"

Brock stared at his phone.

Slid it into his pocket.

Eyed the cock, and almost asked the damn bird to just end him.

Buttercup nuzzled Brock's neck as if she understood exactly what pained him.

If his grandfather ever found out what Brock had planned for the next few weeks, he'd shoot him.

But with each step he took toward the house, he realized fully that he was walking toward something he wanted. Not something his grandfather wanted for him.

And it felt good.

Empowering.

Even if he still hadn't been able to utter "no" to his own Grandfather—his heart still screamed "yes" to Jane.

And for now, it had to be enough.

* * *

When Brock stepped into the kitchen, all heads turned toward him.

Bentley was sticking his finger into a large bowl of frosting while Brant held a cookie over his head.

Jane stood on her toes, trying to grab the cookie from his brother's hand.

And somehow, the ass had found its way inside and was standing by the kitchen table watching.

"Give her the cookie, Brant."

"No." Brant held it higher. "I'm saving her the calories!"

She smacked him on the arm. "It's just one more sugar cookie!"

"You heard her, man." Bentley grinned. "Hand it over or I'm not baking anymore."

Brock was sure he'd heard wrong. He knew that his brother could cook but baking was a whole different beast. "You baked?"

Bentley nodded. "It's not rocket science."

"You baked...cookies?"

"He makes a mean carrot cake, too," Brant added, "Don't be too proud of him; he learned to cook because he found out the cougars liked it when a man knew his way around the kitchen. Think of it as his foreplay."

"You're a conniving bastard. You know that, right?" Brock nodded toward Bentley, who seemed completely unfazed, like it was normal to take up a hobby so you could have more sex.

Brant lowered the cookie to Jane's height and dangled it in front of her face. "If I give you this, what will you do for me?"

"Well, I don't know about Jane, but if you give her the cookie I won't strangle you. So there's that," Brock said in an irritated voice.

"He's got at least twenty pounds on you, Brant. I'd give over the goods."

Jane grinned in triumph as Brant shoved the large cookie into her mouth, patted her head, and glared at Bentley. "Make more."

"Don't pressure him!" Jane said, mouth full of food. "We don't want them burning. I've had four. I could eat them until I get sick. That's how good they are."

Suddenly jealous, Brock frowned hard at his brother. What the hell kind of game was he playing at? Did he know that food was Jane's weakness? He sure as hell did now with all that moaning she was doing every time she took a bite of the damn cookie.

The way she moaned, the way she enjoyed even the simplest of life's pleasures, had him realizing that she wasn't like most women in his social circle—women his grandfather would choose. Those types of women ate salad with no dressing. And Brock had a sneaking suspicion that if he offered one of them a cookie they'd take it as an insult, whereas Jane would ask for more.

A dab of chocolate was on the corner of her mouth. Brock tried not to stare, but he couldn't help it. She looked more delicious than the cookie she was devouring. Without thinking he reached over and swiped the chocolate with his thumb and proceeded to lick the chocolate from his finger.

Jane's mouth dropped open.

He had no self-control where she was concerned and he knew that if he kept tasting her—he'd be completely lost.

He didn't even realize he had moaned until Bentley slapped him on the back. "Problem?"

"You're..." Brock narrowed his eyes as Jane let out another breathy sigh and finished her cookie. "I'm suddenly really grateful for your cookies."

"Was that a compliment?"

Brock clenched his teeth. "Don't get used to it."

Bentley snorted. "Oh, I wouldn't dream of it."

They stared down one another until Jane's moans subsided and she finally was able to speak again. "I need more cookies."

"I will literally pay you five hundred dollars to bake more cookies for us." Brant slapped cash out onto the table. "But make double because Jane is eating them faster than I can get my hands on them."

"What about me?" Brock asked, feeling left out. "I didn't even get any!"

"You hate sugar." Bentley shrugged. Jane let out a loud gasp and covered her mouth.

Strike one.

"No, I just don't like cotton candy," Brock grumbled.

Another gasp from Jane, so clearly that was strike two.

Bentley shook his head slowly. "Maybe it's because your childhood was cut short by the death of our parents? No doubt it caused you to grow up more than us."

The room fell silent.

Brant looked down at his shoes, his face unreadable, while Jane locked eyes with Brock. Her expression was sad—not necessarily pitying, but close enough. God, he hated pity.

Almost as much as he hated being a yes man.

"Hey." Jane slowly made her way over to him. "Bentley said something about horses. Do you think…" Her cheeks burned bright red. "Maybe I could get on one?"

Damn it, she was cute when she was nervous.

Cute was dangerous.

Cute made you want to care.

Cute made you want more than one fleeting night of passion where you left in the morning without saying good-bye.

And suddenly, the conversation he'd just had with his grandfather was thrust into the forefront of his mind. Hadn't his intention been to kiss her senseless when he marched back to the house? It had been, until his brothers had decided to seduce her with baked goods.

"Here." Bentley was suddenly at his side with a small backpack. "I have all the essentials: screw-top wine, cheeses, crackers, grapes, and a few cookies I managed to hide from Brant."

"Bastard," Brant muttered.

Brock took the bag, wondering what Bentley was about, but as always, Bentley was the king of hiding what he was really feeling, which made it damn near impossible for Brock to know if his brother was being conniving or caring.

"Thanks." Brock took the bag and put it over his shoulder while Jane smiled and limped toward the door, opening it for both of them.

"Careful," Bentley said in a quiet voice. "Just"—he licked his lips—"It's private property but you never know… If the press finds you here…with Jane, Grandfather will have a stroke. We already have enough to worry about with the auction looming over the family—the last thing you need is the media somehow catching wind."

Tensing, Brock gave a jerky nod then followed Jane outside, passing a curious Brant on the way.

Jane was next to the barn, the rooster by her feet. It looked like the damn cock had decided he wanted to be friends rather than enemies.

"He's not so bad." She laughed, still standing on one foot and leaning on the barn wall.

The cock flapped up toward Brock. He stumbled back. "Yeah, completely tame."

Jane laughed again. "So, which horse is yours?"

"Buttercup." Brock felt his chest swell with pride. "My grandfather gave her to me right before..."

Her hand touched his shoulder. "Before?"

"Before my parents died. And then after everything happened, he always tried to encourage me to ride her. Grandfather hoped it would bring me out of depression."

"Did it?"

"I'm a firm believer that animals can sense your emotions. Take Diablo, for example. He thinks I'm going to steal his hens and he attacks. Animals have the potential to heal, as long as you remember the cardinal rule." He grabbed a blanket and threw it over Buttercup, then reached for the saddle.

Jane took a step back, her eyes rapt with fascination as he buckled the saddle. "What's the cardinal rule?"

Brock's fingers stopped moving as he looked over his shoulder at Jane. "They're still wild."

Jane's eyes grew wide. "Does that apply to humans as well?"

"Jane, are you accusing me of being wild?"

"Well..." She crossed her arms. "I definitely wouldn't accuse you of being tame."

"I don't think anyone"—he reached for the harness—"has ever accused me of being anything but boring."

"Really?" Jane's eyes narrowed. "No staying out late in high school? Partying in college? Wild raves with that grandfather of yours? Orgies?"

Brock's hand slipped at the word "orgy." Sighing, he gently put the bit in Buttercup's mouth. "Sorry to disappoint, but if I ran for Congress, my grandfather would probably have more dirt than me. I'm clean."

"That's too bad," Jane said, surprising him. "Sometimes my favorite days that I can think back on are the ones where I was dirty."

His heart picked up speed as her eyes lit up with amusement. "You know, mud pies, that sort of thing."

"Sure. Because that's where a thirty-five-year-old man's mind goes: mud pies."

"I figured," she teased, lifting a shoulder in the air.

Damn it, he already felt the familiar strain of his dick against the button of his fly as she giggled and ran her hands down Buttercup's face then brushed a kiss across the velvet of her nose.

Clearing his throat, he attached the backpack to the saddle and held out his hand. "Are you ready to ride?"

It was the wrong thing to say.

Completely.

However, she lifted her chin up, her eyes both challenging and excited. "Are you?"

He let out a groan and tugged her against him. "You know a man can only take so much."

"Cleanliness?"

"Yeah." He eyed her up and down. "That's right."

"So." She linked her arms around his neck. "How do we ride this thing?"

Buttercup neighed.

Jane jumped back on her one good foot, nearly falling on her ass.

Brock smiled and reached for her hips and lifted. "Up you go."

"Ahh!" Jane let out a little squeak. The minute she was in the saddle, her hands found the horn and gripped tight. "It's high."

"You'll be fine."

"Super high."

"I know."

"This horse is tall."

Buttercup neighed like she knew she was getting a compliment.

"I'll be right behind you."

"You better be." Jane clenched her teeth. "You know when Bentley mentioned this, I wasn't imagining I'd be riding Goliath."

"You have no idea how desperately I want to comment on that, but I think it might make you blush again."

She laughed, but it was a nervous laugh, one that said he'd better hurry his ass up before she burst into tears.

He heaved himself up behind her and grabbed the reins and she automatically slid backward. A grunt erupted between his clenched teeth at the soft contact of her ass.

He was going to murder his brother.

This was a horrible idea.

Not because he wasn't enjoying himself, but because he was enjoying himself too much, outside; where anyone could see them, and now he was paranoid. Especially after Bentley's warning.

She moved, just slightly.

Terrible idea.

All he wanted to do was take her back to the house and kiss her—everywhere. Because her mouth, as tempting as it was, wouldn't be enough. Already he'd tasted and wanted more. Her neck, her fingers, her thighs—he wanted his mouth everywhere.

Another slight movement had him inwardly groaning.

His body burned as she thrust back against him. It was all he could do not to take her right here on this horse. Cameras be damned.

"Comfortable?" His teeth were still clenched; he gripped the reins as if his life depended on it.

"Yes." Her voice was wobbly, unsure.

"Shall we see how fast Buttercup can gallop?" he teased.

"S-sure."

"Relax," he whispered in her ear. The temptation to lick her neck was utterly ridiculous, but there it was. "We're going to walk nice and slow."

"I like walking."

"Good." He pulled on the reins and whistled. Buttercup ambled out of the barn, and past the cock who'd suddenly gone silent as the horse went by.

"Oh, oh, wow." Jane dug her nails into his arm, which she'd had in a death grip since he'd gotten on behind her. "This is, this is—"

"Nice?"

She laughed. "Yeah, really nice."

"Do you want to go faster?"

"Maybe…"

"Come on, live a little."

"Where has Boring Brock disappeared to?"

"Eh, I left him back in the barn with the cock."

Jane let her head fall back against his chest as she laughed. "The poor cock is going to commit roostercide. Poor guy will be so bored, what will he do?"

"Did you just call me boring?"

She shrugged and then glanced over her shoulder. "I've just noticed a certain lack of color."

"I wear color," he said defensively, looking down at

his black T-shirt. "I just didn't bring anything like that with me."

"Mmm, I see."

"All right, you've asked for it."

"Oh?"

"I hate to do this, but you better hold on. Clearly I have something to prove."

"Brock—"

"Hold tight, Jane," he whispered in her ear, just as he dug his heels into Buttercup's sides. The horse took off at a gallop. Thankfully, riding a horse was like riding a bike: you didn't forget.

Jane let out a loud gasp. Earlier Brock hadn't thought she could grip him any harder—he was wrong. He'd have nail prints in his arms for days. But she was safe with him; he wouldn't let her fall.

Jane's hair was blowing in his face and it smelled like raspberries. He inhaled deeply.

Trouble. He was in so much trouble.

Because for a moment, the temptation to look beyond the next two weeks was almost too much to resist. There might be a life where he was able to have Jane in his arms like this, where he wouldn't be paranoid about his Grandfather dying over a simple word—or worried that a camera would catch him kissing a woman he actually had feelings for.

He had once loved this ranch,

And she was making him love it again, but she was part of it. The ranch without Jane would just be a house.

She made it feel like home.

Hell, he was so happy he'd even let the cock stay.

Outdoors, of course.

Eventually, he slowed Buttercup to a walk and Jane unclenched his arm.

"What do you think?"

She quickly wiped at her cheek.

He froze. "Damn it, are you crying? Did I scare you?"

"No." She wiped her other cheek. "It's just..." She leaned away from him and he pulled her back against his chest. Not a chance in hell she was going to get away from him. "I felt free."

Brock's stomach clenched.

He knew the feeling.

"Do you feel trapped?"

She nodded.

"Me too," he admitted. She slid her hand into his.

They rode in silence down to the river that divided the pasture and the rest of the property, where they kept a few heads of cattle for beef.

"I blame myself for my parents' death," he said quietly.

Jane gripped his hand as he led Buttercup through the grass. The horse was still breathing heavy from the run.

"We argued. I said no to something my father asked me to do. Something stupid that wasn't even important. And twenty-four hours later they were dead." He stared into her big brown eyes. "I haven't been able to say no again. And I've felt trapped ever since."

"It wasn't your fault. You were how old? Twelve?"

"I said no." He squeezed her hand tighter. "I hate that word."

She blinked down at their joined hands and then back up at him. "Do you still feel trapped?"

"Not right now," he whispered. "Not with you."

Brock slid off Buttercup first, and reached up for Jane. She grabbed his arms and slowly slid down his body.

Their mouths almost touched.

His body burned for her in a way he'd never experienced

before. It was a completely foreign feeling, wanting her not just in his bed, not just in the present, but in the future.

She cleared her throat and stepped back, her smile nervous, pink lips trembling. "If Bentley packs as good as he cooks we should have some good snacks."

He knew that look, the look she was giving him. After all, he wore it often. It said not to prod, not to ask questions, ignore the elephant in the room even though it's sobbing in the corner.

So he obliged her, though it killed him to do so. But selfishly he knew the minute he started digging more into her life, she'd do the same to him. And part of him preferred to keep the future, the auction, all of it locked away, or at least temporarily forgotten.

Where he didn't have to deal with it.

"I'll grab the bag." His voice cracked and he watched as she quickly turned around and started petting Buttercup again.

The moment floated away, and he kicked himself mentally for allowing it to go. After all, moments with her were precious, they were short, and the sand was very quickly sifting through the hourglass.

CHAPTER TWENTY-NINE

She was getting too close.

She was starting to want his smiles, his caresses, his inappropriate remarks.

She craved them.

Not just the attention, but the fact that somehow they were building something together. Just to have it ripped away when she left. When he was auctioned off.

Was it worth it? Pursuing him? Allowing more touches? Kissing? Spending the few nights they had left together? Would it be worth it? Or would she regret knowing what it would be like to be in his arms... Would she spend the rest of her life comparing every other man to him?

Brock's muscles flexed as he pulled the backpack from the horse then patted down Buttercup's side and whispered in her ear.

Holy crap, he was sexy.

He was gruff.

Both a polished CEO and apparently a cowboy.

A regular prince of industry.

With a pauper.

Hah.

She reached for her phone to take a picture of the scenery in front of her then remembered she'd turned it off after receiving all the nasty texts from her sisters and left it in her room.

Brock spread out a small black and red quilted blanket, then grabbed the backpack and dropped it in the middle.

"Wlne?"

She nodded.

He opened the wine and handed her a plastic cup. "So, what do you think?"

"Hmm?" She took a long sip, frowning over the cup as Brock eyed her up and down in appreciation.

"Riding." He grinned wolfishly.

She looked away and smiled. "It was okay."

"Just okay?" He leaned forward. "Careful or you'll hurt Buttercup's feelings."

"Just Buttercup?" She tilted her head.

"Mine too." His voice was gravelly, buzzing with sexual tension as he leaned forward and very slowly pulled her cup from her hands and kissed her on the cheek. His body was braced above hers. "I'm going to taste you again."

"You were right."

"What?" He blinked as if confused.

"You did leave Boring Brock with the cock."

"It irritates the hell out of me that 'Brock' rhymes with 'cock.' Just laying it all out there so you know."

She giggled.

"And now you're laughing, and I'm trying to kiss you."

"Don't try," she whispered. "Just do it, before I lose my nerve and limp back to the house."

"Done," he said just before he slammed his mouth against hers.

With a gasp she hung on to his shoulders to keep from falling backward against the blanket, even though the idea had merit.

His hands reached for her body.

They were a pair: Brock grasping at her in any way he possibly could, Jane holding on for dear life, praying that the kiss could go on forever. It wasn't just his taste, or the possessive way he marked her with his lips with each caress—maybe it was the combination of everything, of the desperation they both felt.

To be free.

His tongue slid against hers and a shiver ran down her body, just as a raindrop fell onto her cheek.

Brock pulled back, his expression heated. "I'm not stopping at one kiss."

Jane brushed the raindrop away only to have another take its place.

Brock glanced up and swore just as the sky opened up and a downpour rained hell all over the beginnings of their romantic picnic.

He jumped to his feet, but Jane remained, her face tilted up at the sky as the cool rain fell against her body, each drop sliding down her skin, making her feel alive, ready for anything.

Maybe the rain was an omen.

A sign.

After all, didn't rain mean fresh chances? Starting over?

Her gaze blurred as she took in Brock's wet form hovering over her. His thick black eyelashes blinked slowly as his hazel eyes locked on hers, never wavering. His full lips were slightly swollen, his chin lifted in defiance—ready to challenge her, maybe?

Or himself?

"Mud pies?" she whispered, needing to break the tense silence with something.

"Mud wrestling?" he countered.

"Tough choice."

"Believe me." He held out his hand to her. "I know."

With a grin she took his hand and stood. Seconds later he lifted her up into his arms and twirled her around the wet grass.

She burst out laughing as he jogged over to a pile of dirt that was quickly turning into mud and set her on her feet. "How do we do this?"

"Oh, I forgot. You were born an old man."

He shoved her lightly, making her laugh like she was a teenager.

"You need to stop talking to the twins, before one or both of them end up dead."

"You'd kill them?" she asked in mock horror.

"It's often a tempting thought, the only thing that used to help me fall asleep at night with a smile on my face." His crooked smile had her heart hammering in her chest uncontrollably.

"And now?"

"Now, she asks." He smiled down at the dirt and slowly leaned over, pulling some mud into his hand and slapping it into his other like he was clapping. "Now, my thoughts are a lot hotter at night, scorching, uncontrollably erotic, and if I'm being honest, damned uncomfortable."

"Hot, you say?" She grinned, leaning down on her haunches to grab some mud.

"Very." He nodded.

"Let me cool you off." She winked, then smeared mud on his face. "Better?"

He bit back a curse then fell against the dirt laughing. "Completely healed of any sort of sexual fantasy, yup, thanks."

"I'm at your service."

He let out a groan. "Just kidding. Still hot."

Laughing, she trailed more mud down his chin with her finger, then captured his lips in hers without even giving a second thought to what she was doing, initiating whatever this was between them.

He cupped her face with his dirty hands, as if she was precious, as if she was everything, and pressed his forehead against hers. "What about now? Not then, but now?"

She frowned. "What are you asking?"

"Now. Give me now."

"And forget about the future? Is that what you're asking?"

"Borderline begging." His voice rasped. "Let me worry about the future. And I swear to you I'll figure something out—but let me taste you now—let me have you now."

Out of fear, Jane hesitated. She wanted him more than anything, but...she wanted more than a fleeting kiss or moment.

"Trust me," he whispered across her lips.

His tone was gentle, desperate.

So she said yes.

Even though her heart simultaneously screamed for her to be careful.

CHAPTER THIRTY

Brock couldn't get the afternoon ride out of his mind. They'd returned to the house soaking wet, and while the twins both gave them looks of complete innocence, he knew better. Hell, he knew their minds sometimes better than he knew his own.

Sending them off had been a complete setup.

To get them out of the house and alone together.

A setup he was grateful for and had desperately needed.

He just didn't know what the next move should be. He knew what he wanted it to be, but ignoring the future was like ignoring a burning house—eventually it was going to crumble around you. And the last thing he wanted was to take her down in the same flames that were going to consume him.

His thoughts darkened, and by the time he was done showering, it was already nearing dinnertime.

Laughter from downstairs gave him pause. The house used to have laughter; hell, it had been filled with it, overflowing to the brim. In fact, nearly all of his memories from before the accident—if he let himself go there—were of laughter.

Memories that no longer refused to stay buried.

But he was starting to realize it wasn't necessarily his presence in the house that was causing them to resurface— but hers.

She brought life back to death.

Didn't she say that was her specialty? Looking at something that others would pass by, picking it up, cleaning it, and making it shine?

His gut still clenched when he thought about his parents' deaths, about his grandfather's orders to marry one of the women of his choosing.

But it was better.

For the first time since he was twelve, it was better.

He took the stairs a few at a time and frowned when he saw that Brant and Bentley both had their bags by the door and were hugging Jane.

"Are you sure you can't stay?" she asked, her expression sad, causing a little kick to Brock's chest.

"Sorry, beautiful." Bentley winked. "We've got women to conquer, millions to make, a world to take over."

Brock rolled his eyes.

Brant barked out a laugh. "Roughly translated, we've been summoned by Grandfather."

"Oh?" Brock asked as he walked into the room. "And what does his highness need?"

"More grandsons to torture. Apparently he's got last-minute auction crap he wants us to take care of," Brant grumbled. "Shit-for-brains Bentley volunteered us."

Bentley rolled his eyes. "The worst he can do is auction one of us off like he's going to do with Brock."

Jane's smile was sad as she glanced down at the floor. "Well, it was really fun. I'm...I'll miss you guys."

"Don't worry, this isn't good-bye." Brant kissed her hand. "Just good-bye for now. Oh, and you can't collect Brock's life insurance unless you're married, so my suggestion is to get hitched before you smother him with a pillow. At least fifty million. That's all I'm saying."

"Great," Brock said through clenched teeth. "Thanks, guys."

"Any time," Bentley said brightly. "Bye, man. I trust you'll be on your best behavior?"

"When is he not?" Brant piped up immediately. "Boring Brock would never do anything to disappoint the family, would you?"

Anger surged, bubbling to the surface as Brock clenched his fists and gritted his teeth.

"That's what I thought." Brant nodded with a smirk. "See ya!"

The screen door slammed.

His brothers were gone.

But as the car started pulling away in the driveway, his anger grew: the anger that he had no control over his life, that in a couple of weeks he would get the same summons, that he had been living this way since he was twelve.

"They're gone." Jane came up behind him and wrapped her arms around his waist.

Brock let out a pitiful groan and closed his eyes. "We're alone."

"It would seem so. I guess I should get back to cleaning then," she said in a teasing voice as she pulled her arms away.

He caught her hands and twisted around to face her. "No."

Damn, that word felt good.

"Did you just fire me?"

"No, I'm"—he gripped her chin with his thumb and forefinger—"I'm reassigning your duties."

She winced.

"That came out wrong."

"Just a little."

"Jane, I..." He slid his fingers down her neck. "Tell me you want this, too."

"Yes."

Never had "yes" sounded or felt so good. He exhaled the breath he'd been holding and took a step back. "Good, then you have two minutes to remove every stitch of clothing on your body and meet me in my room."

Jane gaped and then narrowed her eyes. "What? No *please*?"

"Now." His voice lowered. "Please."

His voice wasn't soothing; it wasn't inquiring. He was taking control.

And it felt incredible.

"Jane." His eyebrows rose. "You have ninety seconds."

She hobbled out of the room with a laugh and up the stairs just as a smirk spread across his face.

His phone went off in his pocket.

He glanced down at the text from Bentley.

Don't be a yes man...unless you're looking in the mirror, then say yes. Or with Jane. Say yes with Jane. We'll keep Grandfather occupied.

Well, maybe his brothers were good for something.

He stared at his phone then put it back in his pocket, and then very slowly took the stairs one at a time, pulling his shirt over his head and dropping it before walking into the bedroom.

Even though he'd told her what he wanted, he was

surprised to see Jane waiting for him, completely naked as requested, a stern expression on her face. It was cute as hell, and he found himself falling a little bit harder in that moment as she arched an eyebrow. Then he noticed she was trembling slightly.

He prayed this wouldn't end badly.

For either of them.

Because his heart was already invested—and if hers wasn't, he was going to try his damnedest to convince it to beat for him.

CHAPTER THIRTY-ONE

Jane shivered as Brock's gaze darkened. His slow perusal of her body left her feeling so nervous she almost ran into the bathroom and slammed the door.

She was shy!

She didn't normally take chances or strip naked because a man had asked her to.

What the heck was she doing? Standing naked in front of Brock, a man she'd only known a few days.

This wasn't like her.

But he made her feel brave.

He made her feel like he was someone she'd been searching for her whole life.

"You're beautiful." He took a step forward, his abs flexing with each inhale. He was shirtless, all golden skin and muscles

"Wait." She quickly covered herself up, then slowly removed her hands and sighed. "I, uh, we need some sort of... rules or something."

"No." He said it so quickly that she nearly stumbled backward. Then he ran his large hands across her shoulders and lower, cupping her breasts gently before moving his fingers down to her hips and pulling her body against his. "Do you want this?"

"Y-yes."

"Then that's all that matters." He captured her mouth again and again, his kiss going from aggressive to soft in a matter of seconds. His hands spread across her ass, fingers flexing against her skin as he deepened the kiss, his lips hungry in their pursuit.

He kissed her like he wanted her.

He touched her like he couldn't get enough of her.

Jane reached up to touch his face. A shadow of a beard was already making an appearance, giving his skin an erotic roughness that made her clench her thighs together.

A small area of chest hair drew her attention away from his face. She trailed a finger down the middle of two impressive pecs to his perfectly chiseled abs. They didn't make men like Brock anymore, ones who weren't waxed and fake, or so thin and wiry that a curvy woman would be afraid of breaking them.

In his arms, she was small, perfect.

"Keep doing that and this is going to be over really fast," he grumbled as she trailed her hands along his sides.

"Sorry." She gulped. "I guess I didn't think my touch would cause—"

"This." He grabbed her hand and pressed it against his erection. "But it's more than your touch; it's every damn conversation, every look, every smile, causes this painful need to be inside you, to fuck society and my grandfather and every other person on this godforsaken planet that dares to tell me what I should be doing with my life rather than being in this bedroom, right now, with the only woman who's ever made me want to say no."

With each word, he seemed to grow beneath her hand, until she was sure he was going to spring free from his jeans.

With a gruff curse, he backed away from her and swallowed. "You do that to me. Tell me you want this as bad as I do."

"I do," she whispered.

He reached for her hips and then slid his hand between her thighs. She let out a moan. "You feel so good."

"Let me make love to you." His voice had changed, shifted, as his fingers started to press into her. "Please?"

Another jerky nod and then she was reaching for the button of his jeans, helping him undress while standing there like a naked hussy.

He shoved off the jeans, almost stumbling into her in an effort to be free from them. His boxers were next.

"Come here," he growled, his mouth hot on her neck. He pinned her hands back against one of the bedposts as he took a nipple into his mouth and sucked. Her back pressed against the hard post as he assaulted her with his mouth, making it impossible for her to escape.

She'd always been insecure about her breasts, thinking they were too small for her curvy body. In fact she'd been insecure about everything.

But Brock didn't seem to mind.

Not at all.

And in the process of him kissing her, touching her, she realized she didn't mind either; not at all.

His face was rough; the friction of it against her skin was one of the most erotic things she'd ever experienced. It was hard to remain standing with all the wonderful sensations flowing through her, and she started to tremble.

"I'm just getting started." He kissed down her stomach, and his gaze moved over her body in what looked like reverence.

Apprehensive, she watched as he knelt in front of her, a wicked grin on his face.

"Wh-what are you doing?"

"You should watch," was his answer, right before he lowered his mouth between her thighs.

"No." She squeezed her legs shut.

It was a bad idea.

But she didn't know that until he reached between her legs again and hooked one over his large shoulder, holding it down, giving him a better angle, making it impossible for her to think as his tongue tasted the most sensitive part of her.

What was she doing?

She was so exposed!

But it felt. So. Good.

Her hips ground against him, her nails dug into his shoulders, both pushing him away and pulling him closer.

He wasn't just kissing or exploring her, but sucking, coaxing, making her so unaware of her surroundings that all she could focus on was him, and how he made her feel.

A wave of anxiety was replaced with pleasure as her body pulsed with the rhythm of his mouth.

And then, she broke.

Shattering not just everything she knew about herself, or about sex, but about how it should feel.

With the right person.

With Brock.

His mouth slid to her right thigh as he released her leg.

"I'm not done," he said, and tremors of pleasure still rocked through her as he slowly backed her up to the bed and lifted her onto it. "Lie down."

She didn't need to be told twice. The minute she lay down she jerked his head toward hers, kissing him as hard as she could, sucking his lips between her teeth.

He let out a hiss, deepening the kiss with so much aggression it was almost painful.

"Brock..." She clung to him as if her life depended on it. "I want more."

His eyes darkened. He pulled away from her and grabbed his jeans. Her heart sank in disappointment; was he leaving? Rejection washed over her, immediately followed by shame.

And then he pulled something out of his pocket.

She was an idiot.

He glanced up at her, taking in her worried expression. "Jane, I wasn't leaving. I just don't think an unplanned pregnancy should be part of this picture."

She just nodded, feeling too stupid to actually use words.

"Hey, look at me." He cupped her face. "Only a complete idiot would walk out of this room right now."

"Which is why it's so surprising you're still here," she teased, finding her voice.

He grinned. "Cute."

"I thought so."

His eyes flashed as he tapped the packet against his fingertips, "Now, stop talking so I can keep exploring, because we have all night, and I'm not nearly as tired or hungry as I thought I was."

"You ate?" she asked, confused.

He glanced down at her naked body. "I had a really, really sweet appetizer." His mouth found hers again. "But I'm a glutton, and I want the main course."

Maybe weeks from now she'd regret this.

But now she nodded and whispered. "Then take it."

CHAPTER THIRTY-TWO

He was going to burn in hell for all the things he wanted to do to her... for the things that he was *going* to do to her.

God, he loved her hips; they fit his hands perfectly. He could spend years getting lost in her curves, in the way she responded with little moans and gasps.

Most of the women he had been with had been older, experienced, jaded, meaning they faked orgasms and screamed so loud you'd think that they were trying to get a part in the next Fifty Shades movie.

Jane's responses were genuine.

This girl, that had held him at gunpoint, called him old, and laughed when he said he'd clean.

His girl.

Possessiveness washed over him as he slid the condom on and watched her eyes grow big. She was nervous.

"Stay with me," he whispered as gently as he could, because, really, truth be told, he was dying, dying to be inside her, dying to feel her, dying to watch her fall apart.

She responded with a jerky nod and he cupped her face,

capturing her lips again and again. They were red and swollen, and her cheeks were flushed from rubbing against his face.

He had already marked her.

He wanted to howl.

Or at least pounce on her and claim her. It was absolutely primitive, the way that he wanted to make every male in the world aware that she was his.

"Relax," he soothed. He could feel the tension flowing off her, and he could only assume it was because she felt it, too. He knew this thing between them wasn't just about sex. These weren't fleeting emotions that would just go away.

His teeth captured her earlobe before he kissed his way down her neck. Slowly, he pressed himself inside her tight entrance, nearly blacking out as her body bucked off the bed. A moan of pleasure escaped her lips as she hooked her ankles behind his back.

She was scorching.

Burning him inch by inch as he gritted his teeth and kept himself from thrusting completely into her and breaking her in half.

"You're so...hard." She exhaled with what he hoped was a satisfied sigh.

"Kind of the point." He let out a dark laugh. "But glad you approve."

"I do." She returned his kiss, grabbing his face, losing complete control as her hips bucked against his.

Brock Wellington was a man of complete control.

A man who knew what was expected of him.

Brock Wellington died in that moment, and was replaced quite possibly with the man he was always supposed to be. Crazed, passionate, slightly drunk on the feeling of the perfect woman in his arms...His destiny felt altered, his world changed.

She met each thrust, her nails digging into his skin as her head fell back against the pillows, her body arching into his, responding, pulling him tighter inside her heat.

Jane let out a gasp as he filled her one last time and stopped—his body throbbing for release.

It was a moment he wished he could freeze in time—the look on her face, the feel of her body beneath his, and the absolute certainty he felt in his heart that this was exactly the future he wanted—for both of them.

A future together.

When her eyes opened, he found he couldn't hold back, not anymore, as with one last thrust she found her release.

His orgasm followed immediately after, and he yelled the first "yes" he'd ever really meant.

For her.

For them.

Brock looked down at Jane, kissed her softly, then smiled.

"What?" She was out of breath. "Why are you smiling at me like that?"

"Because." He shrugged. "We still have nine days alone, unless you count the animals, but I'm going to be more careful about locking doors from here on out."

"Oh." She nodded. "So we're going to have sex like nine more times? Is that what you're saying?"

"Nine? Woman, you'll be lucky to get any work done outside of this bedroom for the next two weeks."

"Oh, no." Her face fell in mock sincerity. "I hope my employer won't be angry with me."

"He may punish you." Brock kept a straight face. "Hard time in the bedroom for not cleaning the bathrooms just right."

She smirked. "Slave driver."

"He really is."

She fell into a fit of laughter when he slapped her ass playfully then rose from the bed to grab a towel and start the shower.

They both needed to wash off the sweat and everything else.

He was in his room, so he at least had clothes at hand, but she would want to put on something comfortable.

"Be right back," he called over his shoulder while she stretched out on the bed. Damn it, he was ready for her again.

He quickly ran into her room in search of sweats or something she could wear so that she wouldn't have to run around naked—even though that's exactly what he wanted. But he knew she'd want to be comfortable, or maybe he just wanted her to be comfortable. Because suddenly all that mattered was her.

His eyes locked on the dresser. He walked over and opened the top drawer and cursed as he pulled the drawer out far enough that it fell.

Jane came running at the sound, a towel wrapped around her body. "Are you okay? What's wrong?"

"Get out," he whispered.

"But—"

"I said"—he rasped—"get the hell out! *Now!*" He kicked the dresser. Jane's perfume flew off the top, smashing at his feet, filling the room with her scent.

Her eyes filled with tears.

And she ran.

Good. She should run.

He couldn't control the rage that filled him. Bracing himself against the dresser, he looked down at the drawer.

It never occurred to him that his grandfather would keep things. Keep memories, store them away for Brock to find.

Plaid shirts.

Harmless plaid shirts.

And stuck between them, the stuffed dog his dad had given him—the day before he'd died.

The day of the fight.

"But I don't want to!" Brock had yelled. "You can't make us move to California! I belong here!"

His father sighed. "Brock, it's my responsibility to keep my word to your grandfather and he needs someone in the LA office."

"Fine." Brock crossed his arms, "Then you go! I'm staying here!" He threw the stuffed dog his father had given him back into his face. "No!" He stomped his foot. "I won't go. I hate you! I hate you!"

His parents died the very next day.

He fell to his knees amidst the broken picture frames that had joined the smashed perfume bottles on the floor and didn't even care that shards of glass were piercing his skin. He welcomed the pain.

The ghosts were free.

And they were relentless.

His parents were gone.

All he had was his grandfather.

And his brothers.

Life would be so much easier if there was a map to get through it, but when he wasn't given one, he'd followed the only family he had left.

And was led to this place.

A crossroads.

He knelt amidst the broken glass and memories for the next hour, feeling guilty as hell, and sad.

Because that was the thing about death.

It haunted the living.

Until they mourned it.

And the more it was ignored.

The bigger it grew.

Until survival was damn near impossible.

It loomed over Brock's body like a vicious storm, and he didn't have a damn clue how to get over it.

Which was why he said the *yes*.

His *yes*es were because of this stupid stuffed animal.

And the picture.

He held onto them for dear life and stared.

An hour later, he realized that Jane had returned, and put a blanket over his shoulders.

When he finally acknowledged her, she handed him a mug of something and lifted a shoulder. "I made it a double."

"I'm sorry."

"I know."

"No, I'm really, really sorry."

"I know." Her smile wasn't present—her strength, however, she wore like a beautiful suit of shiny armor.

"It's not you."

"Drink the whiskey, Brock."

He sighed and took the mug. "Yes, ma'am."

The grandfather clock chimed from downstairs as if to remind them that time wasn't exactly in their favor. They shared a look as Jane reached across the space between them and gave him her hand.

CHAPTER THIRTY-THREE

Jane's hands were still shaking long after she'd left the room and gone back to his. She was insane.

She'd just lost her virginity to a man who already had part of her heart, and he'd just yelled at her and had had what seemed to be an emotional breakdown over a dresser drawer.

The pain obviously had to do with his parents. She wasn't sure if she should push him and get him to open up again or if she should just leave him. One of her major personality flaws was a need to make everything better, everyone happy, even if it was at her own expense.

She'd already showered and was limping around trying to find her cleaning bucket, to no avail, when she felt warm hands brace her shoulders.

Jumping a foot, she nearly fell against the wall before turning around and facing Brock.

The lines on his face seemed more pronounced. He'd never appeared old to her, but in that moment he seemed... haunted.

"Jane, I'm so sorry," he said again, hanging his head.

She shrugged. "We all have our things, right?"

His expression didn't change. Instead he just stared at her, as if she was a complicated math problem, or a Rubik's Cube. His frown deepened. "Jane, it's more than that, it's—"

"Death," she whispered hoarsely, looking down at her shoes.

Brock nodded silently, his chin dipping toward his chest before he exhaled and reached for her hand. "Come on."

She let him pull her away from her work because being with him, being there for him, this complicated man, was the most important thing she could think of doing.

He wrapped an arm around her and helped her walk toward the end of the hall until they came to the master suite.

"My parents' room."

She gasped. "I'm staying in your parents' old room?"

His nod was jerky as his eyes roamed from left to right, as if it was too painful for him to look at any one thing for too long.

He'd cleaned up the glass on the floor but the plaid shirts remained, along with the stuffed dog.

She hobbled over to the dog and picked it up, holding it close to her chest.

"One of my dad's last gifts."

"I wouldn't take you as a stuffed animal kind of guy," she said with a bit of humor, squeezing the dog against her chest.

"I was twelve." He smiled, but it didn't quite reach his eyes. "My parents were often away on business, so my dad always gave me a stuffed animal before he left, a different guard animal each time. I was always so stressed about the responsibility of taking care of my brothers that my dad said it was only fair I have someone to look after me, too, for me to lean on."

Pain sliced through Jane's chest. "What about your grandfather?"

"He's so strong. Always has been." Brock shrugged. "I felt weak telling my grandfather it scared me every time my parents were gone, that every time I waved good-bye I was afraid it would be the last." His smile was sad. "My greatest fear eventually happened. I gave power to it, and it destroyed us all."

"Bullshit." The word escaped Jane's mouth before she could stop it.

"Jane, you don't understand. My dad gave me my dog before he broke the news that we were moving. I said some ugly things, horrible things. I told him no. I told him I wouldn't do it. I threw the dog at him. Said I hated him." Just repeating the words seemed difficult for him, like he was reliving the moments over again.

"I still call bullshit," she said in a strong voice.

Brock's eyes widened a bit.

To be honest she surprised herself a bit, too.

Hugging the dog closer, she shook her head. "That's stupidity at its finest and you know that." Her heart broke for the boy who had held this dog close then thrown it out of anger. Of course he was angry. The ranch had been one of his favorite places. She knew that now.

"Do I?"

"Yes." She turned on her good leg and poked him in the chest. "Believe what you want, but accidents are just that: accidents. And I highly doubt your parents would want you sitting here mourning their loss rather than living your life."

He blinked. "And what would your parents say?"

She gulped, her nostrils flaring. "I took over the family business. I'm pretty sure my dad would be proud."

"And what about the sister situation?"

She broke eye contact. "We all have our weaknesses."

"Is it bad, do you think," he asked, pulling her into his arms, tilting her chin up, "that both our weaknesses just happen to be family?"

Jane slumped against him. "I had really good intentions. Good intentions that turned into this habitual need to make sure everyone around me was happy."

"Everyone except you," Brock pointed out. "Because I highly doubt you're happy making toast for two bitchy sisters."

She smirked. "They are bitches. But they're my bitches."

He chuckled softly. "Don't be angry, but hearing you say that kind of turned me on."

She swatted him with the dog and pulled away. "And you? Do you think your parents would be proud of the way you've allowed your grandfather to rule your life?"

"I think..." He paused. "They would be proud of the way I've kept the family together, and kept the twins out of federal prison, yes."

"And your happiness?" She glanced over her shoulder. "What about that?"

"The thing about happiness is this." He slid his arms around her and pulled her close. "Sometimes it's in the place you least expect it, like in a house full of ghosts and with a girl who carries bleach in her purse."

"How do you know I carry bleach in my purse?"

"You like things clean," he said and smiled. A real smile. "Lucky guess."

She tensed in his arms as she realized how well he already knew her, how he was inching himself into her life and making it nearly impossible for her to stop what was happening between them—not that she wanted to. But the very fact that he had so much power over her already was terrifying.

"Jane, I'm so damn sorry. I hope you know that. You're…you're perfect and I yelled, ruining the entire evening. Holding you in my arms feels so right that I don't ever want to let go." His lips found her ear. "I'm sorry I yelled. I was just taken back, but now that the scent of my father's shirts has worn off, and the dog doesn't look as threatening, I get it. They're just things. Sometimes things catch you off guard, though. I was prepared for the pictures in the house or at least I thought I was, even the blinds— but the dog? It just reminded me of that moment, a moment that I've always wished I could take back. A moment I've always blamed myself for."

She burrowed her head into his neck and sighed. "Now I'm the one who's sorry; I wish I could make the pain go away."

"You already have." He smiled, "Besides, I think I'd rather spend my energy making love to you than fighting ghosts that you seem to be able to push away with one kiss."

"You can't fight a ghost, you know." She tried to ignore the way her body was already responding and yearning for more of his touch. "You make peace with them."

"I may need help doing that. I'm not really sure what peace looks like."

Jane hung her head, fully aware that what she was going to say applied to her—and her situation with her family—as much as it applied to him.

"Peace looks like letting go, Brock."

*   *   *

Jane was behind on cleaning, which meant that she needed Brock's help more than she wanted to admit, because it also meant she had to spend more time with him.

And she wanted to, she really did.

But the more she got to know him the harder she fell, even though she tried not to. Not because she didn't want to fall for him, but because a part of her was afraid that he would leave—or that the end wouldn't be happy. Even though his kisses promised a future, she was still afraid to hope for one.

He was funny—really funny, but in a way that wasn't flashy. He didn't need to be the center of attention, even though he often was. He was happy standing in the background.

Just like she was.

It wasn't fair.

It felt like every time he kissed her, he took pieces of her heart away. And she knew that when he returned to his normal life he would either have to explain her to his grandfather and hope for the best, or realize that maybe a maid wasn't the best type of match for someone like the great Brock Wellington.

She wasn't sure if she could take that loss on top of the death of her father, the realization that her sisters weren't ever going to care for her the way she cared for them, and the start of a life where she might have to go against her father's dying wish. What if she lost Brock, too? It would break her.

She wasn't just falling for him romantically, but he'd become a friend, someone she could talk to. A face she looked forward to seeing every morning and kissing every night.

It had been two days since they'd initially slept together, followed by two more glorious nights in bed.

And now they only had one week left together.

The days were already going too fast, folding into one another. Before she knew it—before she was ready—they would both pack their bags, shake hands, and drive their separate cars back to the city.

"You've been scrubbing that same spot on the floor for the past few minutes," Brock said, casting a shadow over her. "I think you've done the best you can do. Maybe move on? Either that or keep going and you'll end up in China."

She tossed the sponge back into the bucket and turned, hands on hips. "Are you trying to tell me how to do my job?"

"Absolutely." He nodded. "After all, I'm a professional cleaner now."

"One room, Brock. You cleaned one room."

"And it shines. You can eat off those damn floors."

Jane shook her head. "You didn't even finish!"

"Priorities, Jane." He dipped his head, brushing a kiss across her mouth. "I was distracted."

"And now?" she asked, breathless. "You want to distract me?"

"Is it working?" He kissed her again.

"Brock!" She pushed against his chest. "I have to work."

"You're fired."

She gasped.

"Was it something I said?"

Angry, she turned away and kept cleaning. The room filled with tense silence but she kept scrubbing; this time she moved to a different spot.

"Jane?"

Scrub, scrub, scrub. Hot tears ran down her cheeks.

"Jane?" Brock knelt down. "Shit, Jane, don't cry. I'm sorry. I was teasing."

"Well, it's not funny." She refused to look at him. "Did you ever wonder why I took the job in the first place? Yes, it was an escape from my crazy family, but I need the money. Don't fire me because you want more time for sex. I know you were joking, but it just...it just reminded me that we're from two very different worlds. You may think nothing of it, but it's my life, Brock. This is my *life*."

"Damn it, Jane. I would never...You know I care about you. I really was teasing."

She nodded.

He reached for her. "Hey, look at me."

She shook her head.

"Jane..."

"Brock..."

He finally grabbed hold of her and turned her to look at him. His face was apologetic, and so handsome it hurt to stare at him. "You aren't fired." He sighed. "But" —he leaned forward and whispered in her ear—"I think you missed a spot."

With a gasp she threw the sponge at his face.

It splashed against his chest, leaving a wet mark across his nice white shirt. "Oops, it slipped."

"Oh?" His eyebrows shot up. "It seems to me like you took at least two seconds to aim, but sure, it slipped."

"Completely."

"Liar."

She splashed some of the soapy water into his face. "See? All clean."

"One." His voice was calm, too calm. "Two."

"Brock!" She held her hands out in front of her. "Calm down."

"Three." He stood.

She tried to scurry backward, but he was too fast. Suddenly he was on her and the bucket was in midair.

"You wouldn't." She lifted her chin in defiance, just as he dumped the entire bucket's contents over her head.

She couldn't even see, but she could hear his laughter. "Oops."

"You bastard!" she roared, wiping at her eyes. She locked her gaze onto his amused face for a few seconds before running over to the kitchen faucet and grabbing the sprayer.

"Now, Jane!" Brock held up his hands. "Don't overreact—"

She sprayed him directly in the face.

He cursed, blindly reaching for her, and then slipped on the already wet floor.

She burst out laughing and continued spraying him, then yelped when he grabbed her body and brought her down on top of him.

They laughed as he kissed her—softly at first, then more fiercely, his frantic hands gripping her shirt and tugging it off. His mouth fused to hers, his tongue fighting for dominance against hers as his hands slid beneath her shorts and cupped her.

She hissed out a breath as he slowly removed his hands and slid her wet shorts, then her underwear down her legs, pausing at her ankles before he pulled them off completely.

Apparently all it had taken was a few marathon sessions with Brock and she was a hussy now, completely naked on the floor after he'd stripped her bare.

He ran a hand up her thigh, but she stopped him with both hands. A look of confusion washed over his features before she laughed and held up a finger as if to say *not so fast*.

"My turn," she whispered brazenly, unbuttoning his jeans and slipping her hand inside. He groaned out a curse as he moved against her fingers. He was so warm and hard that she felt her own self-control snapping as he gritted his teeth and locked eyes with her.

It was terrifying.

The way Brock looked at her as if he'd never seen anything so beautiful in his entire life—the way he opened up to her both physically and emotionally, and the way he made her feel with just one look.

One look that held promises.

One look that held a future.

"Wait." He gently pulled away from her and struggled out of his wet jeans. When she laughed at his awkward positioning on the floor, he glanced back. "Are you going to just sit there and mock me or help a man out?"

"I think..." She leaned up on her elbows. "I choose mocking."

"I'm killing the moment."

"Actually, I was thinking you were making it more entertaining."

His lips twitched into a smile before he got to his feet, kicked off his jeans and boxers in one swift movement. Reaching for her hands, he brought her to her feet, then lifted her onto the kitchen counter.

The cold granite was a shock to her skin as he hooked her ankles around his naked body. She forgot the sensation when he suddenly froze.

"What?" She asked, cupping his face with her hands then running them down his muscular shoulders.

He swallowed. "I think you're incredible." He leaned in closer, his mouth grazing hers. "I think you're absolutely stunning." His lips teased hers in a draining kiss that had her heart erratically slamming against her chest. "I think that I'll never get enough of this." He kissed her harder. "It's not just your taste..." His lips lingered on the slender column of her neck. "It's you. Jane, it's you."

"It's me what?" Her voice was wobbly with emotion.

"You're everything. I could see you naked every second

of every day, feel your body beneath my hands, watch you explode with ecstasy every waking moment and it would never be enough." He gripped her hips, pulling her to the end of the counter and filling her completely.

She kissed him hard as he moved inside her. Anticipation built until she thought she was going to lose her mind. It was almost more than she could handle.

Because even as they made love she could tell things were shifting yet again, and they were on uneven ground. Both desperately trying to hold onto something they weren't sure they could have. A future that wasn't certain.

Desperation filled her. She longed to be owned by him. To belong to him and only him.

Her head fell back as he stretched her, thrusting inside, filling her over and over again.

"I'll always want you," he vowed, kissing her neck as his hands moved to her hips, thumbs digging into her skin.

"Me"—she sighed—"too."

"Damn it, stop before I lose control."

She kissed him again.

With a primitive moan he buried into her as she drove her hips toward his body in a desperate attempt to feel more of him.

Her release surged across her body and she went limp in his arms.

His body jerked and then spasmed as he brushed another kiss across her mouth.

Sagging against him, she was too lost in bliss to do anything but revel in the feel of him still inside her, his heartbeat as it slammed against his chest, then slowed.

"Hey, Jane." Brock pulled back and looked into her eyes. "The floor's dirty again."

She slapped him weakly against the chest. "Well then, better clean it, Brock."

"I vote to leave it this way, with your ass cheeks imprinted on it. Hell, let's build a monument and—"

She shut him up with her mouth. As they lost themselves in one another she ignored the ticking of the grandfather clock in the living room.

Just like she ignored the wild yearning she had to keep him here at the ranch forever.

*　*　*

Brock ignored his grandfather's calls for the next three days. They were almost worse than the loud clanging of the clock in the living room or the damn cock every morning.

Reminders were everywhere.

Reminders that he only had three more days with Jane.

Reminders that he had to confront his grandfather. The thought of it made him break out into a cold sweat, but the thought of no Jane was like a physical pain.

The hot shower pelted his back, giving him the wake-up call he needed after spending the night in Jane's arms.

It felt right.

Sleeping next to her.

Being inside her.

How the hell could he even date another woman, let alone marry another woman? How could another woman ever measure up to the way Jane made him feel—like he wasn't some lost boy pretending to be a man? She listened to him, understood him, challenged him. God, she was perfect.

"Brock." Jane's smooth voice interrupted his thoughts.

Suddenly she was in the bathroom, completely naked. "Damn."

A blush lit up her cheeks. "Need some company?"

"Need." He exhaled slowly. "Want." Brock held out his hands. "Come here, beautiful."

Her hips swayed as she slowly approached the glass shower door then slowly opened it and stepped in. Her brown hair was splayed across her shoulders, her lips full, ready for him.

"This is a nice surprise," he murmured, pulling her into his arms.

She shivered and then kissed him before saying, "I had a run-in with the clock downstairs and panicked."

He sighed as a heaviness rested on his shoulders. "I'm sorry."

Her face brightened. "We have now."

It felt like his chest was cracking in half. "That we do."

They didn't say any more; words were pointless anyway. Words couldn't and wouldn't solve their problem, and honestly, he just wanted to touch her, feel her.

Brock pressed his mouth to hers and slowly entwined their hands as hot water ran down their naked bodies. Steam billowed around them as he licked a droplet of water from her chin and moved his mouth slowly down her neck until he was facing her gorgeous, lush breasts.

God, would he ever get enough of her?

Her hands hit the glass and slid down to brace herself as his mouth found her nipple—teasing, sucking—he'd never forget the way she tasted or how she responded to his mouth no matter where he kissed her, sucked her.

"Brock." Her chest rose and fell as she gave him a half-lidded stare. "That feels...amazing."

"You're amazing." He pulled back and stood to stare at the woman who'd completely thrown his world upside-down.

The woman he wanted more than anything.

Even if that meant facing his worst fear.

"Come here." He molded his mouth over hers as she reached for him, her greedy hands grasping at him in a way that was enough to make him lose his damn mind.

"Turn around," he said gruffly, gripping her hips without waiting for her response.

Jane gasped as he used his feet to slide her legs wider apart and then bent her forward and thrust into her.

She gasped and then pushed back, meeting his thrusts. "Yes!" Her wet hair slapped against her back. The view from his angle was enough to make any man black out from ecstasy.

"I'm going to—"

"Jane." He clenched his teeth. "Come on, baby."

She cried out, slamming her hands against the glass wall.

And he realized—he couldn't spend a day, a week, a year without this woman falling apart in his arms.

*　*　*

Later that day they fell into their usual routine: she cleaned around the house and he made sure the cock wasn't bullying the other animals.

The hens were more than happy.

The cock glared at him but otherwise left him alone.

Buttercup ate her oats and neighed while the ass roamed free—it was impossible to keep the damn thing locked up. One day Brock was going to put a camera out in the barn just to see if the ass really was as smart as he wanted everyone to believe. On more than one occasion he'd found the damn thing standing in the middle of the living room.

With the TV on, no less.

Always *The Today Show*.

Always.

His days had fallen into a routine, one he liked, one that didn't include going to his grandfather's meetings, making sure he shook hands with men he didn't give two shits about.

Between board meetings, golf, charity dinners—his life had become something he didn't recognize anymore.

Until now.

That Brock—the one who lived in the city, who was boring, and a complete copy of his grandfather—he didn't exist out at the ranch. And yet he was terrified that once he returned to the city, he'd lose what he'd found here, what he'd found with Jane.

With a heavy sigh he made his way back into the house to find Jane staring in horror at the TV.

"The guest list is in for the first annual Bachelor Auction." The newscaster looked like she was going to burst with excitement. "And the names on the list just may surprise you. Here are our picks for the women who will bid the most, though all we can do is speculate. It's still fun to see who might win out and who gets the charity date, along with a chance to steal Brock Wellington's heart! Rumors about the bachelor's disappearance have been rampant and the one that refuses to die is the suggestion that he's taking time away from the speculation to decide who he's truly interested in. Is Brock Wellington planning on settling down? And is he using the auction as a way to find someone who matches him in looks, wealth, and power? We agree that these women are sure to make any man wish he was getting auctioned off!"

Brock gulped as the screen flashed pictures of the women.

"Supermodel Tamara Sanderson, actress Julie Zellman, and co-founder of the country's fastest growing fashion app Di Fashion, to name a few! We want to know, who would you pick? Take the poll and you could win a ticket to the charity ball this Saturday night! Tickets are ten thousand a head; don't miss this once in a lifetime chance to attend Cinderella's ball!"

Brock quickly found the remote and changed the channel, only to discover the story was there as well. Apparently he was breaking news—again.

He hit the power button, and the room fell into an awkward silence.

"Sorry." He locked eyes on Jane. She was hunched over, chewing her bottom lip, her eyes filled with tears. "I'm sorry you had to see that."

"It's okay," she croaked.

"Come here." He held out his hands.

She shook her head and took a step back.

"Jane?"

"I c-can't." She crossed her arms. "I um, missed one of the bathrooms upstairs. I should go clean it and—"

"Jane!"

She turned and ran—well, tried to run, considering her ankle was still hurt. She'd made it halfway up the stairs before he caught up to her.

"Stop." He pulled her into his arms. "Just stop."

"You have to go back." She stared at his chest.

"Yes." It killed him to say so. "But you do, too. As much as I want to stay here forever...we have to face our ghosts. Weren't you the one who said that?"

Jane nodded. "I'm going back to my life, Brock, but... will you be a part of it?"

He closed his eyes and breathed out a curse. "Jane, just give me a few days to talk to my grandfather. It's been a long time coming, but I can't just drop this news on him. I mean, think of his heart and—"

"His heart?" Jane repeated loudly. "Has he ever had a weak heart?"

"Well, he may have had an anxiety attack over me not doing the auction, but we thought it was a heart attack at first," Brock said defensively. "And he's always talking about his impending death."

"Brock, are you listening to yourself? Are you seriously going to do whatever he says for the rest of your life just because you're worried he's going to die the minute you say no?"

Anger swelled in his chest. "You don't get it! He's all I have!"

"What about me?"

"That's not what I mean. You're different."

"I thought I was, but..." She shrugged. "Brock, if you deny him, he's not going to die."

"You don't know that. You can't know that. Accidents happen. Remember?" He shook his head. He knew his argument made no sense, not even to him anymore. "Look, all I'm asking for is time."

"We don't have time. The ball is on Saturday. Today is Thursday."

He gulped and looked away, clenching his teeth together. "Can't you at least give me time? I mean, you of all people should know how hard it is to stand up to family. You've been a doormat to your own sisters your entire life!"

Jane's lower lip trembled as her eyes filled with tears. "You're right. But I'm willing to make that change and it's because of you! I'm willing to fight for me, to fight for us. Are you?"

"Jane." Brock felt like his heart was breaking. "I'm just asking for time."

"Time." She sighed. "Then I guess that's it."

What had just happened? Why did this feel like good-bye? He blinked hard at her. "So, you're okay?"

"No, Brock. I'm not okay. I'm leaving."

"What the hell?" he roared.

"You said you needed time," she fired back. "So I'm going to give it to you. Spend the next few days thinking about what you want, or"—she seemed to shrink inside herself—"if you already know, you can just go back, and tell your grandfather how you feel before it's too late."

"It's not just about my feelings anymore." He sat down and ran his hands through his hair. "If all I had to do was say no to my grandfather, I could manage it." His eyes burned when he took in her sad expression. "Jane, it terrifies me. But for you, for you I would risk it."

She gulped and sat down next to him, sliding her hand up his thigh. "Then what is it? What aren't you telling me?"

"The shareholders want to push Grandfather out. I don't know the exact details but I do know that for him to say something to me, it must be bad. He's using the auction as a way to show a united front—me, him, the twins. The face of Wellington. The publicity alone has made them change their tune, enough that they seem at least partially satisfied. The other snag we have is Titus Enterprises. We've had several..." He tried to think of the correct words. "We've had several sour dealings with them and the board has been itching for a better business relationship with them." He locked eyes with her. "Guess who's co-sponsoring the auction?"

Jane's eyes fell. "Titus Enterprises."

"Right." His laugh was bitter. "And they're absolutely thrilled that the future leader of Wellington is going to take one for the team."

"You," she whispered.

"Me." He nodded. "Wellington, Inc. is everything to my

grandfather. Saying no may not kill him; you're right. But losing this company to a bunch of greedy shareholders who would run our name into the ground would."

"I understand." Jane stood.

"Just..." Brock didn't release her hand. "Give me time to think of a solution that keeps everyone happy...and living." His try at a joke missed its mark; if anything her face fell more.

"Brock." Tears filled her eyes. "You've known me three weeks. You've been with your grandfather, and this company, your whole life." She lifted a shoulder in a half shrug. "I can't expect you to sacrifice everything for a maid."

He sucked in a breath. "You're *not* just a maid."

"Okay, the hired help." She offered a sad smile and cupped his face with her free hand. "I'll wait for you." Tears spilled onto her cheeks. "And I hope you can come up with a solution."

"You don't have to leave."

"Maybe we both should. I'll go back home and face my own ghosts." Her brave smile wasn't making him feel any better. "And you can go try to find a way to keep the company and your grandfather."

"And what about us?"

"We'll be fine." It was a lie. Even as she said it, he knew she didn't really believe her own words. His chest clenched. Did she really have that little faith in him?

Then again, even as he sat there hating life, hating their circumstances, he literally had no clue how to fix them—and still keep her.

She left two hours later.

Brock suddenly understood what it was like to feel truly empty. His parents' death had altered the course of his life— but a few weeks with Jane had changed it as well.

CHAPTER THIRTY-FOUR

Jane held back the tears that threatened the entire drive back to Phoenix. She was proud of herself when she finally pulled up to her house that evening and had managed to shed only one.

New life, new life, new life.

She had to confront her sisters even though it was the last thing she wanted to do. She needed a life of her own, a life that didn't involve walking on eggshells. And Brock was right; would her father really have wanted her to live this way in order to keep the family together? She'd tried. But now, she needed to create a life for herself.

And she hoped to God that Brock would find a way to create one for himself—with her in it.

She'd already called Brock's crazy grandfather and confessed she'd left early, in hopes he would still pay her for the time she did clean. When he asked about her ankle injury she assured him that she only needed half-pay.

He started to argue but she held firm. She wanted to be fair. She hadn't done all the work alone.

Reluctantly, he told her he'd have a messenger drop off her check later that evening.

At least that worked out in her favor.

She'd expected Brock to follow her.

To call her.

To say something.

Anything.

But he didn't chase after her and confess his feelings, and there were no texts from the prince stating that he'd stormed the castle and fixed the shattered happy ending in their future.

Just. Nothing.

She straightened her shoulders and took a deep, long breath, before grabbing the handle to the door of her house.

Locked.

Since when did her sisters lock the house?

Confused, she grabbed her keys and shoved the right one into the keyhole, only to have it go in halfway.

The doorknob looked the same.

Had they seriously changed the locks to piss her off?

Were they that immature?

She knocked as loudly as she could, then rang the door-bell repeatedly.

After a few minutes, during which she seriously considered trying to break the door down, it flew open, revealing a crazed-looking Essence.

"Jane," she spat. "What are you doing here?"

Jane tried to shove the door open. She was exhausted and in no mood to argue. "I live here. Remember?"

"It's been almost three weeks," Essence said in that same irritating tone. "For all we knew you could have been dead. You never took our calls, remember?"

Jane remembered. It had been the most peaceful three weeks she'd had in years!

"I was working," Jane finally answered. "I got hired to do a job and now I'm home."

"Oh, we know." Essence's smile was cruel.

"I don't understand." Jane gulped as dread washed over her. What had her sisters done now? Finally Essence moved aside enough for Jane to enter.

And what she saw nearly made her collapse in a heap.

The news was on.

The cameras were pointed toward the ranch.

And images of Jane and Brock, kissing, were plastered all over the screen.

She covered her mouth with her hands as tears filled her eyes. When she grabbed the remote and changed channels, it just grew worse. Every news station was reporting about the maid who'd seduced the bachelor weeks before the auction.

But the worst part was yet to come.

Because when the camera went back to the reporter, the reporter was standing in front of her house.

With both of her sisters.

"She turned off her phone. We had no idea she was this...conniving. I mean, the auction is days away! She's supposed to be helping out and putting food on the table, and"—Essence wiped away a few fake tears—"she hasn't spoken to us in days. We're so worried!"

The reporter nodded her head and turned toward the camera. "It looks like the bachelor has some explaining to do. After all, he's set to be bid on this weekend, and rumors have been rampant about an impending marriage to one of the lucky ladies. Sources say that he's just returned to the city and refuses to talk to any media outlet, but we did get a statement from Bentley Wellington in the form of, "Leave our brother the bleep alone." The TV bleeped out the curse word.

Oh, Bentley.

The media were losing their minds over the story.

With shaking hands she turned off the TV. Esmeralda had come into the room and both she and Essence started yelling at Jane at the exact same time.

But it wasn't their yelling that caused tears to slip down her cheeks.

Or even the fact that the world probably assumed the worst of her.

It was a simple truth that Brock would have to go through with the auction, and even though it killed her, there was absolutely nothing she could do about it. There was no way his family could survive this scandal and keep Wellington, Inc. under their control—under Brock's control. Wellington, Inc. and his family were everything to Brock—which in turn meant they were everything to Jane, too.

"We're going out," Essence announced even while she was still shouting. "Oh, and the dishes probably need to be done. Good to have you home, sister. Hope it was worth it."

They left in a flurry of perfume and mean-spirited laughter.

Jane stayed on the couch.

And cried.

*   *   *

With her sisters gone and no message from Brock, she wasn't really sure what to do with herself. Dishes were stacked high in the kitchen and a weird odor was coming from the fridge. Everywhere she looked was absolute chaos.

So she did what she knew best.

She cleaned.

Not because she was reverting back to what was familiar, though it looked that way, but because it soothed her, helped her think. And no matter what her sisters did, it was still her house; she was still proud of it and wanted it to look good.

Besides, the only other option was to cry some more and open up a tub of ice cream.

Why hadn't he called?

She was just getting ready to start on the dishes when a knock sounded at the door. Jane jumped half a foot and then ran to the door like her life depended on it.

But when the door swung open it wasn't Brock.

The man standing there, however, looked like an older version of him.

Jane took a cautious step back. "Can I help you?"

The man narrowed his eyes into tiny slits; the moon glistened off his thick silver hair. "I think that's my line."

"I'm sorry; what did you say your name was?" She probably looked horrible, with mascara-stained cheeks and red puffy eyes. The last thing she wanted right now was to have to deal with some psycho news reporter getting a picture of her and splashing it all over the Internet. Not that it would matter.

Because Brock still had to do the auction.

To save his company.

To save his family name.

Ugh. This was such a mess.

Part of her didn't blame him for not calling, but another part was heartbroken he hadn't at least sent her a text or called her and let her know he was fixing things.

"I didn't." The man peered around her. "Mind if I come in? I'm a bit chilled."

Yeah, she wasn't buying that. It was at least eighty degrees outside even though it was starting to get dark.

"Sorry." She started to close the door. "I don't know you so—"

"Ah, but you know my grandson."

"Grandson?" she countered, crossing her arms. After all, she'd never seen this man before, though his voice did sound vaguely familiar. And there was definitely a family resemblance.

The man's mouth twitched before it broke out in a wide smile. "You are well acquainted with...the arrogant one."

"You just described every man I know."

"Yes, well." He rocked back on his heels and glanced down the street before looking back at her. "Some things can't be helped, I imagine."

"Look, sir, I don't care if you're the president of the United States. I don't just let strange men into my house and—" He shoved past her and closed the door.

"Hey, wait a second!" She ran by him to grab her phone, just in case she needed to call the police to give them a play-by-play of her murder, but the elderly gentleman pulled a piece of paper out of his pocket and placed it on her kitchen table.

"I believe"—he nodded—"this was the agreed-upon amount."

Frowning, she glanced down.

It was a check.

Written out to her.

From Wellington, Inc.

Signed by Brock's grandfather.

Suddenly everything fell into place.

Except for the amount on the check: *One million dollars*.

She shook her head.

"No." Jane suddenly felt faint. "I'm pretty sure there weren't that many zeros in the amount we agreed upon." She'd never seen so much money in her entire life.

And it was made out to her.

She could do anything.

Start over.

Kick her sisters out of the house.

Put money in her business!

Hire employees!

The possibilities were endless.

But a million dollars?

Something wasn't right.

"As much as I want to jump up and down right now that you've given me a check with that many zeros, I'm going to have to ask what the catch is." She sat down in a nearby chair and put her head in her hands. "What are you really doing here?"

He seemed to assess her from head to toe. His perusal, almost mocking in the way his eyes slowly took her in, so very clearly seemed to find her wanting—from the way her cheeks were streaked with makeup, to the plain clothes she was wearing—then his gaze fell to the kitchen and the surrounding mess.

Tears blurred her vision.

Yeah, she was making an awesome first impression, wasn't she?

"Jane." He pulled out a chair; it screeched across the dirty tile floor. The man seemed too big to be sitting at her small kitchen table. He folded his hands across the worn wood grain, nearly ruining his expensive suit's sleeve on an open packet of discarded soy sauce. "What would you say if I told you I'd give you a million dollars to never see my grandson again—the arrogant one, about yea tall." He held his hand way up above his head and winked, his indifferent mask slipping to reveal a kind smile. "Carries the weight of the world on his shoulders, prone to barking, yelling, shouting." He shrugged. "And those are just the positive attributes."

Jane attempted a smile, but failed at even that.

"So?" He leaned back, the chair creaking under his massive frame.

Jane leaned forward and uttered a simple, clear "no."

His mouth spread into a wide grin. "Money could buy you everything you need—including happiness. Soon you'd forget about him. It would be so easy, Jane. So very easy to cash this check. Brock doesn't ever need to find out about it."

"My answer"—her eyes never left his—"is still no."

He tilted his head. "Two million."

"Three? Four? Seven?" She countered with a proud smile on her face. "You can't place a price tag on what I've found with him. And my answer is still the same." Her voice was wobbly; maybe it was from the stress of the day or just the fact that Brock's grandfather was trying to give her hush money.

A lone tear slid down her face. She quickly wiped it away and slumped back in her chair. "Sorry, it's just been a really long and horrible day."

"Some days"—he sighed—"are longer than life."

She nodded. Suddenly she was so overwhelmed with exhaustion it was hard to keep her eyes open.

Embarrassingly enough, her stomach chose that moment to growl. She hadn't eaten since that morning.

"Food." Brock's grandfather nodded at her in a knowing way. "Sometimes all you need is a full stomach for things to start looking better."

"And here I thought it was time...or sleep."

He slowly reached out and pulled the check back, then folded it and stuffed it in his pocket. "When you sleep on things, it makes those things disappear until you wake up, more frustrated than before. When you give them time, you allow yourself the possibility of hesitation. I don't believe in hesitation, not anymore." His face fell. "Action, sweetheart. I believe in taking life by the horns and maneuvering it."

"Obviously." She nodded toward the pocket he'd just stuffed the check into. "And what would you gain from sending me away?"

He was quiet for a moment, then said, "In order to gain you sometimes have to lose."

"I refuse to lose him." She stood. "I think you've overstayed your welcome."

"Ah…" He stood. "I guess you're right. An old man needs his sleep and a young woman has a lot to think about."

She laughed bitterly. "There's nothing to think about. I'm not taking the money."

He ignored her, or seemed to, as he walked around the table and wrung his hands. "Here." He reached into a separate pocket and held out a check. This one was written for thirty thousand dollars.

Jane frowned. "I'm sorry. I don't understand?"

"Take what is owed you. From our original agreement." His eyes twinkled as she touched the check with her fingertips and stared at it again.

"Oh." He snapped his fingers. "And one more thing. I'm still auctioning him off, but that doesn't mean you can't bid on him and win. I think I'd like to get to know you better, Jane."

Bitterness washed over her. "It's ten grand a plate and—"

"Is it?" He grinned. "Imagine, ten grand. And look what you hold in your hand." He shrugged his large shoulders. "If you really love him—"

"Who said I loved him?"

"You did." His wise eyes didn't even blink. "When you said no. Amazing the power that word holds...I think, no, I *hope*, that Brock soon understands its meaning the way you have." He hesitated but then took a step forward and kissed her on the cheek. "Good night, Jane. I'm glad I found you."

CHAPTER THIRTY-FIVE

He managed one day, one day of hell before Brock packed up his shit and drove into the city. The ball was the following evening, and he needed to talk to his grandfather. He still wasn't sure how he was going to break the news or how he was still going to keep everyone happy and keep Jane. He just knew he had to do it.

Traffic was hell, so the drive took forever.

And by the time he made it to the Wellington offices, he was advised that his grandfather was out.

He wasn't given a return time, or an address where his grandfather could be found, so he went home.

Only to find his brothers sitting in his apartment drinking.

Well, at least he was home.

"Dipshit!" Bentley opened his arms wide. "So, how was it? Tell me everything. Did you make love under the moonlight? Take long walks with Buttercup? Tease her mercilessly under the stars?" He smirked. "You're welcome, by the way. How did grandfather take it?"

Brock was silent.

Brant rolled his eyes. "Told you he wouldn't do it."

Bentley looked like his head was going to explode. "You bastard! You had her! A beautiful, nice, funny woman who actually *knows* how to do laundry, and you passed her up? For what? A model?"

"Do I know you at all anymore?" Brant glared at Bentley. "You would do the exact same thing."

"Right, but I'm me. This is Brock!"

They both glared at him.

"I haven't had a chance to talk to Grandfather because he's not in the office and not returning my calls. So I came home to shower and think about how best not to give the old man a heart attack when I tell him I'm not going through with the auction. I can't do it. I won't."

"And Jane? How does she feel about all of this?" Bentley asked again, his voice grating on his every last nerve.

"She's probably freaking out over why I haven't called her yet, but I had to close the house down, traffic took fucking forever, and by the time I was able to even look at my phone it was dead." Brock stepped around his brothers and made his way into the bathroom, bracing his hands against the granite countertop. He shook his head. "Why are you guys here, anyway?" He glanced at their reflections in the mirror. Both of them looked guilty.

Bentley's throat worked into a tight swallow. "Grandfather said, and I quote, 'You're next,' so we're hiding...."

"Again." Brant sighed.

Brock's lips twitched in amusement. He would have laughed had his heart not still been busy cracking inside his chest with every breath he took. He just wanted Jane. And in order to hold her in his arms he needed to figure his way out of this clusterfuck.

One of the twins' phones went off.

"Holy shit," Bentley breathed, and dropped his phone onto the glass table before running over to the TV, grabbing the remote, and turning it on.

Stunned, Brock could only stare as the news station showed pictures of him kissing Jane at the ranch. What was worse, he could see her name splashed all over the screen.

This image was followed by the sight of her horrible sisters.

His heart clenched and then a righteous anger, swift and strong, slammed into his body, making his blood boil and his teeth clench.

He'd pursued *her*.

And yet the reporters were making her out to be some sort of social-climbing whore. The more he watched the sicker he felt.

"Turn that shit off. Now," he roared, grabbing his phone. "Fuck!"

"What?" Brant stood.

"My phone's dead."

"Use mine." Brant tossed his.

"I don't have her number memorized!" Brock yelled, chucking the phone back at his brother. "Damn it!" He kicked the sofa. Repeatedly.

"Calm down." Bentley held out his hands. "We can figure this out." He motioned for Brock to sit.

"This is bad." Leave it to Brant to state the obvious. "But we can fix it…"

"No," Brock said in a hollow voice. "I need to fix it. There is no 'we.'"

Bentley scowled. "Do you really think we're going to let you go through this alone? When there's a woman you love out there probably crying her eyes out because she thinks you've abandoned her—"

"Not helping," Brant said in a low voice.

"Let me finish!" Bentley snapped. "Brock." He knelt down in front of his brother. "Think. You're the brains behind most of Grandfather's asinine ideas; there has to be a way out."

Brock sucked in a breath as the pressure of his family settled heavily on his shoulders. It was time to be honest. With both of them. "The auction..." He swallowed. "It's for the shareholders."

"Come again?" Bentley frowned. "What the hell do they have to do with anything?"

"Everything," Brant answered for Brock, then took a seat next to him on the couch, his expression grim. "They're pushing Grandfather out, aren't they?"

"How'd you know?" Brock asked.

"Just call it intuition." Brant looked away. Clearly he was hiding something but it wasn't the time or place to ask how or why. "So, the auction is what? A way to make everyone happy?"

"Good press." Brock stood and began to pace the hardwood floor. "The media's obviously going wild over the idea; we're bringing money in for research and finally playing nice with the Titus family. We're reminding the shareholders about how much the press loves the Wellington name and providing free publicity for the company. It shows we're team players and that the company isn't going to go to shit when Grandfather leaves it to us." He paused. "All of us."

Bentley paled, while Brant kept looking away.

Was it guilt that kept the twins silent? Or something more?

The room was thick with tension.

"Wait!" Bentley jumped to his feet. "Titus Enterprises is sponsoring the auction with us? Right?"

"And?" Brock shrugged. "Grandfather's been pining after them for years. They're basically our counterpart, only the grandsons have actually settled down and made something of themselves, whereas we're all still single and you guys manage to become front page news every weekend."

Brant rolled his eyes. "The fact that Jake Titus is happily married with kids is enough to make me want to throw up a little. The guy was worse than me and Bentley combined. Besides, that marriage doesn't count until he's made it past six years."

But Bentley had a knowing look on his face, his eyes wide. "The point is that Nadine Titus has always been known to have a soft spot for love stories and matchmaking, right?"

"Hunh?" Brock was even more confused.

A smirk crossed Brant's face. "I think that's a solid plan."

"Wait? What am I missing?" Brock stopped pacing.

"Everything, brother." Bentley slapped him on the back. "Damn near everything."

"Will it save Jane?"

Bentley braced Brock with both hands. "And you."

CHAPTER THIRTY-SIX

Jane woke up to her phone going off. She nearly fell out of bed in an attempt to grab it, thinking maybe, just maybe it was Brock.

Instead it was a text from Essence, saying that she and Esmeralda had stayed the night at a friend's house and not to worry.

The thing about it, though? She wasn't worried. Not at all. She'd stopped worrying the minute her sisters had proved they cared about themselves more than her, since she was left, as usual, to pick up the pieces. The press hadn't left her house since news had broken that she was back home, which just so happened to be a few hours after Brock's grandfather left.

Newspapers and TV shows wanted to interview her.

She could understand her sisters wanting to dodge the press, but honestly, leaving had just given them an excuse to do just what they'd normally do.

They'd left a mess in the house.

They'd had no regard for her feelings.

They'd manipulated.

And if she needed more proof of how little concern they actually felt for her, she had all of the text conversations from when she was at the ranch.

Her heart slammed against her chest.

The ranch.

Brock.

She still hadn't heard from him, but at the same time she refused to believe things were over.

Sighing, she was just ready to put her phone back down when it rang.

Fumbling with the device, she pressed answer and had it to her ear. "Jane? Jane, is that you?"

Esmeralda's voice may as well be nails on a chalkboard. "Hey," Jane answered.

"I'm still pissed at you." Esmeralda sighed. "But, whatever. I just wanted to let you know that we forgive you."

"Forgive me?" Jane rolled her eyes. Was her sister serious? "For what?"

"Leaving us."

"I left to take a job!" Jane slammed her hand against her forehead. "Because that's how I make money!" Were they really that dense?

"Right, but you didn't answer your phone, left the laundry, didn't even think to grocery shop. You know I hate going to crowded superstores like Walmart! I had a traumatic experience there! You know that!"

Jane bit her tongue. It was more that Esmeralda just hated doing anything that she thought was beneath her—grocery shopping fit that bill.

"Anyway, we forgive you and we actually wanted to do you a favor. We thought it would be fun to get ready for the ball tonight."

"Did you say *ball*?"

"Yeah, why?"

"The ball that costs ten thousand dollars a plate? That ball?" Jane had a familiar sick punch to the gut. They didn't have the money for it—not at all.

"Are there any other balls where rich men are getting auctioned off?" Esmeralda laughed. "Of course that ball."

"But you don't have that kind of money!"

Esmeralda was silent and then sighed. "Look, I took out a new credit card. God knows you won't be able to marry the guy after you publicly shamed yourself like a whore. Besides, we need money!"

"Esmeralda!" She fought to keep the tears in. "How could you do that? Why? It's just a party! We don't have the money!"

"But you made money at the big job you were just on, right?" Esmeralda laughed. "We'll pay for the rest on the credit card. All we really need is your portion."

"My ... portion," Jane said, fuming. "I don't owe you guys anything."

"You took the job to support the family, right?" Esmeralda said plainly. "So support the family. Plus, think of the networking Essence and I could do at a place like that! We could get so many clients, meet so many people. Really, you would be doing it for us. For all of us. After all, didn't Daddy want us to work together as a team?"

"About that." Jane glanced around her room—at the memories that filled it, the walls with posters of bands and singers, the stickers that still littered her ceiling. "I think I'd rather fly solo."

Esmeralda was silent, then said, "But we love you."

"No." Jane closed her eyes as tears burned. "You love you."

"Jane!" Esmeralda shouted. "Don't do this to us!"

"I'm sorry. I just…I can't. I can't support you spending money, my hard-earned money, on something frivolous. From here on out you're on your own."

"You're a selfish bitch!" Esmeralda yelled. "No wonder he's still going through with the auction. Who would want a frigid virgin for—"

Jane hung up the phone before she said something she could never take back.

Her childhood room suddenly felt too small, choking the life out of her. A memory surfaced of her father.

"Knock, knock." Daddy walked in with an apron over his work clothes. He held a tray in his hand, and a rose was laid across the plate of eggs and French toast. A giant cup of coffee sat on the far right side. "I figured you'd need this."

She didn't trust herself to speak, so she nodded her head and looked away.

"They don't deserve you, sweetheart," he whispered once he set the tray on the bed and tilted her chin toward him. "Girls are fickle creatures. I love all three of you, but sometimes, we say things that are hurtful. Things we don't mean. Promise that you'll see through that and try to keep the family together." He coughed; the tray trembled in his hands as he sat on her bed. "Just promise to try. Family is all we have."

"I promised to keep everyone together," Jane whispered aloud as the memory faded.

But was that what her dad had meant? To be a maid to her own family? No. And she'd already made her decision to stand her ground. So, with shaking hands, she grabbed a suitcase and started packing.

CHAPTER THIRTY-SEVEN

Brock frowned at the text.

She was late.

He tried not to be irritated. After all, he needed her if their plan was going to work.

Brock was checking his phone again when the door to his limo flew open, revealing a flurry of leopard print and expensive perfume. She flashed him a knowing smile and slid across the smooth leather seat. Her bright red lipstick was like a homing beacon in the dark car.

"Well," she huffed. "I'm listening. What exactly do you need from me?"

Everything. He leaned back and took a deep breath, then faced the one woman he knew could help keep his family in charge of Wellington, Inc.

But this wasn't business.

No. This was personal.

Brock exhaled and looked at this woman who could easily destroy a man with a simple snap of her fingers, and said, "I love her."

Her eyebrows shot up to her hairline and an excited smile crossed over her soft features. "Really?"

"Yes." He swallowed. "So damned much I can't lose her. But I also love my grandfather."

"Which leaves us at an impasse." She tapped her chin with a long red fingernail and smirked. "I do love a good romance."

Didn't he know it. Rumors had been rampant over the last few years on how she'd set up her own grandsons and basically forced them into blissful marriages, all without missing a beat.

Which was why he'd come to her.

Wellington, Inc. needed her partnership in order to please the shareholders, and if she agreed to help him with Jane he'd owe her. This would give her more power than she already had, but he knew she'd like that, and he was betting it would make her more willing to form an alliance with Wellington, Inc., if only because she'd feel she had the upper hand.

Besides. He would do anything. Anything.

For Jane.

"What will you give me if I help you?" She sobered, her expression suddenly all business.

Brock met her stare and paused, then said, "A damned good show."

At that she threw back her head and laughed. "Like grandfather, like grandson?"

"I'd like to think I'm less stuffy..."

"Oh honey." Her voice dropped into a husky whisper. "You have absolutely no idea."

Yeah, that was too much information.

"So you'll help me win the woman I love?"

"Oh, I'll help you all right, and I'll do it out of the goodness of my heart." She patted him on the shoulder. "And for the simple fact that while I despise your family as competition, I would be bored to tears without it—plus, that grandfather of yours." She rubbed her hands together and smirked. "He's quite...wonderful, isn't he?"

"When he isn't trying to control everyone and everything? Yes." Brock spoke without thinking.

"Oh honey." She patted his hand. "That's just us grandparents worrying about the future. Besides, something tells me that my involvement will make him happier than you could possibly imagine."

"Oh?" That piqued his interest. "How so?"

Her smile was warm. "Because it will make you happy—and despite what you think—that's all he's ever wanted."

Brock didn't know what to say to that.

She seemed to pick up on his hesitation and shrugged. "You'll have to make sure the media believes it. I hope you haven't been having any secret rendezvous with the girl, or texts since you've returned from the ranch that they can grab a hold of."

He exhaled. At least he'd done that right. "No, no. I've been waiting until I spoke with you. Until you agreed."

She harrumphed. "Well, now that I have, it's just going to get harder. No direct contact." She drew out the word *direct*. "Until the night of, got it? No funny business. The last thing we need is for this to look like a setup."

"I swear, I'll do anything for her."

"I know." She winked. "That's what makes this so romantic." She paused. "You do realize the favors I'll have to owe people, the negotiations that will have to take place in order for this to fully work?"

Brock swallowed back his anxiety. "I do."

"Well, I have been known to manipulate in my day...I guess this just means I'm back in the game."

He suddenly had the sinking feeling that he'd re-created a monster.

"Your grandfather..."

"Leave him out of this," Brock snapped.

"Hmm." She merely stared at him. Hard. As if trying to figure him out. "You know, he isn't as bad as he seems."

Brock let out a breath he didn't realize he'd been holding. "I know, I just...I can't lose her."

The corners of her mouth worked into a bright smile. "Then leave it to me. Trust me to do what I do best."

"And what's that?"

"Why..." She winked. "Everything, of course."

CHAPTER THIRTY-EIGHT

The auction was tomorrow.

Jane tried to ignore the pain in her chest.

Clearly, he was going through with it.

Without her.

Two days had passed and there'd been no word from Brock. She wanted to trust that he was dealing with it, but, really, part of her was already so depressed that she still hadn't heard from him that all she wanted to do was sob into her ice cream and watch crap TV.

With a grimace she walked over to the freezer and pulled out some Rocky Road, then took a seat on the couch. After the fight with her sisters they'd come home, grabbed some of their things, and told her yet again not to wait up.

She was pretty sure they were still going to the auction.

Without her, unless she used the money that was burning a hole in her pocket to buy a ticket to the dinner.

She groaned.

Did she really have a choice?

Her own sisters were sacrificing everything to go.

They'd see Brock.

Brock.

Another groan escaped her lips. Why hadn't he texted her?

Had he stood up to his grandfather?

Was he happy? Sad?

Why the hell did she care? She was sad. She was eating Rocky Road.

With a frustrated sigh she dug her spoon in.

And then.

Her doorbell rang.

"No!" she yelled. "Not more." Probably because even though she was going crazy, the last thing she wanted was another visit from the media. They'd been relentless all day, since it was the night before the auction.

The doorbell sounded again, then someone knocked so hard that she thought they'd break the door down. She shot up from the couch and stomped over to throw it open.

"Bentley?"

"Jane." He smiled. He really did have a killer smile.

"Um? What are you doing here?"

"Getting your sizes, of course," he said as he handed her a garment bag. "For some reason women keep leaving their clothes in my apartment. As if I'd invite them back. Ha. Anyway, let's see if any of these fit."

"Wait, what—"

"Trust me." Bentley shrugged. "Can you do that?"

It was the same thing Brock had said to her.

"But Brock—"

"Trust him, too," Bentley said gently, although his gaze was a bit harsh, as if he didn't have the patience for her to argue with him. "Now, let's get you out of those clothes."

She jerked back and eyed him up and down. "Some things never change."

"Shit." Bentley rubbed his temples. "That came out wrong. What I meant was, let's see if any of these fit. So we can figure out what kind of dress to get. Please?"

"For?" Jane rubbed her arms and stepped back into the house.

"Cinderella has to go to the ball, don't you think?"

She shook her head. "Bentley, this is sweet, *you're* sweet, but I haven't heard from him in two days and, even though I have the money to buy a ticket...." Had she really lost trust in him that fast? When he swore he'd make things right?

"His phone was dead on day one and he's been... advised." Bentley chose his words carefully, it seemed. "He's not supposed to make actual contact with you until the right time. He's working on a solution to this whole mess, believe me. And you've had the media camped outside your house for God knows how long. It's a simple question, Jane. Do you trust him?"

She stared Bentley down. He seemed genuine, but oh, how her heart hurt. "Yes," she finally whispered. "I do." Tears threatened again. "But the company, it's everything to him, and not letting you guys down and his grandfather; don't even get me started on that piece of work and—"

Bentley pressed a finger to her lips. "Do you care for Brock? Possibly love him?"

Tears spilled onto her cheeks. Ah! Why couldn't she stop crying! Three weeks shouldn't have affected her so much—but Brock had found his way into her heart and no amount of tears or logic that he was doing what he had to do made the pain go away or the sadness at potentially losing him. And really, what was she losing him to?

A nameless face? Not really. The messed-up part was that really when she thought about it, she was losing him to his grandfather.

"Thought so." Bentley grinned, bringing her back to the present. He removed his finger and then let out a whistle. To her horror several people piled out of a black SUV and started shuffling into her house.

"Is this necessary?"

His eyes twinkled and that practiced, devastating, panty-melting smile was back in full force. "For a Wellington? For Jane? For the princess of the ball? Absolutely. Besides, my brother would have me by the balls if I did anything as half-assed as sending you to the mall."

* * *

"Should you maybe stop at the stop signs?" Jane gripped the door handle and held on for dear life.

"Speed makes me feel alive!" The driver of the Uber car Bentley had hired chuckled and then took a hard right followed by another hard left that had the tires screeching in protest. "Aha! I knew we were close."

They were in an abandoned parking lot.

"To where you plan on murdering me?" Jane scooted next to the door just in case she had to actually make a run for it. Two hours after taking her measurements Bentley had insisted on sending a car for her. In his words, she needed to pick out a dress.

But still.

No Brock.

And yet Bentley's words bounced around in her head. Trust Brock. Which meant Brock was in on all of this, but she still didn't even know what *this* was.

At Bentley's insistence, she purchased a ticket for the ball. His instructions were clear. "Your money is your own."

What does that even mean?

Should she bid on Brock?

Well, duh, of course; but thirty grand wasn't going to win her anything!

Nothing made sense.

Doubt crept in the corners of her mind.

And then the driver put the car in park and turned it off. "Parking lots are too out in the open, now a parking garage..." He tapped his chin and grinned. "I could commit a crime there, I suppose."

Jane made a mental note to stay out of every parking garage within the city limits.

The van door slid open; a gorgeous Asian woman with bright red lipstick stepped out. "Right off the runway. But some may need adjustments."

Curiosity got the best of Jane, so she got out of the car and peered behind the girl. The back of the van was filled with at least twenty, maybe thirty, gorgeous ball gowns in every color of the rainbow and in every type of material she could imagine. Silk, satin, tulle.

With a gasp, she covered her face. "Those are beautiful."

"I'm glad you think so, sweetheart." Suddenly Bentley walked up, his swagger even more pronounced. "Pick one. Oh hell, pick two. Nothing's too good for my date."

"Your what?" She tried to hide her disappointment, but it was impossible.

Bentley wrapped a muscular arm around her and smiled harder. "Now, I want you to pick one that screams sexy. Brock's favorite color is black—shocker, I know—but he gave me strict instructions for you to make sure it's what *you* want, not what he wants, not what I want, not what anyone else wants but you."

Jane was still stuck on the fact that Brock had given his brother instructions. He had to care. He just had to. And in her heart she knew he did; she just didn't understand why a simple text message or phone call would hurt anything. The media was still hounding her. Maybe he was afraid something would leak? Ugh; and now Bentley was escorting her, instead of Brock?

"Brock knows you're my date? And he's okay with it?"

Bentley rolled his eyes. "Women are so damn complicated." He pointed to the dresses and then back at her. "Just because you're arriving at the ball on my arm doesn't mean you're leaving on it. Make sense?"

"No." Jane shook her head. "Not at all. In fact none of this makes sense!"

"Trust. Remember?" Bentley smiled. "Now hurry up. I have places to be, women to seduce."

CHAPTER THIRTY-NINE

I look like I belong in prison," Brock complained. Brant nodded his head in agreement.

"I'll admit," his brother said, "the stripes are a bit... bold."

"You think?" Brock pointed down at himself. "Do you have anything less"—he scowled as his gaze fell to the striped pants—"loud?"

Jean Paul, the man helping them, gasped aloud.

Bentley and Brant cringed and moved closer to Brock while the personal shopper for Prada began pacing in front of them, a pinched expression between his eyebrows as he started cursing in French.

"Should we tell him we understand him?" Bentley said out of the corner of his mouth. "Or just let him keep going?"

"I hear you!" Jean Paul stopped pacing then glanced up, his eyes hopeful. "I do have one suit left. It's perfect."

"Not to be a jackass, but you said that about the stripes," Brock muttered, glancing back in the mirror and shuddering.

"Here." Jean Paul returned with a black garment bag. "Very new, very classic. A black and white three-piece tuxedo with a black tie. The shirt is a white silk. I'll admit the coattails are a bit long but I think you'll find the cut agreeable to your full figure."

"The hell," Brock muttered. "Did he just call me fat?"

"Good thing Jane loves all sizes," Bentley said helpfully. "Plus more cushion for the pushin'...right?"

"Please stop talking," Brock pleaded while Jean Paul unzipped the garment bag and did a little *ta da* with his hands.

"Dibs," Bentley called.

"Damn it!" Brant yelled.

"Guys, I thought we were here for me? Also: born first, getting auctioned off, you lose." He touched the smooth silk shirt. This, he could wear.

A few hours later, he was back at his apartment, the garment bag hanging in his closet, the rooms silent.

He'd told the twins he wanted time alone, and now he was lonely. Imagine that? Idiot.

He was so damn tempted to just text Jane and let her in on his plan, but Jane deserved more than a text. He wanted to sweep her off her feet, surprise her, do it in front of the whole fucking world. And unfortunately her reaction had to be real—the plan depended on it. If it looked fabricated, people would accuse them of setting the whole thing up.

He picked up his phone and swiped past her contact, even though it made his chest hurt just thinking about the pain he was putting her through by not calling—and hit his grandfather's number.

His grandfather answered on the second ring. "Son, you better be dead. I'm up to my earlobes with ball details. Everything has to be perfect as you know, and the media is in a frenzy over that kiss with the maid!"

Shit.

The media refused to let it go.

Which led to questions about the ball being rigged— which in turn had driven Brock to ask the notorious woman he'd just spent the last hour talking to for help.

Their plan had to look real.

He knew it, for the sake of the company and for Jane.

But that kiss.

He wouldn't take it back.

He couldn't.

It was everything.

His mouth burned with the memory.

"Fruit of my loins!" Grandfather yelled, interrupting Brock's daydream. One more day. Just one more day. "You've caused more drama than the twins together! Child-birth was never this difficult."

"Are you talking to me?" Brock asked. "And you didn't actually birth the children, as far as I know..." He rolled his eyes.

"Good thing, or I probably would have given up and walked out of that damn hospital. Your grandmother was such a saint, pushing out God knows what through her—"

"All right, that's enough bonding for tonight," Brock said gruffly. "We need to talk about the ball."

Grandfather sighed. "It is what it is, that is unless you have something on your mind?"

"Why?" Brock blurted before he could stop himself. "Why would you put the company before me? Before the twins?"

Grandfather sighed. "I guess I would have to answer with a question. Why, Brock, do you always feel you need to put me before you?"

Brock opened his mouth then shut it.

"That's what I thought." Grandfather sighed. "I've seen the news about you and the maid and yet I haven't heard from you. Why is that, I wonder?"

"Because"—Brock cleared his throat—"I've found a way to have both."

"Both?" Grandfather's voice sounded like he was frowning; his brows were probably furrowing in confusion like they always did when he was forced to solve a puzzle that didn't magically solve itself.

"Yes." Brock chuckled. "Both. My family. And my Jane."

"Your Jane, hmm?"

Brock closed his eyes and continued. "I'm keeping my word, to both of you, in the only way I know how."

"Is that why you called?"

"I called to tell you that if it goes badly...if my crazy plan doesn't work out...I still choose her." God, it hurt. Hurt like hell to say that.

He sucked in a breath.

Waited for his grandfather to die.

Waited for the sky to fall.

Waited for an earthquake.

But all the old man did was sigh and say. "Well then. I guess that's that." The line went dead, leaving Brock to wonder if it was another omen for his future.

Death.

When all he wanted was a life.

Life with Jane.

CHAPTER FORTY

The press attention was getting worse.

Well, what did she expect? The ball was tonight. Of course it was getting worse, with speculation about Jane being there even though she didn't have the money to bid on Brock. There were also rumors that she was pregnant with his love child, amongst other things.

It made her sick to her stomach.

Bentley had said that he was going to stop by for some last-minute details, but he was clearly running late. Her dress and shoes were upstairs waiting for her and she still had hours to kill before a team of highly trained professionals—Bentley's words, not hers—would be at her house to do her makeup and hair.

Maybe it was her nerves.

Or the fact that her sisters still hadn't contacted her. They'd said they were staying with a friend, but they'd never stayed away so long. Then again, she'd never made them angry enough to want to before.

Were they still planning on going to the ball? Or at least

trying? Because that was so not the place where she wanted to have a confrontation with them, not that she'd be able to help it in the first place if they wanted to start something.

When had life become so stressful?

Oh right, the minute she'd said yes to a crazy old man and fell in love with his even crazier grandson.

With nothing to do but basically sit on her hands and try not to have a nervous breakdown, she slowly made her way upstairs to unpack from the ranch.

Sadness had kept her from unzipping her suitcase for fear that her clothes and the smell of the ranch would remind her of Brock too much, and it was hard enough as it was to not think of him. He was everywhere—on the news, radio—you couldn't walk down the street without hearing or seeing something about the auction.

With shaking hands she pulled open the suitcase and a smile spread across her face.

She brushed her hand against the plaid fabric at the top of the suitcase and her smile grew.

Maybe all memories weren't bad.

Even if they were painful.

And in all her stress and sadness she'd forgotten something important—something that even if Brock rejected her and never saw her again she wanted to do.

She grabbed the present and ran down the stairs just as a knock sounded. Throwing the door open to a bored-looking Bentley, Jane grabbed a fistful of his shirt and jerked him into the house. "I want his address. Now."

"I don't really think—"

"Now!"

"It's six a.m.!" Bentley yawned. "Six! In the morning!"

"I heard you the first time. Address! Please? It's important!"

"What's that?" He pointed at the object in her hands.

"Something for Brock."

Bentley's eyes narrowed and then a mocking look crossed his face. "Wow, that's . . . romantic?"

"Shut up."

He smirked. "Fine, I'll give you the address if you promise to be on your best behavior tonight."

She scowled.

"No hitting on me, grabbing my ass, flirting, or falling in love. I'm well aware that these past two days have been the best of your life but—"

"Yeah, I'm going to go ahead and stop you right there."

"Sometimes love can't be helped, or explained." He winked. "Okay, fine, you're immune to my charm. Damn aggravating—not that I'd want to steal you out from underneath one of my favorite brothers—but like I said, some things can't be helped and I'm competitive by nature."

"Are you done yet?"

"No." He smiled. "Okay, fine, be ready by six and remember to just . . . go with it."

"Go with what?"

"*It*," he said slowly. "Go with it."

"What exactly is 'it'?"

"You'll see when it or she presents itself. Okay, now I've confused myself. Hand over that weird-looking shirt fluffy thing and I'll make sure it gets to Brock. I'm not entirely sure I can trust you with that address yet; besides, it's for the best."

Well, it wasn't exactly what she wanted, but it would work. "Thank you." She kissed his cheek.

He touched the spot she'd kissed and shrugged. "See? You're in love with me, can't be helped."

"Go away, Bentley."

He tilted her chin toward him. "Give them hell tonight, Jane. And remember, trust him."

And with that he was gone.

CHAPTER FORTY-ONE

Brock woke up to the piercing sound of a rooster. The cock was even invading his dreams now.

Fantastic.

"Wake up!" A pillow slammed across his face.

Twice.

On the third swing, he grabbed it and the person attached to it, shoving them off the bed and onto the floor.

Brant let out a curse. "See if I ever make you coffee again."

"You made coffee? Do you even know how?"

"It was touch and go for a few seconds before I finally just walked to Starbucks." He shrugged. "But it's basically the same thing."

"You're an idiot."

"Thank you." Brant seemed genuinely touched by the insult.

Brock rolled his eyes. "Someone better be dying and why the hell did I hear a rooster?"

Brant held up his phone. "Farm animal app. I'm thinking of buying the company."

"Please don't," Brock grumbled as he got to his feet.

They walked into the kitchen where Bentley was reading the paper.

"Why are you guys always at my house?" Brock snatched a piece of fruit as Bentley slid him his coffee. "Seriously, are you that lonely?"

"Yes," Bentley said without looking up from the paper. "That's why we bother you, because we're lonely." He smirked. "It's more like..." After a long drawn-out sigh, he held out his hands. "We made the mistake of bringing some girls home and..." He flipped his hand into the air. "We may have swapped girls in the middle of the night."

"Oldest trick in the book," Brant snorted.

"Right," Bentley agreed. "But somehow they found out and once we asked them to leave... all hell broke loose. One of them started smashing wine bottles on the floor then chucked one at my head."

Brant bit out a curse while Bentley kept on talking. "We finally got them to leave, but one of them came back and our doorman let her up, the bastard. She spray-painted WHORE in bright red graffiti across our doors."

Brock let out a low laugh. "Oh, that's fantastic. So your apartments are shame prisons?"

"Basically." Bentley didn't look apologetic. "So we're going to hang with you until things die down. I mean, they'll get over it; they always do."

Sighing, Brock took a long drink of coffee and set his cup back down on the table. "You guys can't keep going on like this."

"Sure we can." Brant finally set the paper down. "After all, my life goal includes dying of heart failure during sex."

"It's good to have dreams." Bentley burst out laughing.

"Both of you are going to burn in hell." Brock snorted.

"Hopefully Grandfather will have paved the way by then." Bent smirked. "Now, are you ready for tonight?"

Brock paused, his coffee in midair. "I think so; as ready as I'll ever be. Grandfather doesn't know what's going on; he just knows I'm going to try and keep my word to him while still trying to be with Jane. God, I hope that Nadine holds up her end of the bargain."

"She will." Brant came around the table and sat, propping his legs up on the chair across from him. "She's obsessed with a good love story. Her poor grandsons are proof of that. The woman kidnapped a state senator in the name of love. This? This should be a walk in the park for her."

"Are you going to make a speech before all hell breaks loose? Or just lay it all out there?" Bentley asked.

Brock rolled his eyes. "I have a plan. I'm sticking with it. The end goal is Jane. Anything beyond that? A fucking speech to make people happy? I'm over it. I want her and I've found a way to get her and to make sure that Grandfather's happy. She needs to know I love her. That's all that matters now."

The doorbell suddenly rang and Brock cursed as he stomped over to the door, jerking it open.

"Delivery for Brock Wellington." The messenger had a giant black box. "Just sign here."

Brock signed and brought the box into the house, closing the door behind him.

He opened the box and saw...plaid.

"What the hell is that?" Brant pointed.

Frowning, Brock picked up the homemade plaid pillow and inhaled. It smelled exactly like his father. They were his old shirts.

The ones from the ranch.

A note was stuck between the pillows.

I meant to give these to you at the ranch but I forgot.

I couldn't sleep one night and decided to make them into memory pillows. That way you always have your father with you. I thought it may help fight the ghosts but just in case that doesn't work, I stuffed the dog in the bottom of the box. Rumor has it he's a guard dog.

Love,
Plain Jane

Fingers trembling, Brock dropped the note and took a step back. She'd done this. For him.

She loved him.

"She loves me," he repeated out loud. "God, I couldn't stand another day of this secrecy."

He was having a hard time breathing—swallowing— functioning as a normal human being. All he could do was stare at the box and wonder how in the hell he was going to be able to wait another eight hours until he saw her again.

And tell her how he felt.

And choose her.

For all the world to see.

Funny, how bidders had donated hundreds of thousands of dollars to be at his side, but what she offered him was more priceless.

Because she was the only woman who had offered something money couldn't buy.

Her heart.

CHAPTER FORTY-TWO

Jane gaped at the glam squad currently setting up around her living room. A hairstylist, a makeup artist, and two other people who looked like their assistants were all running around in a rush of excitement.

A glass of champagne was thrust into her hand and then she was shoved into a tall makeup chair, bright lights turned toward her.

"Hmm…" The girl doing her makeup frowned. "The lighting isn't good enough. Someone open up the blinds and a window or something."

A window was opened.

Fresh air blasted in.

Finally, Jane relaxed and let out a sigh.

Getting her makeup done was going to be a dream. She'd never had it done before and—

A second team arrived.

They all had white coats on.

A terrifying hush came over the room.

"She a virgin?" one asked in a cheerful voice.

All eyes fell to her.

"No," Jane said in a quiet voice.

"Waxing virgin," another man clarified, eying her up and down with excitement.

"Waxing? What do you mean, waxing?"

Several people chuckled and then her real hell began.

She was waxed within an inch of her life; at one point tears welled in her eyes. When she complained the esthetician simply held her down and said, "You'll be fine."

"The hell I will!" she roared.

"We've got a screamer," the esthetician said through clenched teeth as another woman entered the living room. She helped to hold down Jane's legs.

"Is this legal?" Jane exclaimed.

"Don't make us bring the duct tape. I've done it before. I don't want to have to resort to it again." The woman had a terrifying eyebrow arch that just wouldn't quit.

And she was only half done.

The last thing she needed, Jane concluded, was to be hairy on one side of her body and smooth on the other.

The anticipation was the worst part. She jumped every time the sugar wax ball thingy was applied, mainly because every time it was spread on her skin it tugged hair and then tugged again.

Two tugs.

So help her God, she was going to die on the waxing table.

She shivered as another tug nearly sent her into a screaming fit. Women did this? And paid actual money for it?

"Don't move unless you want the sculpting and shading to be off," the woman doing her makeup snapped once she was off the waxing table and in the makeup chair.

Was everyone grumpy in the beauty industry? Was that a thing?

Just as she was relaxing again, a brush tugged at her head. "We're running out of time. I need to start in on this...mess."

The lady applying her makeup snorted. "Good luck with that."

"Hey!" Jane said, and another hard tug had her eyes watering.

"It's a lot of hair." The man ran the brush from root to tip. "But silver lining, it's really healthy."

"I don't dye it," Jane said proudly.

"Oh honey, we know." The makeup artist smiled. "It's virgin hair. I can spot it a mile away."

"Is—is that bad?" Jane self-consciously tugged a few strands.

The makeup artist laughed loudly. "No, it just means no hair stylist is going to want to be your first...Too much pressure." She scrunched up her nose. "Now, slump your shoulders again and I'm putting you in the harness."

"There's a harness?" Jane squeaked.

The makeup artist nodded. "It's in my trunk."

"Okay, then." Jane held as straight and still as she could, hardly breathing as the woman did her makeup and the mean, demon-possessed man brushed out her hair.

It was going to be a really long afternoon.

* * *

When Bentley said he'd pick her up at six, what he'd really meant was that he was going to arrive at her house around five-thirty, bring his own champagne, pour himself a glass or two, and then yell at the makeup artist for making her look too beautiful.

He was just being Bentley. Which was a thing in and of itself. The more time she spent with him the more he felt like a brother. A really good-looking annoying older brother who liked to drink and hit on every female he saw.

She had no way of even knowing what she looked like. The team had refused to let her see a mirror. Satan's minions simply said that they were under strict instructions to keep her away from every shiny surface.

Which of course meant that she had three of the squad, the guy included, helping her into her dress.

Nothing about her body was left to the imagination.

Nothing.

Not one small bit.

Her shame was complete when Doug, the hairstylist, was pulling at the skirt of her dress and wanted to make sure that the lining was pulled tight enough so it didn't wrinkle.

Why did it matter?

She'd actually asked that out loud and gained nothing but shocked silence.

They weren't human, these people. They seemed to express emotion only toward inanimate objects: the curling iron, for example. Doug went on and on about its technology for at least a half hour while her makeup artist Leah gasped and moaned like she was... well, like she was having a sexual experience or something.

Doug was lucky to still have a head.

Considering it had been between her thighs about ten minutes earlier, inspecting.

When she'd said something about him looking in places he shouldn't look he very loudly told her she had the wrong equipment to attract him.

"Not that I don't appreciate the view." He slapped her thigh, making her shame complete.

"Stop!" Leah sighed. "You'll make her get all flushed and I did a damn good job on her makeup!"

"Sorry." Doug made his way out from underneath her dress and smiled brightly, his white teeth nearly blinding as he ran a hand over his shaved and tattooed head. "You look killer."

"Thanks." Jane felt a laugh bubble up inside her. "Can I see myself now?"

"Aw, sweetie." Doug lifted her chin with a single finger. "Not a chance in hell. Now off you go!"

"Off?"

Bentley yelled from the kitchen. "She better be ready in five minutes!"

"Ready!" Jane called, turning the corner to find Bentley pouring another glass of champagne. He slowly examined her, his expression blank until his eyes landed on her face. He lifted the flute of champagne in a salute and chuckled darkly before handing her his glass.

"He's going to lose his damn mind," he whispered. "You know, I think I like this sneaking around business."

"Oh?" Jane took a long sip of champagne then looped her hand through his arm.

"Yes." Bentley nodded, then leaned in. "You sure you want Brock?"

"Positive." She giggled.

"Fine." He sighed. "Then I guess I'll just have to pretend to be completely enamored with your sexy ass and gorgeous mouth."

"If Brock heard you say that, he'd kill you."

"Empty threats," Bentley whispered in her ear. "Tonight, he's going to fall to his knees." He pulled back. "The man cares about you—and now? So will the rest of the world."

Jane laughed nervously. "I hope you're right about this. I trust you guys."

"Good." He eyed her up and down again. "Good."

"Are you okay?"

"Fine," he said quickly. Then his smile faded and he locked eyes with her. "Serious moment."

"Um, okay."

"You're absolutely stunning. Don't let anyone convince you otherwise. Hold your head high. You belong there. At Brock's side."

She didn't trust herself to speak. Jane nodded and exhaled loudly. "Thank you."

"No problem." He held out his arm. "Now, let's head to the carriage, Cinderella."

Jane laughed as they walked outside, her heels making a clicking sound against the concrete as her gold dress swished over her hips. At least she knew the dress fit.

She'd picked it out.

It was a bold choice.

With its slit all the way up her left thigh, all she had to do was trip and people would get more than an eyeful.

The plunging neckline covered her breasts then twisted around to her back in a Grecian manner. Everything about the dress was elegant and simple, modern yet very romantic.

Maybe something Cinderella would wear in this century.

Her shoes were a matching gold-strapped sandal, a little high for her taste but still beautiful, with diamond-encrusted buckles across her ankles.

She was so busy looking down at her shoes that when she looked up she was momentarily stunned. "Is that..." She frowned. "Buttercup?"

"Shhh," Bentley whispered. "She's in costume."

"Does she not like costumes?" Jane whispered back,

momentarily wondering if she'd left her sanity back inside the house. Why were they whispering around the horse?

"She doesn't want you to recognize her. Watch." Bentley waved her off. "Oh, look yonder at that beautiful young stallion! Garbed in black and gold with the family crest on its noble hide!" Then the oddest thing happened; Buttercup lifted her head and stiffened into a pose with one leg lifted in the air, head held high.

"No way." Jane's eyes widened.

"She just wants to impress you. Wellingtons are proud that way." Bentley nodded and eyed Jane up and down again, then said, "You're absolutely positive you want the brooding brother? I mean..." He stood chest to chest with her. "Positive?"

His voice lowered.

He smelled amazing.

He wasn't Brock.

"Yup!" She nodded.

"Had to offer you an out." He sighed. "Now, let's go." The door to the gold carriage to which Buttercup had been tethered opened.

"It's a real carriage," Jane said dumbly, glancing around the open, gold-encrusted carriage. It was beautiful, like something you'd see in a historical movie.

Or read about in a book.

It was a real horse-drawn carriage. The seats were a plush black leather, there were two fur blankets with matching pillows on each seat, and it was painted a rich gold with a red *W* in the middle of the door.

Sitting in the opposite seat was Brant. "Wow." He smiled wickedly. "Brock's going to lose his mind."

"Thanks." She blushed and took his hand as Bentley followed in after her. "So I get two dates tonight?"

"Brant doesn't date," Bentley said in a bored tone. "He doesn't like getting women's hopes up."

"Seriously?" Jane frowned. "And one date is enough to make them think you're going to marry them?"

At the mention of marriage Brant's face darkened. He didn't respond. Bentley cleared his throat and slowly shook his head.

Clearly there was a story there, one he didn't want to tell.

"And now"—Bentley quickly changed the subject as the carriage started to move—"you have a gift."

The box was simple.

Black.

She pulled off the lid and gasped.

A pair of glass high-heeled shoes twinkled in the moonlight. Black leather material was braided in an elegant design across the top of the shoe before adjoining the glass heel in the back.

A simple note rested on top of the shoes:

For Cinderella—try not to break a heel at the ball.

Love, Brock.

Her pearls sat neatly between the two shoes, set in the shape of a heart.

How had he gotten the pearls back from her sisters? Did it matter? Tears welled in her eyes. He'd said "love."

Love.

And pearls.

And shoes.

More tears stung.

"Well, I'll be damned." Bentley laughed. "Instead of sending me for shoes, he went shopping all on his own."

More laughter. "Brock hates shopping. Looks like the jack-ass grew some balls."

"Oh, he's always had balls," Jane said without thinking.

Brant snapped his attention back to her. "This is a fun topic, my brother's balls."

Her cheeks heated. "Let's, uh, just put on the shoes. Or I'll put on the shoes and..." She tried to reach her feet but her dress was too tight.

"You're either going to rip your dress or flash us both, which will most likely earn both of us black eyes." Brant rolled his eyes. "Here, let me help."

"Thanks." She beamed as Brant tugged off her heels and replaced them with the beautiful black and glass shoes that Brock had given her.

The shoes were beautiful.

But what made her smile was the fact that they were black. Had it only been a month ago when he'd teased her about black shoes and she'd blurted out information about her underwear?

"Damn, I've never seen a woman so thrilled to have a pair of shoes before," Brant said under his breath.

"It's not just the shoes. It's what they represent." She grinned. "I mean, the thought behind them." Brant's expression was completely blank. "Come on, haven't you ever given someone a gift that held memories? Or a hidden meaning?"

Brant's expression hardened before he offered an easy smile and looked out the window. "I don't waste my time with gifts. Why should I when I'm never with the same woman more than once?"

Bentley laughed softly.

"We're here." Brant held out his hand to Jane and smiled. "You ready for this?"

The carriage stopped in front of Warehouse 215. The entire outside of the structure had been transformed with hanging candles and flowers, making the ambiance magical.

Bentley followed after them and grabbed her other hand. "I believe you have a prince to steal."

Jane pressed a hand to her stomach. "That's not making me feel any less nervous."

The twins merely smiled and escorted her inside.

Directly into the arms of a woman she'd never seen before. She wore bright red lipstick and talked way too fast and before Jane knew what was happening she was showing her license to another lady, who double-checked her name on the guest list.

"Oh look, there you are!" Jane frowned at the flamboyantly dressed woman, who still held onto her arm. She examined the guest list and then nodded. "Okay, now everything looks ready to go!"

"Oh, I almost forgot. Here." Jane handed over her check for thirty thousand dollars. It was all she had to bid with.

The woman still holding onto her arm snorted out a laugh and nodded to the lady with the guest list. "Just add it to her account and we'll deal with it later. Thank you!"

The next person in line stepped up and Jane was tugged away by the pretty, elderly woman. With a giant smile she whispered to Jane, "Wait ten minutes before coming in."

"What?" Jane frowned. "Why?"

"Honey"—the woman's red pouted mouth dipped into a frown—"Cinderella always has to make the perfect entrance." She winked and abandoned Jane just like the twins had.

What the heck was going on?

CHAPTER FORTY-THREE

If Brock had to listen to one more woman talk about the state of the world, or the economy, or the irritating fact that they couldn't park close enough to the warehouse where the ball was being held, he was going to take a cue from his brothers and start downing shots.

Bentley eyed Brock over his whiskey with a smug grin, then lifted his glass into the air in a silent toast.

They were supposed to have arrived with Jane a half hour ago. The twins were here, but where was Jane?

So far there'd been no sign of his grandfather.

Where the hell were they?

Panic set in when he realized that if for some reason his grandfather saw Jane first...What if he said something to her that made her run? What if he was mean to her? Was his grandfather capable of that?

Maybe it was just Brock's own nerves about the plan for that evening. He just wanted everything to be over with. And Jane in his arms.

"He's late," a voice to his right said.

Brock turned and came face to face with the CEO of Titus Enterprises. She and his grandfather were rarely in the same room together.

They couldn't stand one another.

Their fights alone had made national news, when in a fury she'd thrown a pencil at his head during a charity board meeting.

If the Wellingtons were the Kennedys of the south, then the Titus family was the Vanderbilts of the Pacific Northwest. Both companies had set out with the mindset of world domination, and both companies had had their share of scandal.

Then again, with a woman like Nadine at the helm of Titus, it was no shock at all. Her dangerously low-cut silk ball gown had a bright red bow wrapped around her neck and matched her lipstick perfectly. With heavy eyelashes and bright blond hair, she looked to be somewhere around her mid-sixties rather than pushing eighty-nine.

"Well?" Her penciled brows drew together in a furrow. "Where's that damn grandfather of yours?" She rolled her eyes. "Charles never did understand the point of being punctual. Why, last time we went to dinner and—"

Brock's eyes narrowed. "Dinner? You shared a meal? Broke bread?"

"Yes, and I only managed to stab him twice." She adjusted her short black velvet gloves and shrugged one shoulder. "He took all of my silverware before I had the chance to inflict more violence. The bastard just kept pouring me more wine."

"How horrible for you."

"Dreadful man, getting a woman drunk for his own pleasure!"

Brock coughed into his hand. "This isn't awkward, this conversation."

"Boy, ain't nothing awkward about a man and a woman engaging in a nice meal and having the consensual three S's."

Brock stared at her, then toward the door. "I'm almost scared to ask this, but why three S's?"

"Oh." She touched his arm lightly. "How sad. Do you not understand how to woo a woman properly? No wonder you needed my help." She grinned brightly. "You know, I have some incredible lithographs of the Kama Sutra and—"

"No thanks." He took a step away while she pouted.

"Oh, I see." Her eyes suddenly widened. "You haven't conquered young Jane yet. Are you a virgin?"

She yelled the last part. She clearly wanted to embarrass him and create a scene because that's what she did best.

He groaned as he noticed the curious stares from people around them.

"Hilarious," he murmured while she laughed to herself. "Keep your voice down." The last part was said on a hiss.

"Scared of breasts." She nodded knowingly. "Well, boy, they aren't gonna smother you if that's what you're afraid of. Worse comes to worst, hold your breath."

"Great advice. I'll be sure to pass it along to someone who actually needs it."

"Asphyxiation during coitus used to be a thing, you know, back in the seventies."

Why was the woman still talking about sex? God. She was almost more trouble than she was worth. He took a gulp of champagne.

"When I wore the knit tops with no bra."

Brock spit out his champagne in shock then wiped his mouth, while Nadine kept talking about breasts. Then, thankfully, his grandfather appeared.

This was it.

"Such a wicked handsome man." Nadine sighed next to him. "Too bad he has the manners of a bastard son of a whore."

She said it so politely one would think she was almost complimenting him.

Brock glared as his grandfather slowly and very casually made his way toward them. "I trust everything's in order?"

Nadine let out a snort. "Good to see you, Charles." She drew out the 's' in his name and leaned forward, her somehow still perky breasts parted like the Red Sea as her dress nearly came off her chest.

"Nadine," his grandfather said through gritted teeth. "New dress?"

"Yes." She beamed.

"Did you steal it from a teenager?"

"Yes." Nadine scowled. "That's exactly what I did, right after cheer practice, where I performed splits in the air and made love with Johnny in the locker room."

"Bring him up again and I'll strangle you." His grin was still in place but his face was red.

"Johnny?" Brock repeated.

"Your grandfather certainly didn't peak until...after high school." Nadine giggled behind her hand.

His grandfather took a menacing step toward Nadine but Brock stopped him. "Are we ready to begin?" And then his breath caught in his throat as the love of his life waltzed into the room. "Jane."

She moved through the crowd with so much grace it hurt to watch her.

And Brock's heart nearly stopped.

"Holy shit." He sucked in and choked on the same breath while Jane looked down at her feet then up at him.

The glass slippers. Well, his version of them, anyway. *She'd worn them.*

"She's absolutely lovely, Brock, and my my, what an entrance!"

Blood roared in Brock's ears as the entire room fell silent. Jane was looking at him, walking toward him. She was his.

Her gold silk dress shimmered under the lights.

God, she was so damn beautiful. Yet he couldn't make his feet move toward her. He was glued in place, paralyzed, stunned by her beauty.

Beauty that he'd always seen.

But tonight it was perfectly highlighted: her hair was pulled into a low ponytail; the front was braided to the side, covering part of her ear where single diamond earrings twinkled.

The gloves she wore went past her elbows.

Everything about her was—magical.

Her lips widened into a shaky smile as she took a few more steps toward him.

"Well, don't just stand there," Nadine hissed. "You need to speak." Had she just clapped at him? "Go on, shoo!"

Jane bit her bottom lip and then let out a laugh as she finally made it to his side. "There's something really strange about that woman." She pointed her auction paddle in Nadine's direction.

"Don't point. She'll think it's an invitation to come over."

"Too late," Jane whispered. "Sorry."

"Hello, dear!" Nadine spread her arms wide. "I've heard so much about you!" She gave Jane an overly obvious wink, as if asking her to play along and pretend they hadn't already met at the door. "Why, Charles just won't shut up about how you cleaned his home and slept with his grandson when we're—"

Brock's eyes narrowed in on his grandfather, who'd started tugging at his tie like it was choking the life out of him.

The crowd gathered around them.

Good, that's what he needed. He needed people to think Nadine had absolutely no association with Jane whatsoever—though she didn't need to yell all the gory details.

"When you're what?" Brock asked innocently.

"Discussing business," Nadine said brightly. "Why, sometimes it takes all day and night to get just the right contract negotiated." Her eyes lit up. "In fact, Charles, I was hoping to steal you away this evening."

"Leave the rape whistle, the gun, and the Swiss army knife at home, and we'll talk." He nodded to her purse. "Oh, and I wasn't born yesterday. The pens stay, too."

"You know, for being nine years younger, you sure aren't very adventurous in..." Her eyes went from Brock to Jane. "Er, the charity board meetings we're both on...and such."

"Maybe because I prefer for the focus of board meetings to be singular, on one person, rather than...objects."

"Oh, Charles." She sighed.

"Should we leave you two alone now? With the pens?" Brock asked. "Because things just got really weird and I'm pretty sure you're talking about sex with my grandfather, which, by the way, is totally fine, as long as you never talk about it again in front of me or Jane, or any other object that may or may not be scarred for life."

"The cock." Jane nodded.

"Yes, I'm going to have to ask you to refrain from speaking about it, even in front of the ass and the rooster."

Nadine's lips twitched. "You remind me so much of my grandsons. Should we set up a play date?"

"Sure..." Brock backed away slowly. "Let me just see if I can find my Legos."

"Perfect!" She winked and looped her arm with Grandfather's. "Now, we've embarrassed you enough. Enjoy the ball."

Grandfather walked off then paused and turned. "Brock, you promised that you would still participate in the auction." He eyed Jane. "I don't know what she's doing here, but unless she bids on you—"

Brock stared down his grandfather. "I told you I was choosing both. Maybe it's time you let me decide the course of my life."

Grandfather eyed him and then settled his gaze on Jane. When he finally walked away Brock could have sworn his grandfather was laughing, but what did he have to laugh about?

When he looked back at Jane, her face was tight.

"Trust me," he whispered in her ear. "And you look beautiful."

She exhaled, and then pressed her hands to her hips, smoothing her dress as if she was nervous. "It's not too much?"

"It's perfect." He reached for her hand and pulled her into his arms. "Now, you have the shoes, the dress, the pearls." He grinned. "But you're missing one thing."

She frowned. "What?"

"We need to find you a prince."

"Hmm, I don't think I know any princes."

He twirled her in his arms. "I can always go get Bentley. I'm sure he'd step in."

"I don't want Bentley."

"Brant then?"

She smirked. "Nah, he's too handsy."

"Then I guess you're stuck with me." He bent over her hand. "May I have this dance?"

She curtsied low. "I thought you'd never ask."

CHAPTER FORTY-FOUR

Brock's smile melted all her defenses, making her feel beautiful and secure—although she was still a bit nervous. She still hadn't seen her sisters and she feared that they'd approach her and say something hurtful or embarrassing. Probably both.

Brock's smile deepened as he slowly examined her from head to toe.

This man in a suit was a dangerous thing, the way his broad shoulders filled out the black jacket. The style reminded her of something she'd seen in an old historical movie.

Which really did make him the prince.

His auburn hair had a slight wave; it was parted to the side but she knew it would soon fall prey to his hands, since that was his nervous thing: running a hand through his hair.

"I'm glad you came." Brock's voice was deep, his eyes locked on hers. "Even though you're technically here with two other men."

Brock's gaze shifted to her mouth, as if he wanted to kiss her. She strained toward him just as the music stopped playing.

The dance floor wasn't too crowded. People were staring at them, probably because he was about to get auctioned off, Jane concluded.

Her stomach clenched.

"So." She cleared her throat. "What exactly am I supposed to be doing? I feel like I should be helping whatever plan you have here but I'm completely in the dark."

"Well." Brock cleared his throat. "Unbeknownst to the twins, we're actually auctioning them off for charity as well. There will be five bachelors total. Brant, Bentley, and"—he grinned smugly—"Thomas and Lucas Titus. They're Nadine's cousins and when given the option to get on her good side, I knew they wouldn't say no." He paused and then whispered, "I go last."

Jane nodded, careful to keep her smile frozen on her face.

"And then..." Brock sighed. "The woman who bids the most wins a date with me. Each of the top five bidders wins something, but I only have to go out with one of them. Of course, my grandfather still has his mind set on marriage—at least according to the media, but only because it makes sense: rich good-looking woman, rich good-looking man... People are idiots."

Jane's throat went dry.

"But"—Brock pulled her into his arms—"it's not going to happen that way."

"What makes you think that?" Jane asked.

"Because technically it's not going to be a real auction. It's fixed." He eyed her boldly. "I..." He reached for her hands and squeezed them. "I think it's pretty clear who I choose... and it's a girl in a gold dress with seven freckles."

"Eight," she corrected, a bit breathless. "You forgot the one on my ass."

Brock burst out laughing. "I may have to do some inspecting later."

"But, Brock," Jane said, suddenly serious, "what will happen if this doesn't work out the way you want it to?"

"Let me worry about that," he growled.

"But see, that's the thing." She pulled away from him. "I do worry, because I don't want to be the reason people don't take you seriously or trust you, or back out of a deal."

"Jane—"

"You would resent me. Maybe not now, maybe not tomorrow, but you would resent me. I think we have enough baggage between the two of us. The last thing we need is to add more."

Brock's eyes narrowed. "What exactly are you getting at?"

"No matter how this turns out, you have to go through with everything. I mean, if I don't win."

"You will win." His voice was urgent. "And if it doesn't turn out the way I've planned it, then fine. Fuck them all. I love you and I choose you."

"But your grandfather," Jane said in a small voice, her eyes finding the man in question. She could still remember the way he'd tried to convince her to take the million-dollar check and his almost relieved expression when she didn't.

Something wasn't right. She just didn't know what.

"Jane, did my grandfather get to you? Is that what this is about? Did he try to pay you off? Or threaten you?"

Jane froze. "Well."

"Jane." He exhaled loudly and placed his hands on her shoulders. "What the hell did he do to you?"

Her face flushed. "Well, he did offer me money to stay away from you. Enough money that I'd never have to clean another toilet. Ever. But then he seemed relieved when I turned him down." But that made no sense. Why would he go to all that trouble? Something wasn't adding up.

"Jane!" Bentley elbowed his way toward her, his smile wide.

"We'll talk about this later." Brock kissed her temple. "After you win."

Bentley's smile widened as he approached. "She cleaned up well, am I right?"

Jane rolled her eyes and stood up on her tiptoes to kiss Bentley on the cheek. At the last minute he turned so his mouth barely grazed hers. "Sorry, couldn't help myself."

Brock cursed beside her. "Do that again and I'm cutting off your dick."

"Ooh…" Bentley winked at Jane and took a long sip of his champagne. "Remember, I offered to take you off his hands. Until you have a ring on your finger, offer still stands." His gaze heated. "Besides, he's the one with the temper. I'm all about love…sexual healing…"

"I'll do my best." She shoved him away playfully as Brant approached the group. He had three different shades of lipstick spread across his neck.

"Such a selfish bastard. Leave some for us, too," Bentley commented once Brant was in front of them.

Brant eyed her up and down again. "For the record, Brock, I approve."

"Well, that's a relief." Jane stepped into his arms. Brant always smelled like women's perfume. Always. Even at the ranch, which really made her wonder if he didn't just wear it so that other women got jealous?

"Fruit of my loins!" Charles called out to his grandsons. "Gather 'round, my little chickens. The auction is about to start and I have something to say."

The group fell silent.

Nadine's lips were formed into an adoring smile as she blinked up at Charles.

"Tonight, Brock goes to the highest of the five bidders." Jane tried to keep herself from tensing when he looked her way. His eyes lingered on her then briefly flickered to Nadine. "Now that that's settled..." Charles eyed Brock. "Why don't we go to the stage and get things started?"

Brock froze.

Jane squeezed his hand.

"Brock?" Charles tilted his head. "Is everything all right?"

"No," Brock said, and turned to Jane. "But it will be."

CHAPTER FORTY-FIVE

I just love me a man market." Nadine clapped her hands next to Jane, then fluffed up her hair with her bidding paddle. It wasn't shocking at all that Nadine's number was 666.

Jane's paddle was number 1.

She smiled down at it.

When she glanced back up at the stage Charles was making his way across it, smile wide as he approached the podium. "I'm very pleased to bring to you the first annual Bachelor Auction!" Applause erupted all over the building, while a very smug Brock winked in her direction.

Jane inclined her head toward him and smiled. He was really going to do it!

"You." He mouthed the word.

Charles continued talking about the cancer society and why it was so important to donate to a cause so dear to his heart.

Cancer was a bitch. Jane knew that firsthand.

When Charles was done talking, Brock stepped forward. He probably had a speech prepared, but beyond that, she had no idea how she was to proceed except for lifting the paddle to bid on him.

"Jane." Brock gazed across the room toward her. "Would you stand, please?"

Loud whispers erupted from the crowd as Jane locked eyes with Brock and repeated the word "trust" to herself about fifteen more times before finally rising to stand.

Nadine elbowed her sharply in the ribs and whispered. "Well? Are you just going to sit there and gape like a fish? Stand, girl! Present! And for the love of God lift your tits; your slouch is horrific!"

Jane bolted to her feet—mainly to keep Nadine from repeating what she'd just said, only louder—and beamed back at Brock.

Was this part of his great plan?

Because she wasn't really sure how pointing her out to everyone sitting there was a solid idea. Especially since her face had been plastered all over the news as his "before-auction fling."

"The Rosie Breast Cancer Foundation has special meaning to me, and to this young lady here. I only hope that with the money raised tonight, we can help find a cure for such a terrible disease." Brock's smile grew as he continued. "Young women taken too soon, daughters stolen, and mothers."

Choking tears clogged her throat, and Jane had to focus really hard not to break down in sobs. He'd remembered.

"Mothers who must leave their young daughters behind." His smile was sad when he looked back at her. "The auction may be a silly way to raise money; some may say it's stupid, asinine, the dream of an old man popping too many blood thinners." Everyone laughed, including Brock's grandfather. "But it's so much more. This annual auction will bring in millions for cancer research; this *silly* auction may help cure breast cancer one day. If we had this cure today then this young lady right here, Jane, would not be standing alone, without her mother." He smiled warmly. "So today we honor Jane; we honor the fallen mothers, daughters, sisters, wives who could not be present because they were stolen from us."

Tears filled Jane's eyes as a warm hand grabbed hers and squeezed. "I take it you knew Rosie?" Nadine whispered kindly.

"R-Rosie"—Jane fought the lump in her throat—"as my mother."

"Oh, dear." Nadine wrapped an arm around Jane and sighed. "I did not know your mother, but I am one. And us mothers, grandmothers—we're all given that same gene from God. The one that allows us to inflict fear into the most wicked of toddlers, gives us the ability to multitask and still enjoy life, the ability to love through the mud, sweat, tears, the strength to wake up every day and breathe life into the world, to make it a better place—so know when I say this, I do not say this lightly. I say this with the utmost wisdom from years of being a woman." She paused. "Your mother would be so proud, baby girl."

Tears spilled over Jane's cheeks. "Thank you."

"Now." Nadine gave her one last squeeze. "Use all that money I deposited into your ghost account and buy yourself a man."

"Ghost account," Jane repeated. "I don't know . . ." Shaking her head, she stared down the obviously senile woman. "What do you mean, 'ghost account'?"

"Well, the account!" Nadine waved her hand in the air. "The one you signed for when you walked in! Did you think thirty grand would win your man? Maybe his pinky toe." She snorted. "But you want the whole thing, am I right?"

"Um, yes please." Jane burst out laughing. Was this really happening? It was like she'd stepped into a fairy tale.

"Just think of me as your fairy godmother." Nadine winked. "When Brock mentioned that he needed my help, I couldn't transfer the money fast enough. Oh, he'll pay me back one day so it's not like I'm losing out on anything, and even if he didn't— it's for love. Right?" Nadine winked. "Besides, had anyone told you beforehand that we were planning this, your shock wouldn't look real when you actually win. It's why I told him not to text you or make direct contact, why we enlisted Bentley, that rogue, to help. I have plans for him, too. Just you wait."

Everything suddenly made sense.

Bentley. Brock. Trusting both of them, and how Nadine fit in with everything.

"But, I still may not win. I mean if Brock is going to be a high bid...I would need...a lot of money."

"Eh." Nadine coughed into her hand and waved toward the stage. "Dear, I do believe Brock and I have thought of everything. Now, let's have some fun."

Jane looked up to see Brock smiling down at her. "Now, let's get the First Annual Bachelor Auction started." He nodded to his grandfather and took a step back as Charles grabbed the microphone.

"Item number one." Charles paused and then looked up at Brock with a mixture of shock and amusement as he called out from the cards he was holding. "Bentley Wellington."

Someone in the crowd gasped and then several people started clapping. Jane felt herself relax. Brock's plan just might work!

"Five hundred dollars!" Charles yelled. "Do I hear five hundred dollars for Bentley Wellington?" He was shaking his head in disbelief at Bentley, who'd appeared on the stage.

Nadine laughed behind her hand.

There were five men on stage.

Three of them were Wellingtons.

Tears filled her eyes.

They were doing this for her.

For Brock.

Jane raised her paddle out of kindness. Bentley looked ready to kiss her feet and proclaim true love—damn, that man was a danger to women with his killer smile.

"Watch this," Nadine snickered, lifting her paddle.

Bentley went completely pale, and his mouth dropped open as he gave Jane a psychotic, wide-eyed look.

"Bid me up, dear; this is how these things work." Nadine said out of the side of her mouth.

Jane lifted her paddle.

Bentley, once again relieved, exhaled loudly.

Only to pale again when Nadine raised her paddle.

This went on for a good fifteen minutes.

"Most stressful moments of that boy's life," Nadine murmured. "Although I find I'm quite enjoying myself." She lifted her paddle again.

Jane burst out laughing. "You really should put him out of his misery. He looks like he's about to have a stroke."

"Oh, fine." Nadine coughed into her hand, and instantly another paddle rose across the room.

"Ten thousand dollars."

Jane's eyes widened as an elderly lady shouted from the back of the room. "Who's that?"

"My first choice," Nadine smiled warmly. "She'll be so great for our Bentley. He'll have to see past a few things first, but I have faith that it will go great."

Jane frowned. "The lady looks your age."

"Oh, Prudence isn't bidding for herself." Nadine laughed. "She has a lovely granddaughter that needs a little cheering up."

"Cheering up?"

"Going once, twice," Charles said in the distance. "Sold! To Prudence McCleery!"

Nadine sighed. "Yes well, ever since Margot lost her leg she's been impossible to live with."

"Lost," Jane repeated, "her leg?"

"Just one." Nadine shrugged. "She has another. But sometimes when in pain we focus on the loss, not the gain."

"But—"

"Oh look, Brant's up!"

Bentley walked off the stage, sweat marks marring his armpits as he tugged off his tie and made a beeline for the bar. He looked like he'd just seen a ghost.

"This one's a good deal more difficult." Nadine raised her paddle when the opening bid went out, then elbowed Jane to do the same.

Brant's expression was stony. He didn't show his emotions like Bentley did, so Jane had no idea if he was angry or just in his mental happy place drinking shots from some poor woman's breasts.

Brant was walking, talking sex, and so completely unapologetic about it that there had to be a story there.

One she knew she would most likely never get if Brant had anything to say about it.

For ten minutes Brant stood, expression indifferent, until Nadine coughed again and a new paddle flew into the air.

"Twenty-five thousand dollars." A small voice echoed through the room.

Charles gaped and then glanced around the room. "Going once, twice, three times, sold, to number..." He squinted. "Ma'am, I need to see your paddle. what's your number please?"

"Zero, Zero, Five." A gorgeous Hispanic woman with bright red lipstick and jet black hair stood.

And Brant flinched.

Once, twice.

Until finally, his façade shattered and an expression of pure sadness crossed his features, only to switch to red hot anger as his jaw clenched.

"Who is that?" Jane asked Nadine. "She's absolutely gorgeous."

"Oh her? That's Brant's ex-wife."

"What?" Stunned, Jane watched the gorgeous woman smile toward the stage, but not directly at Brant, and then a man to her side grabbed her hand and led her back to the table. "Wait, is she—"

"She went blind, from the accident."

"The accident?"

Nadine didn't say anything else, but Brant moved from the stage past the bar and directly out the doors of the ballroom.

"I sense a story."

Nadine snorted. "You have no idea. That little jackass has had it coming for a while."

You could feel the tension swirl in the room as the next two bachelors were auctioned off in the exact same manner as Brant and Bentley.

Nadine coughed.

Paddles were raised.

The next two bachelors, Nadine's cousins, couldn't have looked more angry if they tried.

"Oh good, Brock's next." Nadine sighed happily. "You know, if you want me to do the inspection before he jumps into the sack with you I'd be more than happy to volunteer."

"I, uh..." Jane laughed. "I've seen under the hood."

"A hussy after my own heart." Nadine grinned. "Oh, the hoods I saw beneath in my day were—"

"And our last item of the evening!" Charles beamed. "My eldest grandson, Brock Wellington."

Jane was just getting ready to lift her paddle when she locked eyes on her sisters across the room. Had they just arrived? She'd been there at least an hour and hadn't seen them anywhere.

They were almost sitting outside, their table was so far away; and they looked pissed, so angry that Jane wanted to crawl under the table and hide. After all, they'd bragged about being able to buy tickets to the ball and still hadn't talked to her since their falling-out.

Served them right.

She smiled politely then looked back to Brock.

"We'll start the bidding at five hundred thousand."

Jane froze.

There was no way she had that much money in her bidding account, right?

"Honey, you're going to have to lift your paddle." Nadine kicked her in the leg.

"But that's so much money!"

"Funding cancer research and securing the love of your life, priceless. Plus I deposited three million into that account this morning. I highly doubt you're going to have any issues. Just toss up that paddle and have fun."

"But—"

"To be fair, it's all Wellington money. Remember, they're paying it back. But I'm charging interest for my services." She winked.

Jane didn't want to ask what that meant. Not by a long shot.

She gulped just as Nadine reached for Jane's hand and thrust it into the air.

Instead of looking upset, Charles beamed in their direction. What? That couldn't be right, could it? "Do I hear five hundred and fifty thousand?"

"You do," came a voice from the back of the room.

CHAPTER FORTY-SIX

It worked.

Or it was working.

Every single time Jane lifted her paddle, his heart jumped in his chest.

God, he wanted nothing more than to run into her arms, kiss her senseless, bend her backwards over that table in front of friends, family, Nadine.

It didn't matter.

He was tired of pretending.

Damn sick of saying yes all the time.

The bidding had just hit one million. He tried not to panic when several women continued to bid up Jane.

He was full-on sweating when it hit two million.

Thankfully two of the girls dropped out, leaving Jane and one of the supermodels he'd just seen on TV.

"Do I have two-point-five million?"

Jane didn't lift her paddle; neither did anyone else.

"Going to paddle zero, zero, one...once, do I have two point five? Twice?"

Thankfully Jane thrust her paddle into the air. "Two point five million."

"Sold!" Charles beamed.

Brock let out a breath and mouthed *thank you* to Jane, who beamed like she'd just won the lottery when it was he who was the winner—the lucky one.

"STOP!" a voice shrieked from the corner. "Stop the auction!"

Oh, hell.

Both of Jane's sisters came barreling toward the stage, the blond one in such a skintight dress she could barely walk, while the dark-haired one had a slinky black number that was nearly identical to Nadine's in cut and style.

"She's an impostor!" the blonde shrieked.

"And who, my dear, are you?" Grandfather asked loudly.

She straightened. "We're her sisters and I can tell you right now, unless she robbed a bank, she has no money. You've all seen the news! This is a setup, a complete setup! Brock obviously gave her money to bid on him! And that's illegal."

"No, it isn't," Charles said simply. "And even if it were, every person had to prove where their money came from at the beginning of the auction when they received their paddles and registered. This is Jane's money. It's not up to us to ask where she got it."

Jane looked ready to crawl underneath the table and hide. Everyone was staring at her like she'd grown two heads. Some women had kind expressions while others were venomous, just like her sisters.

But again.

It was all part of the plan.

And he needed her to trust him.

She'd helped him make peace with his demons.

Now it was time to make peace with hers—in the flesh. Though he hadn't thought it would be this public. He should have suspected as much when he'd donated the tickets for her sisters to attend.

His only goal had been to make sure that they were out of their minds with jealousy when Jane won the bidding—and when they looked ready to attack, he was going to be at her side, holding her hand.

Essence's nostrils flared. "She's a liar! And a fake."

Esmeralda started to fake-cry. "She's such a horrible person. She makes us cook and clean for her and we don't even have money for food most of the time because—"

"That's enough," Jane snapped and marched over to them. "Get out." She pointed to the door.

Brock was just getting ready to open his mouth or possibly slap a woman or two for the first time in his life when Essence backed up. "See? She doesn't have a decent bone in her body!"

Jane sighed and shook her head. "Give us a minute?"

Brock nodded as Jane walked away with her sisters. His grandfather tried to gain the attention of the crowd again, but everyone was fixated on the corner where Jane was currently talking to both sisters, her hands animated and in the air.

Sighing, he started to make his way over to her when Essence slapped Jane across the face.

Esmeralda cupped her hands over her mouth in shock.

Essence looked shocked as well.

Jane cupped her face with the palm of her hand.

Brock was at her side in seconds. "Are you okay, sweetheart?"

"I-I think so." She frowned at Essence. "You slapped me!"

"I'm sorry, I..." Tears filled Essence's eyes.

Jealousy was an ugly thing.

Her sisters stood frozen in place while Jane stared down at the ground, her hand still covering her cheek. "I don't want to see you guys again."

Essence shook her head. "I didn't mean it, I didn't mean to, I just—"

"Leave." Jane's hand fell from her face. "Or I'll have security escort you out. And the last thing you want is to be even more embarrassed than you already are."

"But…" Esmeralda gaped. "We're family! Family sticks together, you've always said that!"

"And I've always been the glue that kept us together. Do you realize how exhausting it is taking care of you guys? I love you but I'm not your maid."

Brock wanted to applaud.

"Could have fooled me," Essence said under her breath.

Brock had had enough. He motioned for security. Within minutes they were at the girls' sides, escorting them out amidst screaming and name-calling.

If anyone wondered who the crazy one was they didn't need to look any further than Jane's sisters.

Jane stood there, calmly taking it all in.

"Would the winner of Brock Wellington please come to the stage immediately," Grandfather said into the microphone.

"I choose you," Brock whispered in Jane's ear. "I will always choose you."

He didn't want to release her, but he knew his grandfather was most likely trying to do damage control; he just wasn't sure how he was going to accomplish it.

Slowly, Jane walked up the stairs to the stage, head held high. Brock followed close behind.

The minute Jane was on the stage, Grandfather grabbed her hand and kissed it.

What the hell?

"This woman, right here"—his grandfather shook his head—"turned down a million dollars to stay away from my grandson."

Brock beamed with pride.

"She's also responsible for the very first real smile I've seen on my grandson's face since he was twelve."

Emotion welled in Brock's throat.

Grandfather's eyes started to tear up. "If all I knew were those two truths, it would be enough." He nodded to Nadine. "Titus Enterprises was always going to sponsor a woman of their choosing in order to partner with the charity—the fact that they chose Jane just proves how smart it was for us to partner with them in the first place. A woman who would turn down money rather than never see my grandson again is a good pick. I'm proud to say that the first Bachelor Auction has been a resounding success."

Stunned, Brock watched as Grandfather pulled Jane in for a hug and then whispered out of the side of his mouth, "Checkmate."

Brock stared at him, confused. "I'm sorry; what?"

"Did you really think you could involve Nadine Titus and not your own grandfather?"

Brock's mouth dropped open in shock. "But she said she wouldn't involve you; she said—"

"That woman." Grandfather shook his head. "Don't trust her as far as you can throw her. But, we'll talk later. What's important is you finally understand that I never wanted you to marry someone I chose. Hell, if that were the case you'd be stuck with someone like that." Nadine was pouring more wine into her glass while trying to talk on her phone and pull lipstick out of her purse.

"But all those conversations, the threat of the auction..." Brock nodded. "I still don't understand."

"Though," his grandfather seemed to say as an afterthought, "I nearly did have a stroke when I saw four more names on the card—it does me proud that you'd throw your own brothers under the bus for charity—and that they'd agree to do it because they know how much you love her." His lips twitched. "Your grandmother would roll in her grave if she knew how badly I'd hurt you. It seems we need to have a very long talk, son, but for now..." He motioned back to the auction and grabbed the microphone. "Now that we have that settled, shall we dance?"

"Take off your clothes!" A shout came from one of the tables at the back of the room.

"Pardon?" Grandfather sputtered. "What was that?"

"Brock Wellington!" Nadine shouted. "This young lady just paid over two million dollars for your sorry ass. You strip, and you strip right this instant!"

"She's drunk; ignore her." Grandfather chuckled awkwardly.

Clearly everyone was drunk, because soon women were chanting "strip, strip, strip."

Jane burst out laughing and shrugged. "Give them what they want."

Suddenly the music came on and the lights started strobing, and it was as if he'd been caught in a horrible version of *Magic Mike*.

Horrified, he was about to walk offstage, but Jane locked eyes with him and suddenly the rest of the world faded away.

Besides. It made her laugh.

And he had said that was all he wanted.

Her.

Her smile.

Everything about her.

Slowly, he shrugged out of his jacket and tossed it at Jane's face; then, with a smirk, he started unbuttoning his silk shirt.

After the third button women started screaming.

Cameras flashed, and Brock strutted toward Jane as he undid the next few buttons, stopping in front of her when the last fell away.

He grabbed her hands and pressed them against his chest.

She helped him out of the shirt and tossed it into the air, amidst screams and whistles.

"I'm going to kiss you now." He grinned.

"I'm going to let you."

Their mouths met in a searing kiss. Too soon she pulled away, laughing as Nadine appeared beside her, phone hoisted in the air, snapping picture after picture.

"Humiliation's complete." He nodded. "Fantastic."

"That is some stallion you've got there." Nadine elbowed Jane. "Come on, stallion, give us a good neigh."

"Grandfather," Brock interrupted before things got even more awkward. If that was even possible. "About that talk."

"Tomorrow." Grandfather's eyes seemed to twinkle. "For now, enjoy that you've bested me." And then he winked, but before he walked away he paused mid-step, looking back over his shoulder. "By the way, you did me proud tonight."

And then he was gone.

CHAPTER FORTY-SEVEN

Were you worried?" Jane whispered in Brock's ear once they were back at his penthouse apartment. She was still trying to get over the luxury and opulence that he lived in. She truly was in a fairy tale, and he was her prince in every way imaginable.

"Never." A hungry kiss followed his confession as he slowly inched his fingers down her back and began undoing her dress. "Especially since I had a Titus on my side."

Jane gasped as he pressed an open-mouthed kiss to her exposed back. Slowly, he pulled her dress to the floor in a pool of fabric. "One day..." Her body felt heavy as she leaned back against his chest. "You're going to have to tell me more about that woman."

"That's part of her charm—nobody really knows the truth. Did she run for president? Did she work for the CIA? Is she a Russian spy?" Brock's hot chuckle seared her skin as his hands reached around her body and cupped her breasts, weighing them in his hands while simultaneously pulling her closer to his aroused body.

"Russian spy? Seriously?" Jane was ridiculously curious but was having a hard time concentrating on anything except the way Brock's erection pressed against her backside—and how all she wanted to do was wiggle closer.

"I don't want to talk about someone who's more than likely seen my grandfather naked." He bit her earlobe then started kissing down the right side of her neck. He turned her around to face him. His eyes were dark with need. "Shocking, I know. But I'd rather be worshipping your body with my mouth right about now."

"That's a good plan..." She touched her fingertips against his lips. "Thank you...for being willing to give up everything."

"In a heartbeat." His eyes flashed. "All of this. I would give up everything for you. Know that when I say I love you it's because you're special, beautiful, caring, unique. You drive me crazy, and now that I have you—I can't imagine ever letting you go."

Tears filled her eyes. "Good. Because I won't let you."

"Oh?"

She slowly started unbuttoning his shirt. He stared down at her with a half-lidded gaze as she removed his shirt.

When he was bare chested but still in his tux pants, she took a step back, crossed her arms over her breasts. "Well, good night," she said.

He blinked at her in confusion.

Then he narrowed his eyes and crooked his finger.

She took a step back, biting down on her lip to keep from smiling.

"Come here." He kicked off his shoes then unbuttoned his pants before tossing them into a heap near her dress. "Jane, don't make me chase you again."

"Again?"

"The ranch." He took a step toward her. "It felt like every day I was chasing you, even when I was telling myself it was a bad idea... Hell, sometimes when I look at you, I wonder if I haven't been chasing after you—the woman I was always meant to be with—my entire life."

"You've really got the whole romance thing down." She couldn't help but smile. "The twins taught you well."

"Final straw." He charged her and tossed her over his shoulder, then tossed her onto his bed. She laughed as she landed with a soft thud, then let him pin her arms above her head with one hand and cup the back of her head with the other. "No more talk of grandparents, brothers, sisters, goats—"

"—cocks," she finished.

"Oh, we can most definitely talk about that." He rubbed his body against hers. "In fact, some might say it's encouraged in the bedroom."

"Is that so?"

He nodded, then slid off the last remaining piece of clothing she had on—if one could call such a tiny strip of fabric clothing—and flicked it to the side.

All that remained were her pearls.

And somehow, that felt right.

"I love you," he moaned, covering his mouth with hers. "I know this should be more romantic, but damn it, Jane, I just want to be inside you."

"I want that, too—" She'd barely finished talking before he was buried to the hilt inside her. Her body purred with pleasure.

"So good." He pressed another hungry kiss to her neck. "You always feel so perfect to me."

"I love you, Brock." She gave him a breathless kiss as she grabbed onto a fistful of his hair and pulled him deeper and deeper until she thought she was going to explode.

"You're mine, Jane." He gripped the pearls, tugging her mouth toward his for another drugging kiss as he swallowed her scream.

"You're mine, too," she sobbed out as he sent her into what felt like a never-ending wave of pleasure.

And Brock Wellington—Boring Brock, the man who'd always said yes when all he really wanted to say was no—screamed out his yes.

And truly meant it.

CHAPTER FORTY-EIGHT

You wanted to see me?" Brock said in a gruff voice. He'd been up all night with Jane, and the last thing he wanted was to be reporting to his grandfather's office at seven a.m. because he had said it couldn't wait.

And that's all his grandfather had said.

It can't wait.

But when Brock asked if it was an emergency, Grandfather had hung up on him. Figures. His grandfather had actually seemed happy last night, happy to see Jane win. Was it possible he'd changed his mind overnight? It was Grandfather. Of course it was possible.

It seemed like every newspaper in the nation had covered the auction, calling it a true Cinderella story. Because of Nadine's connections, inside information had been given to a few key magazines that made Jane look innocent in the whole thing.

And once the media learned Nadine's fairy godmother donation to Jane had allowed true love to win, well, the media had gone wild. How could his grandfather not be pleased with all the attention?

He knocked twice on his grandfather's office door, then finally just let himself in.

And as per usual, his grandfather was seated behind his massive desk, his hair perfectly combed, his suit starched within an inch of its life.

"Brock." Grandfather grinned. "Sit down."

Brock narrowed his eyes at his grandfather then slowly lowered himself into the facing leather chair and waited.

"I didn't know what to do with you," Grandfather began in a hoarse voice. "A part of you died with your parents. Don't deny it."

Brock couldn't. Because it was true. A part of him did die and then Jane went and found it.

"I did a poor job with you three." Grandfather shook his head. "You were so much older than the twins, more mature, that it felt natural you would follow in my footsteps. At the time I didn't realize I was forcing anything on you that you didn't want. By the time I did notice, it was too late. Your fear guided every decision you made—until Jane."

Brock smiled. "Until Jane."

Grandfather nodded his head thoughtfully, then stood and came around the desk to sit directly next to Brock.

His grandfather had never sat anywhere but behind his desk.

It was too familiar.

Not as threatening.

Stunned, Brock watched as his grandfather wiped a tear from his eye and shook his head at Brock. "Nadine asked for my help."

"Wait, what?"

"After you came up with your harebrained scheme to have

Nadine sponsor Jane, Nadine knew that the only way to rig the whole damn thing was to call out favors with each of the wealthiest families bidding. If you haven't noticed, Nadine is a complete mastermind of manipulation. She didn't want to stop with Jane, though—no, that woman's bloodthirsty— the minute she forced me to confess the problems I'd been having with you boys and the shareholders, the entire plan exploded into what I'd like to think of as world domination." He chuckled. "Though Bentley and Brant were never supposed to be a part of the auction—I see now why I wasn't told. I'm surprised they didn't flee the country." He sighed. "I shudder to think of the plans that Nadine has for those two. I do hope you know what you're doing, because they didn't seem happy when they left—though God knows they need someone to straighten them out. They're beyond my reach."

"Why?" Brock blinked in confusion. "Why help Jane? Why help me, for that matter? Why allow Nadine to sponsor Jane in the first place?"

"Oh, son." Grandfather's smile was sad as he reached over and patted Brock's hand. "Did you really think I was such a horrible person for trying to make things easy on you? For taking the choices away from you, the stress? What I thought was a blessing ended up being your curse, and for that I will never forgive myself." He stood. "Asking Nadine to help was smart—the shareholders are pleased, but most of all, I've never been more proud of you in my entire life. You stood up for what you loved—I know that if your parents were here, they'd say the same." He inclined his head. "Last night, I was proud to be your grandfather. You risked everything. For love."

"Yeah." Brock smiled, just thinking about Jane. "All for love."

Grandfather's lips formed an amused smile. "Exactly as

it should be." He chuckled and shook his head. "All right, now leave an old man in peace. And don't think I'm not still watching you!" Grandfather got up and moved to his chair, pointing a strong finger at Brock. "You better make an honest woman out of that Jane. Marry her, give me great-grandkids to spoil. Now you're dismissed."

Someone knocked loudly on the door, then it flew open, and Nadine came stomping in.

She ignored Brock completely, stepped up to his grand-father, and kissed his cheek. "Ready to get those twins settled down?"

"Take notes, Brock." Grandfather's eyes never left Nadine's. "This is what it looks like to sell your soul to the devil."

Nadine and Brock laughed while Grandfather wrapped an arm around her waist and kissed her on the mouth.

"Everyone needs a little sin in their lives," she whispered. Then she looked at Brock. "Shoo! Go find that woman you won, you!"

At that, Brock held up his hands and walked out.

Feeling the lightest he'd felt in years.

CHAPTER FORTY-NINE

Three months later

"It's beautiful!" Jane's eyes filled with tears as the sign in front of her old home was finally revealed. She and Brock had decided it would be best to sell her family home, especially once she found out that her sisters were in such heavy debt that there was no other way out. She knew her parents would understand, and even though the house had memories there was no better charity organization to sell it to.

Her home now belonged to the cancer charity that Wellington, Inc. and Titus Enterprises were working on together.

Her sisters never said thank you.

In fact, they hadn't said much since the ball.

For a while she'd been sad, but then she looked at her new family, the one surrounding her, and realized what a true family was about: Support. Love. Kindness.

The best part was that the charity was using her old house

as Rosie House, a place for families to stay while going through cancer treatments in Phoenix.

And all because of a grandfather with a cold and a keen sense of wisdom when it came to his grandsons and what they needed out of life.

She still had Cinderella Cleaning, but after some encouragement from Brock she hired more staff and took a step back so that she could focus on Rosie House—something she realized she enjoyed because it was about helping people.

Just like her cleaning business, sometimes you needed to pull back the dirt and muck, to get to what was underneath and make it shine. She wasn't a cancer expert by any means, but she knew people, and there was something so satisfying about meeting all of the families and helping them on such a basic level.

"You're beautiful," Brock whispered in her ear. His hot kiss had her knees shaking as her body trembled with desire—and he'd only kissed her neck. The man had a mouth on him. She would never get tired of the way he kissed her.

Honestly, he was her family now—well, him, the twins, and Charles. Her sisters had all but disowned her once the house was sold—she'd tried reaching out but they refused to answer her calls. Brock was convinced it was because they couldn't handle her fame and success.

But she didn't think of herself that way—even if the world did. The headlines after the ball had been insane: REAL-LIFE CINDERELLA FINDS HER PRINCE.

If they only knew what it had taken to get to that place.

She smiled, thinking about the ranch, and all the animals. They were going to spend the next two weeks there.

Charles and the twins were coming by for dinner and then

returning to the city. It would be nice to have the family all together.

"You ready?" Brock asked, his eyes dancing with excitement.

"Yup." She nodded and took his hand as he led her to the waiting limo.

Once they were inside and the car had started toward the ranch, Brock turned to her. He handed her a glass of champagne.

"You left your shoe."

"Huh?"

Brock grinned. "The first time I saw you, you left a shoe; or actually, you broke a shoe."

"Like Cinderella." She grinned.

"Yes." He held up his hand then reached behind him and pulled something out of a bag.

Jane gasped. "That's my black shoe!"

"Size eight and a half black pump. Yes, it sure is."

"You kept it?" Her eyes filled with tears. "Why?"

He smirked. "I'd like to say it's because I knew this moment was happening and I wanted to get laid in the back of a limo."

She smacked him in the chest.

"But I was cleaning out the closet, and found it. I'd stashed it there after I'd slept with it like a complete ass and dreamed about your hair."

Jane sighed happily. "That's romantic."

"There is nothing romantic about sleeping with a stiletto." He grinned. "But maybe this will make up for it." He handed her the shoe.

Inside was a small pale blue box.

Tears filled her eyes as she grabbed the box and slowly opened it.

A giant, princess-cut diamond shimmered back at her.

It was huge.

Bigger than her fist.

Okay, maybe not that big, but at least a few karats. She swallowed a lump in her throat as Brock pulled the ring from the box and whispered. "You left your shoe, and took my heart with you that night, and you've had it ever since... Will you marry me?"

"Yes!" Tears streamed down her face as she threw her arms around his neck and sobbed.

The limo came to a stop and then the doors were opening on all sides.

"Thank God!" Bentley shouted, shoving his way into the limo. He looked like he was already drunk. An expression of pure irritation marred his features before he straightened and said, "If you didn't hurry I was going to propose." He licked his lips and winked at Jane. "Someone's looking good." His smile looked forced—it didn't help that his normally perfect features were marred by dark circles under his eyes.

Brock groaned.

Brant piled in next, followed by Charles.

"Champagne for everyone!" Brant shouted while Charles chuckled and kissed her on the cheek.

"You guys all knew?" she said accusingly.

"I wrote his speech," Bentley claimed, stealing the champagne from Brant.

"He lies," Brant yawned. "Also, the cock died."

All talking ceased in the limo.

"Because it crossed the road." Brant burst out laughing. "Yeah, I may be drunk already."

Well, that explained things. Somewhat.

No matter what the twins did, they were always still getting into trouble, though Bentley had been worse lately, and constantly in the papers for sleeping with married women.

His last conquest had been a senator's wife.

Something was going on with Bentley, but every time she asked Brock about it, it just seemed to make him sad, like his brother had finally lost it. And Brock and Bentley were doing anything they could to get *Brant* out of the house and smiling again.

Which was another problem.

Brant had stopped smiling.

So while one twin was trying to cheer the other up and was most likely in the process of gaining a free first-class ticket to the fires of hell—the other shut everyone out.

Jane focused on both of the twins and said softly, "You two should really stop day drinking."

"Fuck that," Bentley slurred. His eyes were cold when he glanced at Jane, and it sent a chill down her spine. This wasn't the Bentley she knew. The Bentley she knew didn't have a dark or menacing bone in his body. "Sometimes a man just needs to forget, right, Brant?"

Brant clenched his jaw and clinked glasses with his twin while Charles sent Brock a worried look.

"Boys," Charles said in serious voice. "Don't be jackasses. Why, look what happened to Brock. You don't want to force my hand—or Nadine's."

"Brock's the happiest he's ever been," Bentley pointed out. "If I thought that my date would end up half as good I'd get my ass out of bed and actually do something worthwhile."

"Here, here." Brant laughed and leaned against the door like he needed it to help hold him up.

"Besides, nothing wrong with a little ass!" Bentley shouted. "Damn, I miss that donkey."

Jane couldn't hold back her laugh. "You know your family's insane, right?"

"You love them."

"I do."

"And I love you." He kissed her cheek. "So much."

*　　*　　*

Brock walked around the grounds at the ranch, his thoughts scattered as he welcomed the memories of his parents. For so long he'd refused to deal with them. The ghosts terrified him, haunted him, and rather than deal with his memories, he'd allowed the fear of them to define his life.

But pain demanded to be discussed, memories demanded to be remembered.

Jane, a few feet ahead of him, was smiling up at the sky as she looked over her shoulder and gave him a wink.

God, she was perfect.

So perfect.

His father would have loved her.

His mother as well.

He'd grown up with so much laughter, so much emotion that, until now, he had no idea he'd forsaken.

"Brock!" Jane jogged toward him. "What's wrong? Are you okay?"

He stared into her chocolate-brown eyes as the wind around them picked up. Chills ran down his arms as he continued to stare, and on that wind, a whisper called, "Welcome home."

"Yeah." He nodded. "I'm the best I've ever been."

"Even with the twins at the ranch? And your grandfather having an affair with Nadine?"

"Shh, don't ruin the moment," he scolded, molding his

mouth around hers. "Let's just kiss and forget about the chaos of my family."

"Right." She kissed him back. "Because that's an easy task."

Just then a loud voice shouted, "No sex in the pasture!"

"Bentley." Brock said his name like a curse. "We really need to get him married off."

She sighed and wrapped her arms around his neck. "Have I told you I adore you?"

"I have a better idea." He smiled wickedly. "Show me."

Notorious playboy Bentley Wellington has been able to seduce—and dump—countless women. But when he's auctioned off to spend thirty days with shy romance novelist Margot McCleery, Bentley is the one in danger of losing his heart...

Please see the next page for a preview of *The Playboy Bachelor.*

CHAPTER ONE

Present Day

Bentley groaned as the woman, whose name he'd already forgotten a few hours ago, spread her toned thighs over his body and rode him. The scent of her vanilla lotion clung to the air as he slid his hands up and down her hips.

She was just another nameless face.

Another willing female in a long list of women who wanted to have a piece of the notorious playboy Bentley Wellington.

Because that's all he was to her—all he was to anyone. And most of the time? He was completely okay with it—he had to be. A familiar tightening threatened to choke him and completely ruin his morning. He feigned boredom.

And covered his yawn with his hand as she started to increase her speed, her breath coming out in small fake pants that had him sporting a bored grin, as if to say, *Is that the best you can do*? She woke him up? For this?

Her seething glare said it all.

He *was* a jackass.

Then again, it wasn't like she hadn't been painfully aware how much of a player he was. With a smug-as-hell smirk, he winked. "That the best you can do, Sarah?"

"It's Christine!" She smacked his chest and panted as she rode him harder, her skin slapping against his in a way that should have felt good but instead irritated the hell out of him. "You're a complete asshole!"

He gripped her hips and quickened her movements with deep thrusts. "But..." Another punishing thrust. "I'm a handsome asshole." Her lips parted on a moan as he leaned up and finished what she'd started. "Right?"

"The last thing you need," she said in a breathy whisper, "is for me to stroke your ego."

"Aw." He made a face and pulled free from her body. Bored. Angry that she was speaking. And maybe a little bit sick of himself, if he was being completely honest. "Play fair. I'm always in the mood for a good stroking."

Her bright blue eyes flashed before she rolled off his sweaty body and out of the bed. "I'm leaving."

"That was fun, Sarah," he called after her. "We should do it again sometime."

She screamed in fury, and two minutes later the door slammed.

Frowning, he sat up on his elbows. Now, that was a bit of an overreaction. Whatever. Whenever one left, there were at least a hundred waiting in line, willing for a glimpse or even just one small taste of what he had to offer.

His sexual appetitive was huge—and legendary. But basically Bentley had a problem with boredom. He hated marriage, commitment, dating...really, anything that sounded like long-term.

Because long-term meant exactly like it sounded.

Long.

Term.

Like a contract he couldn't get out of. And the last thing he needed was to allow someone in—someone who would want to share all of his demons, or worse—free him from them.

The door opened again and clicked shut.

"Back for more?" He chuckled and pulled the covers over his naked body, waiting for whatever her name was to come back in and finish the job she'd started. Damn it, he could have sworn her name really was Sarah.

He snapped his fingers. No, no, Sarah had been the night before. Amazing mouth. Jet black hair.

He hardened again just thinking about how she'd used her long silky hair to—

A shadowy figure stomped toward his bedside with clenched teeth and a furious look in his eyes. "Shouldn't you be on your way?"

"On my way?" Bentley repeated, fisting the sheets with his hands. His grandfather was a giant pain in the ass. "To hell?" Another nonchalant shrug, because that was what his grandfather was used to. He was the younger twin by a few seconds, the one who would never amount to anything—though not for lack of trying.

A dull pain flared in his chest, as if his grandfather was standing on his ribs rather than towering over him from the side of the bed.

"Don't be a jackass." His grandfather's mouth twisted into a disappointed frown.

"Prudence McCleery spent ten thousand dollars for your services. You're due to arrive at their country estate today and make good on your promise."

"Right." Bentley hadn't forgotten. How could he, when

he'd been nearly scarred for life two weeks ago as every rich woman in the greater Phoenix area had tried to win him at auction? The charity event had been his grandfather's grand plan to get his brother Brock married off, but Bentley and Brant had stepped in to help save Brock for the woman he was truly meant to marry.

He'd assumed some bored, rich, trophy wife would take him home, have her way with him, then slap him on the ass and send him on his way.

Instead, a woman with bright green eyes and equally bright white hair had lifted her paddle—and basically purchased him for a weekend getaway.

Bentley liked older women, just not *that* old.

Thankfully he'd found out later that he wasn't being bid on for the silver-haired woman at all—but for her granddaughter. And suddenly the past, *his* past, became the present as images of a girl with bright red hair burned his vision.

"I tried." Grandfather's shoulders slumped. "I tried to do right by you boys. Maybe I was just too focused on grooming Brock to lead Wellington, Inc. to realize how horrible you and your brother have turned out."

"Thanks?" Bentley offered with a grimace. It wasn't like Bentley didn't work for what he had, he just didn't work very hard—a fifty-million-dollar trust fund had a way of doing that to a man.

After all, people worked to make money.

They worked for success.

And he already had those things.

A nagging voice shattered his confidence, the same voice that reminded him how he used to be a man who'd had dreams an actual purpose, direction.

And that same voice reminded him that his life had become a boring cycle of using women and hiding who he really was from the world.

Because the last time he had tried to be himself, he'd been shattered.

His world had been shattered.

It wasn't worth it. It was easier to be the rich, good-looking, bored playboy who listed fucking as an actual hobby on his résumé.

He'd been called black-hearted.

A manwhore.

A woman-shaming, prostitute-loving gambler.

Hell, he'd been called it *all*.

And he always shrugged it off. Nothing touched him, at least not typically, but today his grandfather's comment snaked its way around his throat and took hold.

"The VP of marketing stepped down this morning," his grandfather said thoughtfully. "I want to hire within."

Bentley froze; his heart hammered against his chest. On the outside, he was calm, rational, thoughtful, but on the inside, he was freaking the hell out. "Oh?"

"Yes." Grandfather leveled him with a perceptive stare. "I don't suppose that would be something you'd be interested in... You do realize you'll have to take 'fucking' off your list of hobbies in order for me to actually process your résumé."

Bentley smirked. "It was a joke."

Grandfather's eyes were granite as he narrowed them. "It wasn't funny, nor was it professional."

"Brant thought it was funny."

"Your brother doesn't count." Grandfather's mouth twitched like he wanted to smile but thought better of it. "So... what do you say?"

"Are you saying that you'll give me an actual position within your company?"

With a heavy sigh, Grandfather nodded his head once. "The board, of course, won't like the idea."

"They can go to hell." Bentley clenched his teeth.

"It might help your image"—Grandfather's body was rigid as he spoke—"to be seen doing charity work."

Hell. It would do more than help. But he had a life in Phoenix. One that on most days he actually enjoyed, or at least liked.

And he was a creature of habit.

"Or don't take the job and keep sleeping with every woman who will spread her legs in hopes you'll get her pregnant and be forced to pay child support."

Low blow.

"I'll go." Bentley sighed. It wasn't like he had a choice, not if he wanted the job, not if he wanted more purpose outside of what he already did for the company, which was basically just smile for pictures and wave when they had charity events and expensive dinners. He was a pretty face. The only work he'd ever done for Wellington, Inc. had been an internship right after college, and he had been bored out of his mind—it had been too easy, but his grandfather had refused to promote him to a position that carried any real weight. So Bentley had quit. Because that was what he did when things didn't go his way. He quit.

"Of course you will." Grandfather straightened. "You're going to be late."

"Does it matter?" Bentley snorted.

"Punctuality always matters." Grandfather stood. His thick gray hair was swirled into one sweeping curl that fell across his forehead. Bentley and Brant might be playboys, but Grandfather had an Instagram page dedicated to that very curl. And he was pushing eighty-eight.

Grandfather lifted a brow. "Well, boy? Aren't you going to pack?"

Bentley clenched his teeth until he felt like they were going to crack. "I'm naked."

"Ain't nothing I haven't had the great displeasure of seeing before." He unclenched his fists. "Now get your shit together before I cut you off and give your trust fund to your brothers, and hire Brant for the VP position."

"You wouldn't." The words rushed out before he could stop them.

"I would."

"You hate me."

"I love you." Grandfather sobered. "You're twenty-seven, Bentley, time to stop playing around and actually take responsibility for your actions, starting with Prudence McCleery's granddaughter."

"Margot," Bentley whispered without thinking.

"What was that?" Grandfather cupped his ear.

"Nothing." A vision of red luscious hair that went on for days burned before his eyes, and bright green eyes and freckles. At sixteen she'd been breathtaking but quiet, too shy for someone like Bentley.

Hell, she'd been too good for him.

Too nice.

Too proper.

Too perfect.

And now...too sad.

CHAPTER TWO

*H*is eyes whispered a promise his words had failed to do."
Margot read the words out loud as the sound of her fingernails tapping against the computer keys filled the room. " '*I
love you,*'" *he declared, tucking his beaver hat under his
arm as he took a step toward her waiting arms.*"

She hesitated and contemplated the computer screen. I
love you? Was that it?

She had exactly forty-seven chapters of historical crap.

Crap she had to turn in within thirty days if she had any
hope of meeting her deadline.

She glared at her computer and tried again. The scene
was pivotal; it had to be perfect, it needed to be believable.

Then again, what was believable about a rich rakish duke
falling for one of his scullery maids, only to discover she
was really part of the gentry? Even if she came from a good
family, it would still be frowned upon. It wasn't accurate,
and it bothered her, but it was romantic, and that was why
she'd decided to write it.

It was a horrible idea.

But that was what sold.

Rakes and rogues.

And poor sad wallflowers who somehow magically became the object of their affection.

It was complete BS.

She'd been that wallflower.

She *was* that wallflower.

And nothing, not one thing, had set her apart from the other girls. Men might say they wanted character, they wanted something different. They claimed they wanted the girl next door, childbearing hips, whatever. Their actions, however, and the women they actually dated, said it all.

Skinny.

Botoxed.

Implanted.

Airheads.

Margot slammed her hands against the keyboard and stood in a huff.

It was *his* fault.

Because he was late.

Not that she wanted to see him, anyway.

But still, it grated on her nerves.

In a moment of complete insanity, her grandmother, God bless her, had bid on one of the country's most notorious playboys in an auction set up for cancer research.

Unfortunately, her grandmother had won.

Margot still remembered the phone call from that night.

"I've landed you a man!" Her grandmother yelled loud enough for half the country to hear. *"Paid a pretty penny for him too! Oh, muffin, you'll love him, he's strong, and—"*

"You bought"—Margot pressed her fingertips against her temple—*"a man?"*

"He was spendy, too." Grandmother slurred her words

a bit. "Cost at least half of what I was willing to spend, though."

"Half?"

"Ten thousand dollars isn't too steep!"

Margot choked.

Grandmother laughed.

"Are you drunk?"

"I had the whiskeys, yes." Her grandmother sighed happily. "Such a delicious burn. Did you know Titus Enterprises just closed a deal on Honey Whiskey, Incorporated? Nadine's such a dear, she even brought me a few bottles. Has her sights set on McCleery Whiskey too, but we'll cross that bridge when we get there."

Margot groaned and sat down on the bed. "A few bottles?"

"Ten," Grandmother slurred. "Or was it twelve? Did I have two? Ha-ha."

"Grand—"

"You know him! This man."

"The man you paid ten grand for? That man?"

"Your new friend."

"Thanks, but I don't need you to buy me a man. I can find my own man," Margot said through clenched teeth.

"How's that working out for you, love?"

"I'm busy!" she snapped.

"You're sad."

"I'm—" Margot clenched her left hand into a fist and refused to stare down at her one good leg. She flexed the toes of her left leg and tried not to stare at the right. "I'm not sad. I'm fine. I have my books. I have my house. I have my work—"

"You have wild tomcats, too, and cats are a bad omen."

"How much whiskey did you say you had again?"

"Whiskeys. Plural," Grandmother corrected. "Now, he's going to report to the estate in two weeks. He'll arrive at nine in the morning. I told him to be punctual. And you're to give him the downstairs blue room during his stay."

"His stay!" Margot yelled. "He's not staying anywhere!"

"Of course he is," Grandma said in soothing, albeit slurred tones. "It's part of the package. Hah, not his package, but the package. I bought him, and once old Wellington discovered what I meant to use him for, he gave me more than the weekend that was up for bid. You get him a full month."

Margot sucked in a breath.

"I know! Thirty days!"

"Did you say Wellington?"

Please don't say Bentley. Let it be Brant—he always had a teasing smile—or Brock, the serious one. No, it wouldn't be Brock; didn't he just get married?

"Bentley Wellington!" Her grandmother shouted with glee, confirming Margot's worst fears and causing her eyes to search the room for her bottle of Xanax. "Lovely man. When he keeps it in his pants, which, let's hope for the sake of my great grandchildren he doesn't—"

Tears burned the back of Margot's eyes as she blinked away the blurry vision of a boy she'd always wanted.

And never had.

He was a man now.

Featured in Forbes, among other magazines.

He dated supermodels, celebrities, pretty women.

Not her.

She glanced down at her right prosthetic leg. The amputation had been made right below her knee, so while her thigh looked normal, there was no foot, no ankle, no toes.

Definitely not women like her.

"Oh, must go, I'll fill you in later on the more pertinent details." Her grandmother hung up before Margot could protest.

Why would Bentley even agree to be auctioned off? It made no logical sense. He was either that bored, stupid, or doing it for good PR. God knew he needed it, since he'd allegedly been having an affair with a senator's wife; not that the rumors were ever confirmed.

And now she was going to be stuck with him.

Margot shook her head at the memory of his smile and wandered over to the window. A sense of dread filled her as a red sports car sped up her driveway, scaring the crap out of every small creature in its way and kicking up enough dust to make the road nearly impossible to see.

Bentley Wellington had arrived.

ACKNOWLEDGMENTS

I could list all the hundreds of people who made this book possible. And I often do. I thank everyone in my life and I still always forget someone. It's ridiculous. It takes the whole world (or at least it seems) to get a book off the ground.

First, I'm so thankful that God has given me this incredible opportunity—all honor and glory *always* go to him first. Second, my family is amazing for putting up with me when I'm on deadline! My husband took our son on *a lot* of walks when Mama was "typing" furiously at her computer trying to finish this book!

My amazing PA, Jill—more of a sister to me than anything: Thank you for your tireless hours working with me and thanks for being just amazing in general.

My beta readers, *sister* Kristin Van Dyken (Vayden, her books rock!), Liza Tice, Jill, and Jessica Prince (more awesome books): Thank you for always being honest with me!

To Bae (you know you who are) and Wife (aka Lauren Layne): Thanks for keeping me sane on most days and not thinking I'm crazy when I send you wine texts at noon that go, "It's almost five in New York, right? RIGHT?"

Erica: the best agent in the world. No, seriously, guys. I fully think she would take a bullet for me (let's not ask her though, just in case, LOL). She is one of the hardest-working agents out there; I still pinch myself when I think about how lucky I am to have her in my corner. If she ever breaks up with me, I'm stalking her (You know I would too, Erica).

Amy: *Hehe*, this is our first "real" project together. I was terrified. I know how honest you are. But I also know you *know* what you're talking about. Thanks for taking an "OK" book and making it spectacular, because I truly feel like you made magic. You completely shoved me off a cliff and out of my comfort zone, and for that I will always be thankful. You are absolutely fearless when it comes to editing, and I'm so blessed to also be able to call you my friend.

I'm so happy to be back with Forever Romance.

Dani and Inkslinger PR: Thanks for all your hard work with getting this book ready, and bloggers, GAH! You are incredible; thank you for all that you do! I know I don't say it enough!

Readers: There's a reason you distracted me from deadlines; I literally just want to hang out with you guys all the time and talk about *all the books*. Thank you for being so loyal, so dedicated, and just being like family to me. I love you all so much!

I hope you enjoyed Brock's story! Look for more of the Bachelors of Arizona in the next book, where we see Bentley get his ass handed to him ;)

Hugs,
RVD

ABOUT THE AUTHOR

Rachel Van Dyken is the *New York Times*, *Wall Street Journal*, and *USA Today* bestselling author of Regency and contemporary romances. When she's not writing you can find her drinking coffee at Starbucks and plotting her next book while watching *The Bachelor*.

She keeps her home in Idaho with her husband, adorable son, and two snoring boxers. She loves to hear from readers.

Want to be kept up-to-date on new releases? Text MAFIA to 66866.

Fall in Love with Forever Romance

WICKED COWBOY CHARM
By Carolyn Brown

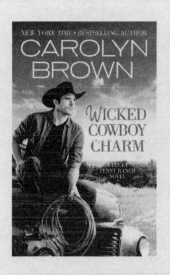

The newest novel in Carolyn Brown's *USA Today* bestselling Lucky Penny Ranch series! Josie Dawson is new in town, but it doesn't take long to know that Deke Sullivan has charmed just about every woman in Dry Creek, Texas. Just as Deke is wondering how to convince Josie he only has eyes for her, they get stranded in a tiny cabin during a blizzard. If Deke can melt her heart before they dig out of the snow, he'll be the luckiest cowboy in Texas...

THE COTTAGE AT FIREFLY LAKE
By Jen Gilroy

In the tradition of Susan Wiggs and RaeAnne Thayne comes the first in a new series by debut author Jen Gilroy. Eighteen years ago, Charlotte Gibbs left Firefly Lake—and Sean Carmichael—behind to become a globetrotting journalist. But now she's back. Will the two have a second chance at first love? Or will the secret Charlie's hiding be their undoing?

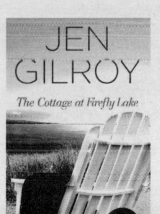

Fall in Love with Forever Romance

TOO WILD TO TAME
By Tessa Bailey

Aaron knows that if he wants to work for the country's most powerful senator, he'll have to keep his eye on the prize. That's easier said than done when he meets the senator's daughter, who's wild, gorgeous, and 100 percent trouble. The second book in *New York Times* bestselling author Tessa Bailey's Romancing the Clarksons series!

THE BACHELOR AUCTION
By Rachel Van Dyken

The first book in a brand-new series from #1 *New York Times* bestselling author Rachel Van Dyken! Brock Wellington isn't anyone's dream guy. So now as he waits to be auctioned off in marriage to the highest bidder, he figures it's karmic retribution that he's tempted by a sexy, sassy woman he can't have…